Lady of the Dead
By
Gretchen S. B.

Gretchen S. B.

Acknowledgments

I wanted to give my thanks to everyone who helped me get this manuscript into a book. Thank you to my lovely beta readers for reading this story before an editor touched it. Special thanks to the 'fearless leader' who urged me to publish the way he had and for answering each of my random questions. Thank you to the editors at The Author's Red Room for making this story readable. Also, I have to thank each and every one of my 'cheerleaders' over the years who have encouraged me to write out the stories dancing around in my head. Last but not least I want to acknowledge 'He who must not be tagged.' If it were not for his support, I would not be publishing anything.

Chapter 1

"The Night World stole me from reality. No, a better way to put it is that the Night World weaned me from the normalcy of what most people would consider the real world," Gwen began by way of explanation.

"That's an interesting and very selective memory of events you have there," Viking said, raising a blond eyebrow at her. "In fact, that is not how I remember it at all."

Gwen glared. "Storebror, are you going to let me tell my story or are you going to be a nuisance?"

Viking smiled but before he could say anything he was interrupted by Raider, his second-in-command.

"Viking, the boy asked her about her past, let her tell it her own way so we can get on with the game. You know how the new guards become so enamored with our Lady of the Dead. Let the boy get it out of his system." He laid his cards on the table, folded his arms and nodded at Gwen to continue.

Gwen rolled her eyes. She hated that title and Raider knew it. She had tried desperately over the years to convince the Warriors sent to guard her to call her by her name instead of the title, that really creeped her out. Gwen did not just talk to the dead, but to the entire Spirit World. She wanted to meet who ever had come up with that title and kick him in the balls.

Sighing, Gwen turned to Kegan, one of the new men sent to guard her. The fact that he still used his birth name told Gwen that he was less than two centuries old. When Warriors became older, they tended to make up their own names, like Viking and Raider.

"Anyway, I was seven and once again helped out of the house by my Fairy friends..."

Kegan waved a hand. "Fairy friends? There's no such thing as Fairies."

Gwen glared at him until he looked away. Yeah, he was definitely young. Older Warriors would not give in that easily. Gwen looked at Raider.

"What is it with you men and interrupting?"

Raider grinned at her. She had known him since she was seventeen, ten years now. Gwen had harbored a minor crush on him when they first met, but had found out what he was in his first life and the feelings had faded. A first life is what Warriors called their first century; everything after that is considered their second life. Raider's first life consisted of raiding tombs in the 1700s. The young Gwen had been crushed that the gorgeous man before her was not only far too old for her, but a professional thief as well.

Raider kept his light brown hair a little shaggy and his sharp jaw clean-shaven. His broad nose showed signs of a bad break. The break must have occurred very young because at thirty a Warrior's body became too strong for scarring like that.

When Raider did not respond to her, Gwen continued. "A small child is not going to understand that a being from the Spirit World is not a Fairy. My Fairy friends and I went to play down by Green River; they knew the paths to take to get all the way down to the bank. I was playing in the water when some of the Fairies picked me up and started dunking me." Gwen did not like the next part. She still had nightmares. "At first it was fun, but then I was under too long and I needed air. The Fairies would not let me up to breathe. They were trying to drown me."

She knew her voice was emotionless. Though it had been the first traumatic experience in her life, it was not the last. The attacks only grew worse as she aged. When Viking's hand slid onto her left arm, Gwen knew he was thinking of those later attacks as well. His one little gesture calmed her down. She was safe now. Viking always made feel her safe, even when the odds were against them.

Shaking her head to clear it, Gwen continued her story. "Suddenly I was up in the air and huddling against this huge chest. He was yelling at the Fairies, speaking in a language I didn't know. Nevertheless, I knew he was there to help me. I could feel that he was a good guy. He made the Fairies leave and has protected me ever since."

Gwen smiled at the man she called Storebror; he smiled back and withdrew his arm. She never told the rest of the story. He had given her a necklace that belonged to his mother, who had been his village's wise woman. It protected the wearer from the illusions that the Spirit World could cast. He told her he no longer needed it and that it would be more useful to her. His mother taught him many things about the Spirit World. In the world Viking grew up in, that was rare; men simply were not taught those things. He helped Gwen in ways no one else could have and she learned over the years that he did not share that part of his life with anyone. She respected that and kept his secrets. After all they had been through together in twenty years, it was the least she could do.

"I don't understand what you call him. What does Storebror mean? I don't know that word." Kegan was looking from Viking to Gwen in confusion.

Gwen made a mental note; Kegan's phrasing made her wonder if perhaps English was not his first language.

Before she could answer, Viking did it for her. "It means Big Brother in Norwegian. Since that is where I am from, Gwen wanted to learn the language. Only she is allowed to call me that." Viking's pale blue eyes narrowed on the other man in warning.

Before anyone could respond, the door to the lounge swung open hard enough to hit the wall. One of the other four new guards stood in the doorway, a young looking redhead whose name, Gwen was embarrassed to say, she could not remember.

"Lady of the Dead, the Alpha of the Northwest Pack seeks your assistance."

Gwen clenched her teeth at the title; she was going to resort to death threats soon if they did not knock that crap off.

"In what capacity?" she asked instead.

The redhead looked at her in shocked confusion. Apparently, he expected her to simply jump into an unknown situation. He must be young too. Why did the King send so many young Warriors this time?

Raider answered the redhead's unasked question. "Gwen needs to know how you received this information before acting on it, Stanley."

Several thoughts went through Gwen's head at the name before Stanley recovered.

"He called your shop and told Poet that you were needed at East River Park for a kidnapping case."

Gwen, Raider, and Viking burst from their seats, Kegan following. If Carter Tuckman had called the shop, he was not calling in his capacity as Alpha of the Northwest Wolf Pack. He was calling in his capacity as Lieutenant Carter Tuckman with the King County Police. That was a big deal.

Gwen took the lead, but since both Raider and Viking were Warriors, they caught up with her by the time she reached her storefront. Raider moved in front of her and Viking in back, to protect her from harm in any direction.

She slowed her walk to a stroll as they reached the actual store. Gwen craned her neck around Viking to see that the newbies were now behind them. She stopped altogether, forcing Viking to do the same to prevent from running her over as she spoke to the four men.

"Stay put! A show of force will scare the customers and as a police matter, you can't be there anyway."

It looked as if several of them would argue, but Gwen felt Raider appear over her. "She's right, go back to what you were doing."

There was some grumbling before they all went in various directions.

Gwen muttered under her breath only loud enough for Viking and Raider to hear. "Seriously, they've only been here two weeks and already they're like overactive puppies. They can't be that bored yet."

Both men chuckled as the three of them walked into the store, half-full of customers. Viking leaned down to whisper in her ear; he was over a foot taller than her, so it was a ways down. "You should hear the stories Poet's been telling them. All action and adventure. He's getting them all riled up."

Gwen rolled her eyes and looked at the man in question. Poet stood behind the counter with a pleasantly calm expression on his face. He had been assigned to her with the first detail.

In the early years, she and Viking had struggled and, by some miracle, held their own. As she neared adulthood, Viking requested that Raider join them as the attacks increased. Raider had been appalled when he arrived at just how much activity Gwen and Viking fought on their own, and he petitioned the King to send a detail of Warriors to help guard the Lady of the Dead. Poet had been one of the four men sent just before Gwen's eighteenth birthday. The details were in three-year stints and Poet had requested to stay permanently. Gwen never knew his reasoning, but she liked him so she did not push the issue.

Poet inclined his head to them as they made their way across the store. Poet had been born somewhere in the Persian Empire. He was very secretive about his past, which meant that was all Gwen knew. He kept his ink black hair just shy of his waist, and as usual it hung in a braid down his back. The diamond stud in his nose was just big enough to be eye-catching.

Poet drew women like insects to light. He possessed an exotic look and a faint accent that made him intoxicating, and he loved it. Gwen possessed an immunity to it, which puzzled him. For the first two years he saw it as a challenge, but now he seemed more interested in figuring it out.

Gwen smiled back at him as she leaned over the counter. Poet followed suit, leaning in until their faces were less than six inches apart. She gave him a disapproving look. Gwen knew what he was doing, he liked to make the new details think they were an item; her discouragement only seemed to egg him on.

"What exactly did Carter say that sent Stanley running down the hall?"

Poet gave her an open-mouthed smile and ran his tongue over one of his canines. All four of Poet's canines had been filed centuries ago to resemble snake fangs. He made it look like an unconscious gesture but Gwen knew it was for show.

"There was a kidnapping from East River Park two days ago and it was the third in a month. A child of four, male."

Despite his demeanor, Gwen watched Poet's eyes go flat; he was pissed. Cases involving children and women did that to him. Gwen itched to know why, but she knew better than to ask any Warrior in America about their past.

As recent as the early 1800s, North America was the dumping ground for Warriors who had broken laws. It had been, for lack of a better comparison, a penal colony. In less than two centuries they had developed a hierarchy and policed themselves into a society. It now resembled the other nine Warrior kingdoms. Gwen always kept in mind the older Warriors here had dark histories that all of them wanted left alone.

"Did he mention where he wanted us to meet him?"

Carter solicited Gwen's help on multiple occasions. Sometimes without official approval, and those cases were trickier.

"He is at the park now with several other officers. They have officially asked for your help, which means they brought in our dear lieutenant because they know you work with no one else."

Gwen watched him for a beat. Poet was leaving out something. Nothing important—he was not stupid—but there was something in his expression that let her know he was playing with her. The child was more important so she turned to leave the store. Thinking better of it, she turned back to Poet, who was smiling at her playfully.

"And stop filling their heads with nonsense. We haven't had that much action in years."

Poet laughed as she turned back to the door. It was a rich laugh, full and throaty. Gwen noticed almost every female in the store automatically turned to look. Gwen shook her head and headed the six blocks to the park.

They were about a block from the park when Raider cleared his throat. "You are aware that it sounded like you were talking to Poet about sex right?"

Gwen could hear Raider trying to keep the amusement from his voice. She mentally rewound the conversation and snorted. "Crap, he's going to try harder to appear couple-y isn't he?"

Viking grunted from behind her. "Pretty much."

Gwen sighed. "Great."

Raider's back stiffened slightly; if Gwen hadn't known him so well she wouldn't have caught it. He was thinking something he was not comfortable with.

"Spill it, Raider."

His shoulders tensed. Warriors were always uncomfortable when she read them well, and she didn't ignore unconscious gestures the way they did. Gwen didn't get it.

"I do not think he does it for the reasons you believe he does."

That gained Gwen's full attention. She had been prepping herself to drop her mental shields. "Why do you say that?"

Raider let out an uncomfortable sigh. "Why must you always ask questions?"

Gwen knew he was not actually expecting a response so she did not give him one.

"You were too young to notice the inner workings of the first detail. This is fine. Poet claims you as his with every new detail to avoid any of them from trying you out. I believe he is protecting you and them from any animosity that would come from one of them sleeping with you."

Gwen could not decide how she felt about that. Part of her was offended. Part of her was confused, and part of her was contemplating the concept that Poet was thinking that far ahead of the game. "Is that why he stays with us?"

Both men were silent for a full minute before Raider's unsure tone floated over his shoulder. "I do not think so. I have never asked him his reasoning. It is not my business."

It was the typical response Gwen received from both Viking and Raider. She had gotten used to it; she did not like it, but she wasn't going to push it.

Viking interrupted her thoughts. "We should table this conversation for later. Gwen needs to prepare herself for this so we are not caught off guard."

And just like that, the conversation ended. Gwen learned long ago not to argue with Viking. Sure, *she* could argue with him, but he did not take it from his men. They would not go against a word he said. Even if she wanted to keep talking, Raider wouldn't. She worked on preparing her shields as the parking lot came into view.

Viking had slowly taught her how to build her shields when they met. He told her once she had the best he had ever seen, and he said it with such pride.

She would have to lower her shields to be of any help at the park. Since she was not calling to any particular spirit, she needed to be open to everything. It was dangerous and only within the last two years had she been able to lower her shields without drawing unwanted attention and still protect herself. She had not told Viking but she knew he picked up on the change; in true Warrior fashion he didn't ask her about it.

He had been her mentor for their first ten years together, but then she begun to surpass him as her abilities reached maturity. Viking did not like it. He wanted to be able to protect her from the world, but he had known it would happen at some point.

Gwen developed a secondary shield. She thought of it as a chain link fence. She could see out and things nearby could see her, but the energies would not come in contact. She put up her secondary shields, because it was draining to keep both shields up at all times. She had not fully mastered it, so the process took time. She built it link by link. That was why the Warriors were there; she was not aware of the world at large when she concentrated on her abilities, or when her shields were down.

Many hundreds of years ago, the Warriors, as the largest organized group in the Night World, took it upon themselves to protect the Lady of the Dead. There was only one born every hundred years. They were valuable and could become very powerful. Therefore more often than not, they were killed, or turned to do evil things in the world. Gwen had been very lucky Viking found her.

As they crossed the parking lot, Gwen barely registered Carter walking toward them. She shut the world out as she closed her last remaining links, trusting Raider to ward off intrusions until she was finished.

As the last link closed, Gwen felt the pulse of power that let her know she was completely shut in. She raised her head and expanded her focus to the men in front of her.

Gwen stepped forward to Raider's right, careful not to touch him. The shield may ward off the Spirit World, but anything in the real world was fair game. She could pick up all sorts of things if the other person did not have mental shields of their own. Viking moved to her right, but stayed slightly to her back. She smiled innocently to the scowling man who stood beside Carter. They had never met before, but Gwen could tell from the way his eyes shot right through her that he already did not like her. Gwen moved her gaze to Carter and gave the Wolf a genuine smile. Inclining her head as she did so, he might not be asking for help as Alpha, but he still deserved her respect.

Carter inclined his head in return; he knew better than to shake her hand at a crime scene, they had made that mistake years ago and Gwen now knew things about Carter he would never want her to.

Carter gestured toward them as he turned to the other man. The gesture was dismissive, showing Gwen that Carter did not particularly like his colleague.

"Captain, this is Ms. Gwen Erwin, our local psychic."

Carter knew what she really was, but never alluded to it as a cop. After all, things like them did not exist in the real world.

"With her are her associates, Raider and Viking. Guys, this is Captain Russell Tate. He is the lead on this case, since the kidnapper started in Pierce County."

Gwen felt for Carter. Cases that crossed county lines were a bear for the cops.

She nodded politely to the Captain. "It is nice to meet you, sir. I hope I can help you."

Captain Tate snarled at her. He looked about sixty, and she would have thought he would have more tact than that.

"You probably can't, but since King County wants to waste its resources and not mine, it's none of my business."

Gwen mentally rolled her eyes. This was going to fun. She dropped her smile and let her eyes go flat as she concentrated all her attention on Tate. She was sick of people like him. They were there for a child, not his ego.

"Mr. Tate."

Gwen purposefully dropped the title and watched both Warriors stiffen; they knew what she was about to do, and didn't agree with it.

"We can do this one of two ways. You can tell me about your kidnapper and the missing child and we can get closer to finding them. Or, we can have a pissing contest and I can scare the crap out of you. Your choice."

There was a flash, just a flash of curiosity and fear in Tate's face before he settled on angry. Not the right move. Before he could say anything, Carter stepped in front of him, drawing Gwen's attention. He might not know what she was gearing up to do, but he had an idea.

"The boy is Michael Anders, age four, and he was playing in the park with his two older sisters: Ann, age ten and Beth, age six. The girls were on the slide, Michael was in the sandbox. By the time they were ready to go, he was gone. That was four-thirty on Wednesday. The toys he played with were gone as well and there was a white rose on the edge of the sandbox, taped down to prevent kids from taking it. It's been a signature left at every crime scene. He wanted us to see it.

"He has a seven-day cycle. Day one: take the kid, always ages four to six. Day four: kill the kid. Day five: cops find the body. There is a two-day gap before it begins again. Michael is the eighth kid, third in King County. There were four in Pierce and one in Snohomish. Peirce was able to find his nest on the last day five, forcing him out. He found a new place before they could track him."

Gwen nodded and tried not to vomit. She could not think about that many dead children. It would weaken her and draw unwanted Spirit World attention.

She took a deep breath before speaking. "I need a picture of the child and the kidnapper, if you have it."

Carter was already prepared; he pulled a small photo from the file he was holding, but did not turn it to face her. "We don't have a photo of the kidnapper, just a general description. He is about five-foot-eight with straw colored, short hair and about sixty pounds overweight. He sometimes wears frameless glasses."

Gwen nodded again as she filed that away. Carter turned the picture so Gwen could see it. He knew her routine well enough to know she would work better if she did not touch the picture. The imprint of all the emotions the distraught family felt would be coating it like tar.

Michael looked small, almost skinny, as he beamed up at her. He had an unruly mop of black hair and squinty brown eyes. Gwen memorized the features. She would have to project the image at the spirits she spoke to and she could not afford to get it wrong.

"Okay." Gwen sighed.

Carter slid the photo away and moved so she could walk by him without touching. Gwen stepped past the group and went into the actual park. As she strode to the children's play area, she removed her middle necklace from under her shirt.

Gwen wore three necklaces at all times. The longest, clearly made for a person larger than her, hit between her breasts. The leather strap was smooth from centuries of wear; the metal circle held an intricate pattern that Gwen had never been able to identify. It was the necklace Viking had given her, and she did not really expect to understand it.

The shortest chain was a simple pointed Celtic cross. The first detail made jokes about her wearing such a young symbol, until they had seen the faith-backed cross protect her. Then it was never mentioned again.

The necklace she removed from her shirt was a metal pendant with the image of a male hand clutching a raised sword. It was the international symbol for the Warriors. The hand was red, which specified America. There were symbols around the outside; Gwen was told it was a spell of protection. Should she ever be in danger, the nearest American Warriors would come running. Under the hand in scrolling letters was her title. The necklace had been a gift from the American King for her eighteenth birthday. When she wore it outside her shirt, the Night World knew who they were taking on if they messed with her.

Stepping onto the rim of the sandbox, Gwen pushed her power through her chain link shield. She swayed as the world slid into view. It did not seem to matter how many times she did it; it stole her balance every time.

She could see spirits floating around with no real purpose, all of whom snapped to attention. They were close enough to feel her presence. Gwen hoped no one became hostile. She opened her arms, lifting them away from her body, and spoke low enough the Spirit World, and Carter, would be the only ones to hear her. Being a Werewolf meant he could hear every word she said, but he never admitted it aloud.

"I am seeking a boy who was taken from this place during the daylight hours, two suns ago."

A sizable majority of the entities moving toward Gwen went back to their business. Most average spirits could not manifest in the daylight.

Three shapes began to move toward her; they were semi-manifesting as two women and a man. Gwen could feel power rolling from them and the hair on her body stood on end. The amount of power they possessed was frightening. She only came across beings this powerful when something was preparing for attack. Gwen stiffened; Raider and Viking might not be able to help her right away from as far back as they were. Panic began to course through her; she would put money on these being the spirits of three dead Magical Practitioners. There was no way Gwen and two Warriors could fight them off and win.

"Viking!" Gwen called in a stage whisper. The Warrior himself would not be able to hear her, but Carter would.

Magical Practitioners or MPs were true witches, humans who could do 'not so human' things. MPs could be good or bad. Gwen did not recognize these three, which meant in life they had not been local. Female MPs were stronger than male MPs; two females together would be trouble.

Gwen began to call up as much of her power as she could. She did not understand why Viking had not reached her yet. There would be only one chance for her to land a hit before they attacked. She would have to pick one to center on and pray she could get a scream out before the other two could do too much damage. Her breathing was shallow and rapid. Luckily, practice made it possible for Gwen to squelch her growing panic.

The three figures hovered about a foot from the ground. They were wisps of white, revealing their shapes. The wisps would dissipate and move, like most strong spirits Gwen encountered. But these three maintained their faces almost perfectly. That was uncommon and unnerving.

They stopped two yards from Gwen. The female in the middle spoke, though spoke is not quite the right word. There was no sound; she just knew what they were saying.

"We mean you no harm. We have been here three days. Waiting for you, Lady of the Dead."

Gwen held back her shudder as warning bells went off in her head. Just because they claimed not to be a threat did not mean it was true.

"We mean you no harm," The spirit repeated with more emphasis this time. *"You have our word. We know the child you seek."*

Gwen knew MPs did not offer their word unless they meant it. Magic hated those who went against an oath. But she had no idea if that fact still held in death. Her muscles relaxed minutely with relief but the adrenaline still flowed through her system.

An image of Michael playing in the sandbox was projected into her head. That should not have been possible with her shielding. These spirit MPs were very powerful. More powerful than most MPs Gwen knew. Reigning in her fear at the possible consequences, she maintained eye contact. Showing fear to the Spirit World could get her attacked. If they said they meant her no harm, odds were it was the truth. That did not mean it was true for other beings. With Viking's necklace, even the most powerful of beings couldn't slip a lie past Gwen. But Gwen had never come across spirit MPs before, and she hoped all the normal rules applied.

"We saw the man take the boy. Are you sure you wish to seek the boy?"

Gwen felt the world go quiet; somehow, her answer would affect more than just her and Michael.

"Why do you ask me this?"

A sense of approval came to her from the spirit MPs. *"We were drawn here by what took the boy. This is no mere man who stole the boy you seek. An old power is behind it. You have no need to involve yourself in this war."*

Viking had told Gwen stories of spirits that spoke to his mother like this but it was the first time she ever come across anything similar.

"What happens to the boy if I walk away?"

"He will die." There was no emotion to those words; it was just a fact and nothing more.

"I can not let that happen."

"Very well. We will help you. Come with us." The three of them turned in unison and began floating toward the far end of the park.

"What about payment?" Gwen knew MPs did not work without payment. She would rather know the payment for their help now than get stuck later.

All three shapes stopped moving. Without facing her, the same woman answered.

"You will suffer payment enough in the coming war. We have no need for payment from you. Next time though, we will ask something of you." They started moving again.

That scared Gwen. Something very bad must be coming if MPs were denying payment. Gwen could not quite suppress her shudder as she stepped off the sandbox and followed the three wispy shapes. A good part of her wanted to turn around and hide behind Viking, as she had done as a child. But if there was a chance to save Michael, then whatever happened was worth it in Gwen's eyes.

She was now betting these MPs had somehow stopped Carter from hearing her call. Part of her yelled that they were far too powerful for her to be alone with, but she dismissed it. The child was more important.

Not wanting to walk beside them, Gwen stayed a pace behind. They were walking farther and farther away from living beings. Gwen tried desperately to hide her nervousness. They passed spirit after spirit; every single one ignored them, and she never experienced that before. These MPs were obviously powerful enough to keep everyone else at bay. Gwen's anxiety grew stronger with that thought and increased the farther they got from safety.

The three MP spirits stopped at the edge of the park. They moved to her left side so that she could see the low fence and the street clearly.

The main female moved her arm, motioning to the street, an image of the kidnapper and Michael dodging traffic as they crossed played in Gwen's head. She knew what he looked like now, the direction he had gone and she watched him slide into a red Ford truck. She memorized the plate before the image vanished. Gwen turned to the spirits to thank them but the female held up her hand.

"Do not thank us. That would put you in our debt. We have a gift for you."

Gwen paused for a moment. Her inner alarms began to ring. Something bad was coming. "What is it?"

"We will open up a door in your head. Unlock some power to give you a fighting chance for what comes ahead. It is your power; you would tap into it eventually, we are merely unleashing it before you are ready. A great boon was given for this to be done. We will give you a chance to call your guards to you so that you will not be prey for beings lurking nearby."

Gwen did not even think. Terror seized her as she wrapped both hands around the Warrior's pendant and mentally screamed for Viking.

The two other spirit MPs placed wispy hands on each of the lead female's shoulders. The female reached out impossibly fast and her hand went through Gwen's head. Gwen let out a scream before feeling herself crumple to the ground and black out from pain.

Gwen came to with a barely tolerable headache and multiple aches informing her that her body held a number of bruises and scratches. She was in her bed and heard a female voice chanting words in an ancient language. As soon as she concentrated on the voice, Gwen recognized it as Sivia.

Sivia was an Immortal Princess, and rumor had it she was promised to the current High King of the Immortal court, though Sivia herself denied it adamantly. Sivia was one of very few Immortal royals to live outside the compound. The princess was well known among the Night World for her healing skills, not physical, but metaphysical. If Gwen's detail called Sivia, then her injuries must have been extensive.

Gwen waited for a long pause in Sivia's chanting to sit herself up, placing her back against headboard. When she opened her eyes, Gwen saw that she and Sivia were the only people in the room.

Sivia kept her brown hair in a shaggy pixie cut, in rebellion against the long hair preferred at the Immortal court. Her petite frame held a layer of lean muscle from picking up various fighting techniques. Her hazel eyes looked at Gwen appraisingly.

"How do you feel?"

"I've got a hell of a headache, minor bumps and bruises, but other than that I seem fine."

Sivia seemed to take that under consideration before sighing. "When I was able to get to you, your shields had been ripped to shreds and you were sending out energy like a neon sign. You were attracting all kinds of attention. You are lucky the Warriors got to you in time and the wards on this building are so strong. A little too lucky, really." Sivia watched Gwen a moment before continuing. "Your Warriors are a bit banged up though, best be nice to them for a bit. Plus, shock waves from things testing the wards won't die down for a day or two, so don't go wandering alone. I've left some loose leaf tea I need you to be drinking for the next three days. I've also left those instructions with Viking because heaven knows he has the best chance of getting you to follow through. It tastes like crap, but drink it anyway and I'll be back to check on you in three days, so I'll know if you've followed my instructions or not." Sivia gave her one more appraising look before standing up and leaving the room.

Gwen had very little time to gather her thoughts before Viking, Raider, and Poet strode in. Raider came in last and shut the door behind them. Poet carried a matching black teapot and mug. Gwen rubbed her face before grabbing the mug Poet held out in front of her. She could already smell the tea, and knew it would be horrible.

Poet smiled down at her as he set the teapot on her bedside table. "Don't worry; I've been put on tea duty. So I'll be making sure you drink the doctor-recommended amount."

Gwen groaned and rolled her eyes. Poet appeared unharmed, but Viking and Raider had scratches and gashes on their arms, necks, and faces. Raider looked as if at some point he had bled from the scalp. It was not the worst condition she had seen them in and they would heal within the next few hours, but it still bothered her. Gwen hated seeing them hurt.

"What happened?"

Raider snorted and folded his arms over his chest. "Shouldn't we be asking you that question?"

Gwen couldn't round up enough emotion to get annoyed. She was too tired.

Viking mirrored Raider's stance; his blond curls had been ripped from the queue he usually had at the nape of his neck. "You called, plain as day. But you somehow managed to call just me. I took off and Raider evaded police questions before following. When I got to you, you were on the ground. I could feel you, like when you were young, no shielding at all. Then beings began to descend. I scooped you up and ran straight here. Raider followed right behind me, fighting things off from behind, which as you know is hard when we cannot see most of the beings coming after us without our pendants on. It isn't as if we had the time to activate them."

Gwen knew that was a lie, at least for Storebror. He could always see the Spirit World, but that was not common knowledge.

"Thankfully we were close enough to the shop. We will probably get some unexpected visitors over the next few days. The new guards are on alert to keep an eye on the wards. As long as they hold, you should be fine."

Gwen sat there staring into the face of the man who had been her protector for past two decades. Viking was telling her if the wards did not hold, things would get messy fast.

Viking cracked his neck but continued to look down at Gwen. "Now, tell me."

Only over the last year or so did Viking allow Poet to be in the room while Gwen discussed spirit events. With one this big, she half expected Viking to kick the other man out.

"I was standing on the sandbox when three spirits of MPs approached me…"

"Whoa, what?" Raider held out his hands in shock.

"Two female, one male. They were Magical Practitioners. I could feel it, but they were spirits."

Gwen watched Poet and Raider exchange shocked looks, but Viking kept his eyes on Gwen. His jaw was clenched; he did not like that news. Not that she blamed him, she had never even heard of such a thing.

"They said they could help me find the boy and led me to the far edge of the park. I need to talk to Carter; I saw the kidnapper and his vehicle. The MPs said they had a gift for me, but it would leave me vulnerable so they gave me a chance to call for help. I called Viking, then one of the MPs reached for me and I fainted."

There was silence in the room for several minutes. All three of them watched her.

Viking's growl drew her attention. "You trusted three spirit MPs? Gwen, think of the possible consequences." He vibrated with frustrated anger.

Gwen couldn't do much more than blink at him; she just did not have a reaction in her. "They gave me their word that they meant me no harm."

"They stripped you of your shields!" The growl grew louder.

"They let me call you first," she countered.

Viking glared down at her, taking deep breaths, but he did not say anything else.

"It did not matter anyway. I called for you, they blocked me. I called your name loud enough for Carter to hear it. Clearly he didn't."

The glare grew to a snarl, but Gwen knew it was not all for her. It had been more than a decade since a being was able to block her from him. The last time, she had needed seven stitches by the time he reached her.

Poet strummed his lower lip with his thumb, an unconscious gesture of his. "I see several holes in that story."

When Gwen did not answer, Viking shifted his weight.

Gretchen S. B.

"Gwen, what did you give to the MPs as payment for their services and this very stupid gift?" Viking sounded more worried than angry about her response.

Gwen took a deep breath. "I didn't, they said it had already been paid for."

The three men exchanged suspicious glances. She didn't blame them. MPs just didn't work like that.

Viking dropped his arms. For a moment, Gwen thought he would accuse her of lying.

"Very well then, Carter is downstairs. He is quite worried about restitution for getting the Lady of the Dead injured. I will send him up to speak with you. Then you will sleep, but I expect you to finish that pot before then." He gave her a meaningful look before he and Raider left the room.

"You know there can't be restitution, I was working with the police, not the Pack," Gwen shouted after them.

She heard Viking chuckle from the hallway. "I know, but that has not dawned on Carter yet."

In that moment she worried Viking might be taking his anger out on Carter. Gwen chugged half the cup down and almost gagged before looking at Poet. He was watching her with a worried expression.

"None of us like it that you keep such things to yourself. How are we to help you if you become so secretive?"

Gwen did not intend to share more about her developing powers. Some things she preferred to keep to herself, and she wanted privacy wherever she could get it. Though how Poet knew she was holding back, Gwen didn't know. She emptied the mug before answering him.

"I believe all of you are rather secretive as well. I never keep anything back that could get us hurt. Besides, you and I both know you do not always mention when you sense trouble."

Poet was something of a bloodhound when it came to danger. He could sense it coming far in advance; mostly he kept it to himself unless he deemed the problem big enough.

Poet poured more tea into the mug and simply watched her until Carter came into the room, closely followed by Viking.

Carter was looking her over, face full of concern. "How are you, Gwen?"

Gwen smiled; Carter could be a real softie. "I'm fine. I have a vehicle and plate number for you."

That got his attention. Carter's back straightened and he slowly pulled out his notebook. "And how did you manage that?"

Gwen knew he did not mean anything by his words. She just was not usually that precise. "You don't want to know, Carter."

He raised both eyebrows. "I do, actually, but my curiosity isn't important."

Gwen nodded. "It was a red Ford truck with Washington plates." She rattled off the number. "Your kidnapper, he isn't fat. I think he's lost weight since he left Peirce County." Gwen took a deep breath; this next part was going to be tricky. "Alpha Tuckman…"

Carter's head slowly came up and his wary eyes met hers. She purposefully used his title to let him know she was not talking to him as a cop.

"Yes, Lady of the Dead." His voice was cold and flat.

Gwen could see both Viking and Poet straighten.

"My sources have informed me there is a war coming, if it has not started already. I believe you would appreciate the warning. The man the police are searching for is harboring something darker and stronger than himself." She felt it coming off the vision the MPs gave her; something very dangerous was connected to this kidnapper. It was like a Spirit World tick, sucking energy off the man. Gwen felt the Wolves had a right to know. Odds were if she didn't tell him, the Warriors would not think to.

Carter watched her for several beats. "You're sure of this?"

Gwen nodded.

Carter bowed low before her. "I thank thee, Lady, for the warning. I will be sure to let our people know."

"Thank you."

Without another word, Carter walked from her room. Gwen had no doubt that by dawn, all of the Seattle Night World, if not the entire state, would be on the alert.

Viking looked down at her from the foot of the bed. "What is this about a war?"

She could sense his aggravation with her for not sharing that sooner.

Gwen shrugged as she downed the last of the wretched tea. "I don't know. They just said that there was a coming war."

Viking watched her as if waiting for more, before signaling to Poet to leave. "I need to tell the king all this. It is not normal Night World behavior. Sleep, and tomorrow I will let you know what he says." Then he followed Poet from the room.

It was not long before full exhaustion hit Gwen and dragged her to sleep. But before exhaustion took her completely she could feel beings outside rippling and testing the wards. Nothing powerful enough to get through, just strong enough for her to notice with her shields as shredded as they were. Gwen's groggy mind wondered if this would be the last full night's sleep she would be getting in a while. Then she made a note to call Lucia to have the MP reinforce the wards again.

Chapter 2

"What exactly do you mean by war?" Cesar asked his youngest general through the phone.

Viking was not one prone to exaggeration, so when the man said the Lady of the Dead had been told of a war, Cesar immediately began maneuvering America's Warriors in his head. Being the end of the country, the west coast held the highest Night World population in the North American Kingdom, so logistically it could be a nightmare.

"She said she doesn't know. She received the information from the spirits of three MPs."

That also worried Cesar. MPs, more than any others in the Night World, went out of their way to make sure they moved on after death, to ensure others could not use their magic. MPs working from the Spirit World was an idea he had only distantly heard about. He had been getting word of more hostile activity in western Washington, but as long as it did not reach the Lady of the Dead, Cesar had not seen reason to worry. The rumor of war and the Lady of the Dead warranted his personal involvement.

"I will come check into it myself."

Cesar knew the protest was coming before he heard Viking make it.

"No, Cesar. That's not necessary, and if there is someone about to start a war, our king should not be in the thick of it."

Cesar knew Viking's intentions were good, but the comment still offended him. He had never turned from a fight in his life.

"Do not be insulting, Viking. I will come, but I agree, the king will not be there. Few know what I look like; no one on the detail but you. I will come under a different guise and look into this. If someone is trying to start a war with us, I want to squash it personally."

———————————

Cesar took the first flight out to Seattle from Montana. Only his three generals knew where he really was. As far as his Warriors were concerned, he was in Montana and the rest of the Night World did not have a clue. This was the way he liked it. It gave him an advantage over others.

He was now standing in the shadows in front of the penthouse apartment belonging to the Lady of the Dead. She owned the five-story building just outside Bellevue. The bookstore store and café took up the bottom floor while the other four floors were remodeled into apartments for her and her detail. Though Cesar had sent her the money to buy and renovate the building four years before, he had never been here. All he knew was that the business was successful enough that she had already paid back more than a third of it. Cesar had never met the current Lady of the Dead, but he made sure to be informed about her. From information the details brought back and the reports from Raider and Viking, Cesar had a pretty good image of young Gwen Erwin.

After discreetly making his way into the building, his decision to come himself was affirmed. Cesar activated his Warrior pendant prior to entering the building. It let him get a glimpse of the Spirit World around him. As he walked up, he was surprised by the sheer volume of beings pounding against the very strong wards around the building. Viking assured him such attacks would die down after a few days, but Cesar felt the other man understated things.

He decided to appear to Gwen first, claiming to have been sent by the king to look into matters on the coast. Cesar did not foresee matters taking more than a few days and then he could go back to his Montana solitude.

The elevator opened and for a moment, Cesar forgot to breathe. She was beautiful. Her auburn hair hung straight around a slightly rounded face with a small pointed chin. Her eyes resembled a cat's, he was sure he had never seen irises so pale. She was not petite but still delicate, and her lower lip had a natural pout. She appeared young and innocent.

Cesar understood why so many of the warriors sent to her detail commented on her appeal. She was a Warrior's dream, small and crying out for protection, but everyone knew she would fight right beside them.

She sensed his presence and the peace dropped from her face. She scanned the hall. He saw the fire in her eyes, and her right hand eased to her thigh. Cesar knew, thanks to Raider, that she kept a long knife Viking had given her years ago strapped to her leg. The image brought a spike of lust. Cesar would relish the chance to disarm her. His own thoughts surprised him. The Lady of the Dead was off limits.

"I know you're there. Come out where I can see you." She swept the hall looking for him.

Cesar had not become king without learning a few tricks, and hiding himself in plain sight was one of them, it helped that the only light was from the two windows and the elevator. Sighing, he stepped forward, knowing the movement of his trench coat would get her attention.

"Forgive me, my lady. The king sent me. After the news of your latest trouble he wanted a less biased opinion on the matter."

Cesar felt the delicate brush of her power feeling him out. It was not any stronger than a light spring breeze, but he knew if he was deemed a threat that breeze would become a wind storm.

"Prove it."

He held back his smile of approval as he held out his right hand to show her his palm. All Warriors had their symbol tattooed to their right palm; it was the easiest way of identifying each other from a distance.

She watched him skeptically for a moment then stepped off the elevator. "Do you have a name?"

The Lady of the Dead crossed in front of him to get to her door. He reminded himself could not sleep with her. He found out long ago that as king, any woman he took to bed was put in harm's way, so he refrained. It was hell, but he did not want innocents in danger. Not to mention she was spoken for; several men in the details reported stories of her and Poet's relationship.

"Augustus." The name flew out of his mouth. Why had he given her his birth name? He had not intended to, but it slipped out.

She paused with her key in her door and looked up at him. "As in Cesar?"

Cesar was surprised she made the connection, most beings her age did not. "Yes, but I would prefer you call me August. I am not terribly fond of the man I was named after." Where had that come from? No one had ever called him August in his life.

She nodded and unlocked the door. "Fair enough, I'll call you August if you call me Gwen."

Cesar loved the way she said his name. The last part hissed out if her mouth. He could see why Poet liked her so much; with the other man's affinity for snakes, it was no wonder the two were involved.

Gwen let them both in and motioned to her stainless steel kitchen as she relocked the door. "Help yourself. It's heavy on fruit and fish but there is some Monk's alcohol in the fridge."

Cesar was surprised by that. Warriors were red meat eaters. He expected that to have rubbed off on her. He was also not sure why she would have Monk's alcohol in her house. The idea was appalling. Warrior bodies did not respond to normal alcohol. Monk, one of the Warriors out of Europe, created his version several centuries ago; it could knock a Warrior out of his chair. For a human, it could kill.

"Why do you keep Monk's Poison in your home?"

She turned around and gave him a look that said he was asking a stupid question. "Think of whom I live with. It would be rude of me to not have it in supply. Plus, Monk gives me a discount on account of the title. We serve it at the bar downstairs too. There is almost every other type of booze in the pantry too, if you would prefer that. I know some of you Romans prefer wine." Gwen crinkled her nose delicately; apparently she didn't enjoy wine anymore than he did.

Cesar almost did not believe it. He walked over to the pantry and opened it up. He was appalled by the amount of human alcohol. How could Viking let a young woman of status possess that much liquor? He had been told Viking seemed to have a way with Gwen no one understood. What else were they letting her do? Rules were looser out here than Cesar realized. He was going to have to fix that.

"If you didn't care for Augustus, why not go by something else entirely? You seem a bit old to still go by your birth name."

He knew her question was driven by polite curiosity and had been warned she asked many questions, but for some reason her calling him old made Cesar bristle. He closed the pantry and saw her sitting in one of the two large red leather chairs in her living room. The thing engulfed her. Why did a small woman need furniture that big? Cesar strode across the room, removed his coat and placed it on the back of the chair across from her.

"I do, the others will know me as Roman." It felt better to be back on course. Roman was Cesar's right hand man, his highest general and best friend since they were boys. They were similar enough in looks that the lie could be convincing.

Gwen was giving him an appraising look. Something about it bothered him. It was as if she saw more than he wanted her to, but he knew her powers were not that developed.

"How bad things must be," was all she said.

Cesar raised an eyebrow. "I beg your pardon."

Gwen's left arm came up and began stroking something under her sweater. It was an absent gesture. Cesar's guess was that she stroked her Warrior pendant.

"How bad things must be for the king to send his right hand to us."

Cesar could not help his surprise. She knew who Roman was. He knew she had never met the other man, but he had not expected her to know Warrior hierarchy.

"Viking shares a lot with you."

She actually snorted. "Not about that he doesn't. I'm more cunning than I look, apparently."

There was a pounding knock at the door. Cesar had heard the footfalls come off the elevator, but Gwen simply got up and went to the door as if expecting it. Cesar knew he was missing something and he did not like it. As he came around the front of the chair, Viking walked through the open door and Gwen shut it behind him.

While her back was turned, Viking bowed his head to Cesar in respect.

"Storebror, do you know who this man is?"

Cesar was shocked; somehow, she had called Viking to come check him out. He was unaware she was able to do that. If he had not told Viking his plan, Cesar's cover would be blown.

Gwen came to stand beside her guardian and looked up into his face. Was she looking for a clue in Viking's expression? Cesar began to regret not coming out here sooner. The Lady of the Dead was a precious person to Warriors the world over. He had been too lax on this. She was the first of her kind born in North America. Other leaders had clamored to move her to the old world; Cesar barely managed to keep her.

Viking's expression was blank but softened when he looked down at Gwen. "That would be Roman. Our king's right hand man. He answered my call yesterday."

Cesar noticed Viking was careful to lie as little as possible. He had been taken the call. He always took calls from his generals personally.

Gwen looked from Viking to Cesar. "I see. He needs a place to sleep. Someone needs to volunteer to be his sleeping buddy."

Viking jumped in. "He will stay with me. Since only three of us have presentable apartments, and Poet, as usual, has company."

That threw Cesar; he heard Poet and Gwen had been a couple since she was twenty-one. How could the Lady of the Dead allow Poet to have other women?

He felt anger on her behalf, but did not show it. "There is no need. I will sleep here."

Gwen looked at him in shock and Viking looked every bit a protective father.

Before either could speak, Cesar continued. "Do not worry. I am merely to stay as close to you as possible while Viking and or Raider are not around. If that means sleeping on the couch, so be it."

Viking was ready to argue, but Gwen snorted and gained both their attention. "If you really want to sleep on the couch, that's fine, but I have two spare bedrooms that might be better."

Cesar nodded his thanks and Gwen headed down the left hallway, presumably to ready a room.

Viking was giving him a murderous look Cesar was not sure he'd ever seen from the other man outside of battle. If this was any other situation, Cesar would have disciplined his young general for insolence, but he found Viking's over-protectiveness more amusing than anything else.

When he spoke, his jaw was completely clenched. "I will go round you up some clothing."

Before Cesar could thank Viking and let him know he'd brought a duffel bag with him, the other man was slamming the door.

Cesar made his way down the hall after Gwen. He had been in houses smaller than this apartment. He found her exiting a bedroom door only to motion him to follow her into a room across the hall.

It turned out to be a bathroom. When he stepped into the doorway, she opened the mirrored cabinet.

"In here there are spare toiletries, and there is guest soap and shampoo in the shower."

Then she brushed past him and headed back into the room she exited earlier. Cesar followed her, trying to process this group's dynamic. It was clear Viking did not want him here, especially so close to Gwen. She however, did not seem phased as she played the proper hostess. When he entered the bedroom, Cesar was surprised to find that he liked it. The room had been done in forest greens and browns. He was surprised by the lack of femininity in the apartment as a whole.

"Okay, this is where you'll crash."

"Thank you. Your flexibility is much appreciated."

Gwen snorted again and looked up at him with her hands on her hips. For the first time, her eyes held anger. "I don't have much of a choice, do I? I mean, my entire life I have to make concessions for Warriors." She sighed and rubbed the bridge of her nose. "I'm sorry. That was unnecessary."

Cesar's need to comfort her was overwhelming, but he had no idea how. Like most Warriors, Cesar had very little contact with women. The only woman he actually knew was Arianna, his third general's wife, and it had taken him almost a century to get used to the daughter of a Russian fur trader and an Indian woman.

Gwen's hand dropped and her face was calm again. "Never mind, it's just hard to be who I am in this century. Don't mind Viking, he's my older brother, my protector, and my mentor. We are the most important person in each other's lives. So of course, he hates men. He'll get over it."

She spoke of Viking with more love and affection than Cesar expected and smiled as she finished. He could see why Viking would give her allowances. She was clearly unhappy and Viking wanted things to be as easy on her as possible. Other than the few times when she was younger and would disappear for an afternoon, there was never a report stating her unhappiness.

Cesar did not quite want her to leave on such a sad note, so he said the first thing that came to him. "I was led to believe you and Poet were a couple?" He cursed himself afterward. That would only come across as nosy or a come on.

Luckily, Gwen did not seem to see it as either. She stopped walking and rolled her eyes, clearly holding back a laugh.

Gretchen S. B.

"Everyone in the Night World thinks that except me, Raider, Viking, and Poet. I have a sneaking suspicion Poet finds it funny or it's revenge for when I said I had no interest in sleeping with him. Either way it's a rumor no one cares enough about to squash." She smiled before heading down the hall.

Cesar was surprised at the relief he felt. He knew he could not sleep with her, but was glad no one else was either. Not long after, Viking appeared silently, handing him nightclothes and clothes for the following day. Cesar did not bother mentioning he brought three days of clothing with him.

Chapter 3

Gwen had not slept well. There was someone she didn't know sleeping in one of her guest rooms, which bothered her enough. To top it off, the guy was very attractive.

He had smooth black hair he kept back in a queue at the nape of his neck, Gwen was pretty sure it was long enough to brush his shoulders. His brown eyes were almost black. August possessed one of those natural tans that screamed Mediterranean heritage. His lips were a little thin, but Gwen never liked thick lips on men. He was a few inches shorter than Storebror, so maybe six foot. August appeared to be thick and chiseled.

Gwen shook her head. She could not be thinking about him again. She needed to be thinking about the dreams she was having. The last two nights she dreamed about the woman she called Oracle.

Oracle appeared in Gwen's dreams on and off since she was a child. She instructed Gwen on how to use her powers as they developed. Gwen never told anyone about Oracle; something about the older woman bred secrecy. Not that Oracle asked Gwen to keep quiet, just to use discretion.

Oracle was a woman in her mid-forties. She had riotously curly blond hair and clear blue eyes. Oracle always wore a blue dress that matched her eyes. When Gwen was young, she asked Oracle how old she was. The woman chuckled and said such things were unimportant.

The last two nights, though, Oracle had been agitated. She kept telling Gwen that these new abilities needed to be harnessed and soon, but Gwen couldn't concentrate. Oracle had been almost furious when Gwen woke up the third and final time. It was hard to do any kind of training when she kept waking up in the middle of it.

So, Gwen got up, showered and now made a pot of coffee. The world could not function without coffee. It was six a.m. and still pitch black outside, but February did that. Gwen was rarely up this early. She was usually in the store at nine or ten and stayed until about seven, unless she had a booking elsewhere.

Much to Viking's chagrin, Gwen gave readings to customers and sometimes was invited to be the entertainment at parties. She was the most prominent psychic in the Northwest. She loved it. That was the only reason Viking did not fight her about it. Tonight she had a bachelorette party to go to. She was to have a Warrior escort with her at all times. With it being a party full of drinking women, there had been arguments on who would go with her. Gwen knew better than to get involved with fights like that.

She poured a cup of blissfully black coffee and sat at her cherry wood kitchen table. She was surprised when a few minutes later, a fully showered and dressed August walked into the main room.

Gwen found him distractingly hot enough she was grateful she hadn't spilled coffee all over herself.

"Is that all you will be having for breakfast?"

The question was a little condescending and Gwen straightened. "Of course not, but coffee comes first."

He watched her a moment longer before opening her fridge and grabbing the carton of orange juice from the door. He rummaged around until he found her cups then had the gall to pour two glasses.

"So it is true what they say about Washingtonians, that you live on your coffee." He set the carton on the counter and came to sit across the table but not before setting one of the glasses in front of her.

Gwen glared at it before glaring at August's calm face. "I am fully capable of getting my own food."

He smirked at her and Gwen felt a spike of lust. "Of course you are. Perhaps I was just being gentlemanly."

She continued to glare at him as she finished her coffee then got up to grab breakfast. Gwen was not big on food this early in the morning so she opted for a smoothie instead. On her weekends, she made a big batch of smoothie so she could eat it throughout the week. It was all fresh fruit and veggies with the protein powder Storebror demanded she add in.

She reached into her fridge and grabbed two sixteen-ounce re-sealable containers. Popping both tops, she set one in front of August and one where she had been sitting before refilling her coffee.

As she sat back down, she saw August looking at her with amused interest. "This is just liquefied fruit. Is this and coffee all you consume in the mornings?"

Gwen laughed. "Usually yes. I'm not much for mornings and there is a vitamin-protein powder in there so your caveman nutritional needs will be taken care of." She took a long drink from her smoothie. It was a good batch this week, heavy on peaches and mangoes. As she set her glass down, she saw August was watching her with a smile.

"What?"

He gave a chuckle before taking a sip. "You obviously enjoy the taste quite a bit. It was evident on your face."

Gwen felt herself blush, reached for her orange juice and drained the glass. She wasn't sure how to respond. The rest of their meal was silent and Gwen fought to avoid looking at the attractive man across from her. She just was not used to having men that attractive sitting across her kitchen table. If he were anything other than a Warrior, she would be flirting her butt off.

After she finished, she brought everything to the sink and rinsed it. When she turned to grab a travel mug August was right there holding his own dishes. Gwen jumped.

He appeared just as startled but did not move. "My apologies, I was simply waiting until you were done at the sink."

When he still did not move, Gwen took a step back so he could stand at the sink. She then reached around him and watched his back tense. Interesting, he did not like people at his back. There was no other indication that it bothered him. Filing that away for later, Gwen grabbed the closest travel mug from the cabinet and walked to the coffee pot to fill it.

"Do you truly drink an entire pot by yourself? Every day?" He sounded astonished.

Gwen looked over her shoulder as she clicked the machine off. August was leaning against the sink watching her. She screwed on the lid and turned to face him.

"It was half a pot actually, but yes."

He just looked at her in surprise until she started laughing, then his face blanked.

"I'm sorry, but that's just not as uncommon as you seem to think it is." After a pause, she could not tell what he was thinking so she changed the subject instead. "I'm going downstairs to the store. You are more than welcome to stay up here if you like."

August folded his arms and looked at her sternly. "I am to stay with you."

Gwen just rolled her eyes. "All right then, let's head out." Without waiting for him, Gwen headed for the front door.

As they went downstairs, Gwen went over her mental to-do list. No events were in the store today. Luckily, Lucia was able to stop by last night to reinforce the wards, and even she was surprised by the number of beings hanging around outside. Gwen sincerely hoped she could manage to avoid Poet today. She couldn't handle any more of Sivia's wretched tea. He had tracked her down several times yesterday to watch her drink the entire pot. Poet was usually her partner in crime, so unfortunately he knew all her hiding places. Putting him on tea duty was genius of Storebror.

Gwen sighed. Her reading schedule was quite full today and there was inventory to get done. Maybe she would get lucky. She snorted to herself as they walked through the door separating the staircase from the main floor. There was no way she could outmaneuver Poet and she knew it.

Resigned, she pointed to the two doors across the hallway from where they stood. "The door right in front of us is the lounge, you are free to hang out there if you want. The door next to it is the office. There are three computers, each on a separate desk. You can also kill time in there today."

August blinked down at her. "I am to stay near you if one of your three main guards are not around. I am going where you go."

Of course he is, Gwen thought. If nothing else Warriors were their sense of duty. She would be lucky if he didn't feel the need to sit in on her readings today. Sighing, Gwen continued to walk down the hall to the front of store.

"All right then, just try not to be too suspicious about it. I don't want customers getting unnerved by my six foot shadow."

"Noted." There was no hint of humor in his voice.

Gwen was tempted to comment but held her tongue when she saw how long the espresso line was. Without any warning to August, she darted across the room to pitch in during the morning rush.

Chapter 4

Cesar had been pleasantly surprised by the store. It was open twenty-four hours a day and from what he gathered from conversations he overheard, this was one of the two main Night World locations in the state. He was glad his people created a safe place for others to go. From the steady stream of customers throughout the morning, he gathered it wasn't just the Night World that found the store a haven.

There was both a bookstore and a café. Much to his surprise, Gwen and two human psychics performed fortune telling for customers in private rooms toward the back of the bookstore. At first he would have followed her in, but the look she gave him over her shoulder told him he did not want to have that particular fight. So instead he stayed in the back of the store

He saw several Weres of various flavors, a gang of Warriors still in their first life, and a female MP who put a book on reserve. A few Reoccurring Immortals came in for brunch. There was never less than a dozen customers in the store, not counting those in the café.

Gwen introduced Cesar to the staff when they came down a little after six a.m. The café had a line out the door and three frantic employees filling orders. One of the females and the male were twin Werehawks, with the usual names of Skye and Meadow. They were both in their first year of college, which made them impossibly young. The third was a Reoccurring Immortal in graduate school named Lexa. He hadn't asked her what she was doing there.

Reoccurring Immortals were beings who were reborn over and over and every puberty they remembered every past life they had ever lived. Reoccurring Immortals tended to reincarnate in the same social circle over and over, mostly with others of their kind. These circles were known as families. It was very strange to see one alone.

Manning the bookstore were two young Werewolves in their early twenties. The taller of the two, Kern, was very quiet. Cesar grew to appreciate that as he realized how chatty Walker, the other Wolf, was. Cesar spent a good deal of time avoiding conversation with the second pup. Gwen seemed to find that hilarious.

Gretchen S. B.

At nine a.m., Poet came in to relieve Kern. Cesar found himself wishing it had been the other Wolf. Poet set himself up at the register before turning to stare directly at Cesar. It was eerie. The two men had met once in the early 1700s when Poet pledged allegiance to Cesar. Cesar was hoping the other man's memory was not that good.

Poet tilted his head and lifted his right palm in Warrior greeting, showing Cesar his tattoo. Cesar raised his palm in a matching gesture. It had been a long time since he greeted anyone in this manner. As king, only other kings would greet him as an equal, but since no one was to know his true identity, Cesar faked it.

Lowering his hand, Cesar made his way to the register. Poet appeared to be assessing Cesar as he approached. He stopped on the other side of the counter but before he could introduce himself, Poet grinned.

"So you're the general causing all the fuss upstairs. You put both Viking and Raider in quite a mood with your sleeping arrangements, mostly Viking. I imagine he'd like your head. I am Poet by the way."

He grinned wider and Cesar saw the other man's sharpened eye teeth.

Cesar raised an eyebrow; he did not remember Poet being this easygoing. "Should I have slept outside her door? I have my orders." Cesar felt his interest increase as Poet laughed.

"No, not at all. I mean sure they'd be less upset, but Gwen wouldn't have stood for it. She would have put you in an extra room anyway."

Cesar nodded. That was good to know. "You do not appear upset. Are you not her lover?" He knew the answer but he wanted to hear Poet's response.

He was not disappointed as Poet let out a melodious laugh. "Oh excellent, word has gotten around, has it? That has to be the highlight of my week, thank you." Then he lowered his voice and some of the mirth left his tone. "No, we are not, but if ever asked in public, I always confirm. She does not need young Warriors jockeying for her affection. Nor do I need the headache Viking would cause should such a thing ever happen. She gets to date nice normal boys her age, who usually run off after meeting Viking anyway."

Cesar smiled. He was pretty sure that scenario had not occurred to any of the others. "I'll keep it to myself."

Poet saluted him before turning a charming smile on a gaggle of middle-aged women wanting to pay for their items. Cesar shook his head at the women's unanimous response to Poet's attention before walking away from the counter.

Viking, Raider, and two other Warriors came down to the store before noon. Viking and Raider ignored him, but the two younger men glanced at him with great interest before walking around to discreetly check the building's wards. Cesar inwardly smiled at the uproar he'd caused.

At about noon Gwen came out of a reading and Walker yelled across the store. "LUNCH ORDERS!"

Several patrons jumped and Gwen rolled her eyes. "Must you do that so loud?" She only spoke loud enough for those with supernatural hearing to catch it.

Walker actually looked sheepishly at her from where he was across the room talking to a pretty, young female Werewolf.

Gwen came to stand next to Cesar and waited until he was looking down at her to speak. "Two days a week, we send Walker out at the end of his shift to get food for the employees. I don't know where he's going, but you might want to go with him to pick your food."

Cesar cringed at the thought of going anywhere with that talkative puppy. It must have shown on his face because Gwen laughed.

"All right, all right, scratch that."

She made eye contact with the boy and he headed toward them. When Walker finished scribbling on his notepad he looked up expectantly.

Gwen smiled at him. "Where are you going today?"

"Piggilio's is celebrating his thirtieth anniversary, so he's discounting orders today and tomorrow."

Gwen made a noise Cesar couldn't decipher. Her hand was up to her mouth and her expression was a happy shock. "Oh that's great! Congratulate him for me and ask what we can do for him to celebrate."

Gretchen S. B.

Walker bobbed his head. "Will do, boss."

Cesar did not quite understand all that but set it aside as Gwen turned to him. "Piggilio's is a deli farther down the block. He's one of the best I've ever seen. So any of your deli basics apply, plus some Italian and French specialties." Then she turned back to Walker. "Full muffilata unless there's gumbo left, please."

Walker wrote it down, then turned to Cesar.

Cesar had no idea what to order, each deli had different strengths and without going he didn't have a clue. "I'll just have the same."

Walker looked surprised a moment before walking away.

Cesar's curiosity got the better of him. "Was that wrong?"

Gwen shook her head and smiled. "No at all. Piggilio makes his gumbo very spicy. I'm the only one here that really orders it."

"Why is that?"

She shrugged. "I grew up on Creole food. My Granny is from southern Louisiana and she lived with us when I was growing up. I guess everyone else is afraid to try it." Her eyes had wandered with that last sentence. "And my noon is here. Look, you should talk to Storebror about tonight. If you're going to be my shadow, you're going to have to run it by him. He's the one with the plan." Then she walked away to greet a middle-aged woman who dripped with money.

It did not take long to track down Viking. Both he and Raider were sitting at a tall circular table in the cafe with coffee cups in front of them. Neither looked happy to have Cesar approaching them.

He didn't give them a chance to speak. "I was told to speak with you about what Gwen was doing tonight." He lifted his eyebrow in question.

Raider groaned and cursed. "I forgot about the party."

Viking frowned further. "I had not." He turned back to Cesar. "She is using her fortune telling skills at a bachelorette party tonight." The other man did not sound thrilled. Cesar didn't blame him, it sounded horrible.

"What are the odds she would cancel such a thing?"

"None." Both men answered at once.

Cesar looked at Viking. "And who goes with her on such...?" He couldn't quite find an appropriate word.

Viking and Raider exchanged looks. "Usually one of us and one of the other guys. They love the idea of drunk women."

"And you do not?"

"Not particularly. Party duty means costumes. Raider and I do not do costumes."

Cesar was appalled. Grown Warriors in costume. "Why must you wear costumes?"

Raider shrugged. "It's a gimmick. Gwen figured it would make more money for us. She was right, we make a hell of a lot more."

Cesar grimaced. "Why do you let her do such things?" Cesar did not like Gwen parading herself around for customers and police. Viking had let his protection become way too lax.

Viking's eyes flashed momentarily, but he knew better than to snap at Cesar. "I would never let harm come to her. She is entitled to live her life as she sees fit, within the confines fate built for her."

His general would not back down, Cesar knew it. The man had been his own leader far too long. That needed to be addressed later. Cesar put his mind to the topic at hand, as much as he hated the idea. "I will be more than willing to replace one of you, since Raider and I are about the same size."

Both men exchanged looks, neither wanted to wear costumes, but neither wanted Gwen without one of them either.

Viking looked back at him. "Then you will take Poet with you."

Cesar nodded. "Agreed."

Viking nodded. "She will need to be there at seven, so be ready at six and Raider will help with your costume."

Cesar inclined his head before walking back into the bookstore. He needed to put more thought into how to rein in this unruly part of him kingdom.

The afternoon passed slowly until Cesar was roped into helping a young pregnant Panther restock and count inventory. The Panther was heavily pregnant and very vocal of her appreciation. Sissy was pleasant and easier to talk to than Cesar expected. It was her first child and she was understandably nervous considering the father was a Werewolf. That made the child a Shapeshifter instead of a true Were.

Shapeshifters could be more powerful in many ways than their Were cousins. They changed into any of the animals in their lineage. However, they were very unstable. They didn't have just one animal half to contend with. Every Shapeshifter Cesar met had been crazy. They were universally not trusted and for centuries killed almost on sight. A Shapeshifter child was still something Weres everywhere feared.

Fifteen years ago, a mercenary Wolf started an agency to police Shapeshifters. He had two Shapeshifter sons and knew the struggles they faced. He hired Shapeshifters as bounty hunters to police their own kind. It worked so well that the genocide stopped in most countries and their services now included all Night World beings.

When six rolled around, Raider came to grab him and instructed another employee to help Sissy. They walked silently up to the fourth floor where Raider, Viking, and Poet each had an apartment. As they stepped off the elevator, Poet was leaving his apartment. Cesar got a look at what he would be wearing and groaned.

Gold arm bands went from Poet's wrist to elbow and there was a matching torc around his neck. His hair was down and he had outlined his eyes in kohl and had a diamond in his nose. The only clothing he wore was gold banded, black, loose pants. Poet looked like he'd stepped out of an Arabian fantasy book.

At his groan, Raider snorted. "Yeah, I don't envy you. But at least you don't have to wear the make-up. Poet, where are you going?"

Poet grinned at them before stepping into the elevator and pressing a button. "To help tie up my mistress." Then the doors closed on his grinning face.

Raider scrubbed at his own face before unlocking his door.

Cesar seemed the only one bothered by Poet's comment. "Tying her up?"

Raider dropped his keys on the counter before opening a closet door and rummaging. "Yeah, the party tonight is for a local socialite, lots of money and such. The theme is Arabian Nights, and we happen to have costumes for that. Gwen's outfit, though, is a two-person job. The top is one step up from a glorified sash and oddly enough Poet claims to have experience with that kind of thing." Raider pulled out a dry cleaning bag and handed it to Cesar. "Bathroom is the first door on the right."

It didn't take Cesar long to change, since there wasn't much to the outfit. Looking at himself in the mirror Cesar felt like a romance novel cover. Rolling his eyes, he grabbed the clothes he had been wearing off the counter and headed back to the front of the apartment.

Raider had a beer in his hand and was leaning against his kitchen counter. "Just leave the clothes, I'll take care of them. You can head downstairs. Gwen and Poet shouldn't be too much longer."

As he waited for Poet and Gwen, Cesar set up his game plan. He had an idea of how things ran here but he wasn't any closer to finding out what was going on that would be big enough to cause a war.

When Gwen followed Poet into the room, Cesar's mind went blank and he couldn't quite remember why sleeping with her was a bad idea.

Her auburn hair was in cascading curls, her eyes were lined similarly to Poet's, and her lips were a bright red. The cloth posing as a top was the same black fabric as his pants. The bodice hugged her generous breasts, then formed an X below them and must have crossed in back because the two thick strips came around to cross again under her navel and over the top of a matching thin, flowing, full length skirt. Her clothing had gold trim, the same as he and Poet. She had a diamond stud in her nose and one in her navel. There were several bangles on her wrists, and she was lifting the skirt as she walked, which showed off bangles on her ankles as well. Her right arm had an arm band shaped like a golden snake coiled to strike. Golden hoops hung from her ears and the upper section of her left ear had a gold band running through it.

Cesar had not noticed those piercings before. Part of him wanted to frown on the modern liberties she had taken with her body. The bigger part of him was too turned on to work up any real complaint. She was breathtakingly exotic. Which of course was her point.

"All right, he's here. To the van." She left without waiting for a response.

At Gwen's words, Cesar snapped out of his stupor. Poet's smirk told Cesar the other man saw his reaction. It also told him he wasn't the first to react so strongly to Gwen's costume. Neither of them spoke as they followed her out. Cesar was grateful, he did not particularly want Poet teasing him all night on top of having to watch Gwen's enticingly swaying hips.

Chapter 5

Gwen had not expected August to handle himself so well. He didn't seem to enjoy the drunk women hitting on him all night and discouraged several from groping him but he hadn't been rude. August even did better than Raider usually did. Gwen was definitely going to tease her friend about that later. August was a distraction at best in the costume he wore. Poet looked good, and fit the part perfectly, but something about August without his shirt on set Gwen's libido buzzing. She was grateful every time she could use one of the hanging curtains to block her view. The sight of him made it hard to concentrate.

Now, all she wanted was to sit on her balcony with some mint tea and take in the night. It was the first day of the full moon, which meant Gwen was drawn outside. Only Viking knew that for some reason the full moon called to Gwen. When the moon was full, Gwen was at her strongest. She could draw upon what seemed like a bottomless well of energy. At the same time, it could make her drunk with power, and an easy target. Viking made a habit of sleeping at her place, or vice versa, on nights with a full moon. But as she stepped off the elevator, Viking was strangely absent. Did Viking think August's presence was enough?

Neither of them said anything as she unlocked the door. When he walked down the hall toward the room he was staying in, Gwen felt marginally slighted; he was extremely attractive without a shirt after all.

Gwen filled her steel tea kettle and walked back to her room to change. The only real thought driving her was to get outside under the moon. To breathe in and bathe in all that natural power.

By the time she had changed, and removed her makeup and jewelry, she could hear the kettle beginning to whistle. She jogged into the kitchen to remove the kettle, not wanting to disturb August with the noise. She softly hummed to herself as she poured the water over the tea bag and put the kettle on the cooling burner.

She had barely curled into one of her black leather balcony chairs when August stepped out and sat down beside her. Gwen glanced at him momentarily; she was a little bothered that he was interrupting her alone time, but he didn't seem interested in her in the slightest. They both sat there in silence for at least ten minutes before he finally spoke.

"I was charged with watching a Lady of the Dead once, during the 1600s, for a year. Not long before I was exiled to North America. She had an affinity to the full moon as well. She said it sang to her. That no matter what she was doing, the full moon would always have her attention. Is this true for you?" August turned and looked at her for the first time since walking onto the balcony.

"Yes...not exactly the same, but similar."

"It makes you feel stronger."

"Yes, how can you tell?"

August shrugged. "The way you hold yourself, the energy around you. Your eyes seem more vivid."

Gwen wasn't sure how to respond to that, so she didn't. Instead she lowered her strengthening shields just enough to see the wards. There was a drastic drop in the number of beings trying to break the wards, which was a relief. Many seemed to have given up by the time she left for the party.

It seemed August was not quite ready to lapse back into silence. "I need to know about the spirit MPs and about this war they spoke of."

Gwen shrugged; she wasn't quite sure how to explain it. "The Spirit World does not work like ours. Just because we have a war does not mean the Spirit World is involved, or even realizes it is going on." She raised her hand before August could speak. "Yes, those spirit MPs knew, but that is an exception, not the rule."

Then she watched his face. August's sharp features lent to a hard and mysterious air, but Gwen wasn't entirely sold on that idea. Perhaps he had been that hard person so long even he believed it was all there was to him, but some how Gwen knew it wasn't.

"Are there ways to verify what they said?" His voice was blank, but she knew what he was asking.

Gwen drained her cup and set it on the cement. He wanted her to open up and find those MPs again. She wasn't sure that was a good idea. "Maybe. I might not be able to do what you're asking, but I might get you something."

August looked at her curiously but didn't say anything. Gwen straightened and leaned back in her chair, hands folded in her lap, and stared into the moon. She had never actually tried to use her gifts during the full moon before, not intentionally. Both she and Viking hadn't thought it wise, but for whatever reason, she wanted to try it. Gwen dropped her shields and threw her energy out like a net, searching for news of a war. The power and strength was like nothing she had ever felt before. Her net stretched so much farther and she could feel so much more. She could sense the Spirit World for miles and somehow she knew that if she wanted to, she could speak to any being she sensed. Gwen could feel herself becoming drunk with power; it was overwhelming and she felt so alive.

Then she hit a bump and it turned to face her and snarled, raking a clawed hand against her net. She felt it across her stomach and the shock crashed her energy back to her so fast she jerked. Her breathing was ragged, but at least that thing hadn't followed her back. Her energy pulse drew more beings to the building, but luckily, the wards were reinforced.

She had not been able to get a good look at its face before it struck. All she had seen was black swirls that felt powerful and malicious. The thing was eager to take out its aggression on anyone that noticed it.

Her breathing was ragged and her head was swimming a little from the power coursing through her. She felt like a light bulb about to burn out. Without thought she stood up and holding his necklace through her shirt she leaned over her balcony to the one below, Viking's. It hurt, but she called out to him with her power. Only she and Viking knew she could do this. Gwen saw several of the beings hovering about focusing on her use of power, but she ignored them. This was too important.

"Big Brother!"

"What? What is it? I can hear your panic."

"Need you...call Carter...found boy...please, need you."

Gwen let go of the necklace as she felt her head go fuzzy. That was new. What had she run into that hurt her so bad? Had she short-circuited herself in the effort?

"GWEN! Talk to me. What happened?" August sounded panicked.

She honestly had forgotten he was there. Gwen turned around and reached out to lean on his arm. Beings were floating up the building toward them and she wasn't quite strong enough to hold them off at the moment. "We need to go inside."

Gretchen S. B.

He grabbed her and she leaned on him heavily. It was like she was hungover and had just had the crap beaten out of her. To his credit, August didn't ask any more questions, just guided, and half-carried, Gwen inside. Viking burst into the apartment as August was shutting the balcony door.

Viking took one look at her and before she knew it he had scooped her up and was carrying her to the couch to set her in his lap. He muttered in his native tongue, which didn't happen often. He stroked her hair as he switched to English.

"Tell me, Little One. What did you do?" Concern was heavy in Viking's voice, but the daggers he shot at August didn't get by Gwen.

She sighed and gave Viking a brief recounting of events. When she finished, Viking seemed considerably calmer.

"Since I haven't heard any fighting, the wards will hold until I can get Lucia out here again to strengthen them around the balconies and not just the walls. I will set up extra lookouts just in case. Why did you have me call Carter?"

She considered it a plus there was more curiosity than concern.

"The thing that attacked me, it was with the boy, Michael. It was in the same house. It was a strong being and I got the feeling it was in control of the kidnapper and it wasn't working alone."

Gwen turned to look at August, who had not said a word since Viking appeared. He was still standing, ramrod straight, by the balcony door. His face was an intimidating blank.

Her next words were for him. "That is where your war will come from. That thing had so much malice, not all of it his own. That much hatred wouldn't remain contained very long."

August watched her for a moment and Gwen squirmed under the scrutiny. Then his gaze flicked to Viking. "Get your men up here. I need to have words with you before the Wolf arrives."

Gwen could feel Viking tense, as if to argue, but something in August's continued stare stopped him. She felt him maneuver and pull out his phone. Within seconds he was speaking.

"Grab Poet and get up here." There was a pause. "She seems fine, but we may have bigger problems." Then he hung up the phone and slowly began transferring Gwen to the couch. "Gwen, when Raider and Poet get up here, relay the events to them and get their take on it. Maybe one of them will have an idea about the thing you saw, because I have no clue. And make sure you drink more of that damn tea."

Within five minutes Gwen had switched two guards for two others and was once again explaining what happened. To her frustration, Poet brought a pot of Sivia's tea with him.

She worried about what was coming. As far as attacks went, it had been very mild and not a need for concern, but she couldn't shake the sense of foreboding. Her worry was only made worse by August and Storebror going off in private. What had spooked August enough that he and Viking had to talk alone? Gwen couldn't help the sinking feeling in her chest.

Chapter 6

"We have a problem," Cesar said as soon as he and his general were locked in the other man's apartment.

Viking snarled. "You think?" He paced his living room like a wild beast.

Cesar understood the feeling. To be that angry and have nothing to lash out at only made things worse.

"We've never had that happen, that I know of, anyway. That thing, whatever it is, has to have a lot of power backing it to be able to knock her power back into her body." Viking only paced faster as he spoke.

Cesar chose his words carefully. "Rogues. This could be rogue Warriors. I have information that a group of them may have banded together."

Viking stopped dead in his tracks and stared at Cesar in horror.

Rogue Warriors were Warriors that chose not to follow the formal hierarchy the North American Warriors set out for themselves. Cesar and Roman had spent the last two hundred years monitoring or eliminating the ones left. However, no one knew how many there were. If rogues banded together, they could be using others in the Night World as well.

"How long have you been aware of this?" Viking couldn't seem to decide between shock and anger.

Cesar shrugged. "Only recently, maybe four months. Last I heard they were in Canada somewhere, but it would not surprise me if they had moved."

Viking seemed to settle on angry and folded his arms. Cesar was glad. Anger he could use.

"Why did you not tell me this?"

Cesar looked his youngest general in the eye. "In taking care of Gwen, you did not need to know. Had matters progressed to a more active level I would have told you. I am telling you now."

Viking seethed for a moment longer, but before he could lash out, Cesar cut him off. "That was not the problem I meant, however."

Cesar watched Viking blank his face. "Tell me."

Cesar took a deep breath. This would not be easy. "When Gwen finished calling you…"

Viking opened his mouth but Cesar gave him a look and he closed it.

"Don't bother denying it. I am not stupid. I don't know how she did it but I have no doubt it happened. I was almost yelling at her to get her attention. She turned and grabbed for me saying she needed to go inside. I obliged."

Here came the difficult part. Cesar looked Viking in the eye again. This was going to cause problems for them both.

"When I grabbed her arm so she wouldn't fall, I felt the Flash."

Color drained from Viking's face and he backed onto his couch. He didn't try to speak until he was sitting.

"Are—are you sure?"

They both knew Viking wasn't really asking. There was no mistaking the Flash.

The Flash happened to a Warrior the first time he touched his mate, flesh to flesh. It was described as a bolt of lightning that boiled the blood and shot through the entire body. It was an unmistakable identifier for the Warrior. The problem was, a Warrior only had three days to bed his mate. If he didn't, the Warrior in question would be driven insane by the overwhelming lust that came over him in that three day period, or as it was usually referred to, the Maddening.

During the Maddening, the Warrior would experience physical pain when away from his mate. He would lose his senses should she be injured or touched by any other male. Warriors tended to stay away from those in the Maddening or in the first stage of mating when all the Maddening symptoms hadn't lowered to the tolerable level mated Warriors dealt with. The first stage of mating could last anywhere from three months to a year, depending on the Warrior. The more the Warrior bedded his mate in that first stage, the easier it would be for him to handle the symptoms.

If a war was coming, and Seattle was going to be center stage, the North American Warriors could not afford to have their king in Maddening or the first stage of mating, especially to a being as well known as the Lady of the Dead. If she was a target before, she would be doubly so now.

Gretchen S. B.

Cesar could feel his blood starting to heat. He knew it took about an hour after the Flash for the Maddening to kick in. He had to figure out a way to fight it. He was the king of the most dangerous Warrior Kingdom in the world. He could hold the Maddening at bay. He could hold it off long enough to make sure of Gwen's safety, then he'd have to explain things to her. He would live with whatever she decided; he would not push himself on her.

Viking let out a long string of curse words and Cesar snorted.

"Yeah I'd say that about covers it."

Viking ran a hand through his hair. "You can't hide this. The other Warriors will notice, and the Weres will smell it. I am happy for you, but I also want to beat you within an inch of your life. She is the closest I have come to family in a thousand years."

Cesar didn't say anything. There was nothing to say. He knew Viking had lost his own three younger sisters to a raid on their village while Viking had been away, along with one of his nephews. Viking had never been able to find the other one and rescue the boy from whatever slavery he had been forced into. It was why Cesar assigned Viking to Gwen. His general yearned for a sense of family, and he would know how to care for a young girl.

Since the Warrior gene passed only to the oldest son, many Warriors lost what little understanding they had of women. Viking's attachment to his sisters had never faded, making he and the Lady of the Dead perfect for each other.

"I understand, trust me. I would not have wished for this timing."

Viking gave Cesar a look that said he caught his meaning. Cesar wasn't sorry about the event, just the timing.

"At least she is already used to being guarded, right?" Viking smiled falsely as he spoke.

Cesar rolled his neck. "I will fight this as long as I can. You are not to tell her. I will not have this influence her decision. Becoming queen of the most dangerous Kingdom puts her at more risk. It is not a life someone blindly steps into."

Viking frowned at him. "You cannot fight the Maddening. Don't be stupid. Gwen is a smart, caring woman. She grew up in our world. She will understand. Keep your queen a secret, and when the first stage is over, she can always live separately. I do not want to kill you for doing something so foolish."

Cesar gave his general his most commanding look. He would not be moved on this. "No, once she chooses to be my queen, there will be nothing else. No separation or going back to our old lives. Swear to me you will not tell her."

Viking clenched his jaw. They both knew Cesar wasn't giving him a choice. "I swear to you, my king, that I will not mention this to your mate."

Cesar nodded, relieved. He wanted Gwen to accept him, not the circumstances.

Viking yanked his phone out of his pocket and pressed a few buttons. The speaker began ringing.

Cesar recognized Roman's voice immediately. "Viking, this had better be damn important. I was sleeping."

Viking looked at Cesar as he spoke. "The king has begun the Maddening."

One loud curse repeated over the phone non-stop for several seconds, followed by silence. "Oh, please tell me it isn't who I am thinking it is."

Viking let out a fake laugh. "Oh, it is."

There was more cursing. "Hey Cesar? You there?"

He and Roman never used their birth names in front of others.

"Yes, Roman, I am here."

"Do you need Apollo and I to fly over there?"

Apollo was Cesar's third general. Though Cesar appreciated his friend's worry, having all four of them here with a war coming could be catastrophic.

"Not at this point." Cesar then filled Roman in on everything else.

When Roman remained silently thinking, Viking filled the silence.

"He intends to fight the Maddening. He thinks he can hold it at bay. He thinks he can fight it off long enough to court her. He does not want her to know what is at stake."

Cesar glared at Viking, but the other man ignored him.

Roman's snorted over the phone. "I would expect nothing less." His voice was laced with amusement and disgust. "I will see

Gretchen S. B.

what I can dig up about recent activity over there. Good luck, my friend." Then Roman hung up.

Viking shoved his phone back in his pocket and began walking past Cesar to the door. "We need to get back. Carter should be here soon if he is not already." Cesar followed his general out, neither spoke as they headed back to Gwen.

They walked into the apartment to see Carter had already arrived. His jeans and t-shirt told Cesar the Wolf was off-duty. Viking shut the door behind them and the Wolf stopped talking. He looked directly at Cesar, his face blanked. After a beat, Carter took several steps from the couch where Gwen sat.

The action told Cesar the Were smelled the Maddening on him and was giving his mate space. It was a curious move, because as the Alpha of his Pack, Carter had rank in the Night World, therefore he could have stayed where he was. By moving farther away, the Alpha was telling Cesar he knew Cesar's true identity. That was interesting.

"Carter!"

The Wolf looked down at Gwen when she spoke.

"The boy is on Fourth and South Bend Avenue. It's a pale blue rambler."

Carter nodded and went to leave. His unquestioning acceptance of Gwen's word showed Cesar just how much clout she carried in this little sector of the Night World. Gwen leapt up after him and grabbed the man's arm to stop him.

Several things happened at once. Cesar felt his temper shoot up. Viking went very still. Carter froze and his eyes shot to Cesar; the Alpha was trying not to panic Gwen by overreacting to what was apparently a common gesture. Raider had been standing, so none of it escaped him. His eyes widened and he moved his arm to get Poet's attention from the couch. Both men turned and watched Cesar, wide-eyed, as he struggled to control his breathing and not rip Gwen's hand from the Were's arm. The urge was stronger than Cesar thought it would have been so early on. Fighting the Maddening was not going to be easy.

The look on Gwen's face said she had caught the tension in the room but didn't know what caused it. Thankfully she dropped his arm. "Carter. Bring as few Night Worlders in as possible, and the ones you do bring should be well protected."

Carter gave one last look at Cesar before turning to Gwen. "Why is that?"

Gwen gave a quick confused look at Viking before answering. When Cesar looked at his general the other man's face was blank. Gwen was trying to read information from Viking and he wasn't giving her anything.

"There is something attached to your kidnapper. It's strong and bad and feeding off him. When you take away his meal ticket he is going to be pissed. Either he will be looking for someone else to ride or he'll take it out on those he can easily see."

Carter watched her for a moment as if processing her information. "Are you telling me our kidnapper is a member of the Night World?"

Gwen actually seemed to think about that. "No, he isn't. A being like the one attached to him takes time to bond with an average person. There is a lot of effort and time that goes into it. They are easier to corrupt, but they have to be open to hearing the being first. I got the impression that this thing has a plan. It knows what it's doing and it will need to find an easier victim."

Carter folded his arms and looked at her questioningly. "Won't it take time then to detach itself from this guy?"

Gwen ran her left hand through her hair. Cesar was momentarily distracted by the movement as hair brushed against her bare arm. She was showing far too much skin to be around this many unmated males. Her dark brown tank top was ribbed and hugged her body. It stopped just short of her navel; there were about two inches of bare flesh before the matching drawstring pants hung from her hips. At least the bottoms were somewhat loose.

Cesar was able to snap his control back when he heard Gwen's voice.

"I don't know. There isn't really a handbook for the Spirit World, and if a previous Lady of the Dead left one, I haven't seen it." She shrugged.

Carter waited a beat before inclining his head to Gwen. It was a gesture only fitting of a leader or their mate. Gwen gave him a confused and disgusted look.

"Thank you for the help, Gwen." Then Carter turned and made eye contact with Cesar, giving a commiserating smile before walking past them. "As always, thank you for the call, Viking."

Gretchen S. B.

As the door shut behind Carter, Gwen's face became angry. She turned and backed up so she could see all four Warriors. "Someone tell me what is going on right now or so help me I will take it out on your hides."

Viking snorted and folded his arms. "You couldn't."

Her eyes narrowed on Viking. Cesar felt a spike of lust. "Try me."

Viking mimicked her stance but smiled. "You think I can't feel how weak you are."

Gwen straightened indignantly. Cesar wasn't sure what they were talking about. All four of them were several times stronger than Gwen, and to his knowledge, Ladies of the Dead didn't have offensive abilities.

"Fine keep your secrets, He-men. I'll find out another way." Then she pivoted and headed toward her room.

Cesar assumed that was bad, because Raider started cursing. Poet jumped over the coffee table to land in her path. Cesar saw the other man reach out to touch her, but hesitated, then dropped his hands. Poet knew he couldn't touch her. It wasn't lost on Gwen because the action seemed to make her angrier.

"Get out of my way, Poet," she growled.

Poet shook his head. "Absolutely not. I will not help you run away this time. It's too dangerous right now. Not with beings injuring you and things crawling up the walls."

Cesar saw red. She had been running away. He was never told of this. Slowly he turned his eyes to Viking. They had been endangering his mate. "She has run away before."

To his credit Viking remained blank. "Yes. Several times. We either find her or she comes back on her own. She needs time alone every once in a while."

Cesar was seething. He should have been told this. What else had his general been hiding? "NO."

"What do you mean, NO?" Gwen now focused her anger on him.

Good, he wanted to be the focus of all that wild energy. Cesar didn't stop the challenging smile he felt sliding onto his face. His anger had a new focus, domination.

"You hold no power over me. I am strong enough now that I do not need to stay against my will. I have learned to hide myself from the world. It has been years since the Warriors have been able to track me down."

The fire in her eyes was more than Cesar could take. Without thinking, he leaped the couch and table and was staring down at her from inches away. She had a moment of shock before her anger flooded her face again.

Cesar gave her a dominating smile that was all teeth. "I could track you, woman. There's nowhere on this Earth you could hide from me."

Her eyes flashed at him and she took a big step away from both him and Poet. Her hand went instinctively to the pendant under her tank. "Oh really?" She spun in a circle and vanished.

Cesar roared. His mate had run from him. Every fiber of his being burned to give chase. He wanted nothing more than to hunt her down and mount her. That thought stilled him and he came flooding back to himself. She shouldn't have been able to do that. In fact as far as he knew, only Immortals and a few MPs could do that.

There were several curses from behind him and Cesar spun around to look at Viking. The other man looked just as shocked as Cesar was.

"She should not be able to do that."

Viking looked at Cesar when he spoke. "She can't. I've never seen her do that. I mean, obviously she just did, but she hadn't mentioned any kind of abilities that didn't fall into the Lady of the Dead category."

Cesar felt his face blank and folded his arms. "Except communicating with you."

Viking actually looked surprised. "Well, yes."

Raider started swearing and held up his hands. "I knew it. I knew she was talking to you. The two of you always knew things you shouldn't, and I knew it wasn't because she was the Lady of the Dead because I've watched over two of them and neither could do that."

Viking rubbed the back of his neck. "It's the necklace I gave her. It was given to me by my mother. She was our wise woman. The necklace has been mine so long it has my imprint. At some point in the early years, Gwen unconsciously figured out how to call to me. Once we realized what she was doing we worked on her doing it purposely. It grew from there."

Cesar wanted to be angry about not being given this information earlier, but a part of him understood Viking wanting to keep it to himself, so he left it alone.

"Can you track her by it?" he asked instead.

Viking shook his head. "Not since she was a teenager. When she fully developed her shields they blocked me too."

Raider and Poet exchanged glances. Cesar had always known Viking possessed abilities that were outside of the Warrior realm. They helped make him such a fine general.

"I'm just going to point out that, uh, displaying the Maddening like that didn't really help matters. It was all under control."

The whole room glared at Poet for his comment. The man just shrugged.

Raider shifted his gaze to Cesar. "How many days in are you?"

"Not even an hour."

There was lots of cursing. "You're this bad after less than an hour? How long has it been since you got laid?" Raider raised his hand. "Don't actually answer that. Damn man, the king is going to be livid about this. Who's going to tell him?"

"He already knows." Viking's voice was blank as he answered his second in command.

Raider raised an eyebrow. "Does he now, and what does the high and mighty have to say?"

Cesar held back his smile at the snide remark.

Poet gained everyone's attention with a loud scoff. "Oh cut the crap." He started walking past them all to the front door. "We need to find Gwen and we need to do it now. We also have to find this being she kept talking about and whatever power is supporting it. I can without a doubt say Raider is the only one in this room that doesn't know we have the king in our presence."

Cesar saw identical shock on both Raider and Viking's faces.

"It would have been stupid of him to not come himself. The first Lady of the Dead in North America, that's a lot of pressure. If his general tells him there's a problem, he sure as hell is going to come take care of it himself. Now who has a plan?" Poet just looked at all of them.

They were all too shocked to respond right away. Cesar didn't know how Poet had known the truth. Maybe the other man recognized him, but the others hadn't. He also knew Viking was a general. No one knew who Cesar's second and third generals were. That way they could gather information unnoticed. Poet had also known Gwen was the first North American Lady of the Dead, that wasn't common knowledge either. Their locations were always kept a secret. How had Poet known all that?

Viking watched the other man warily. "How did you know all of that? Have you been spying?"

Poet actually laughed before giving Viking a bitter smile. "No, I have no need to. You forget that most of us were exiled here for our crimes and a good number of us deserved it."

Something in the man's tone made Cesar wary. What could the man have done that could gain him information?

Cesar made eye contact with Poet. "We will be discussing this more when there are no longer more pressing issues."

Poet's face blanked and there was silence for a beat.

Viking gave a heavy sigh. "All right. We'll split up. Two will stay here. Four will go after whatever that being is and the other four will hunt down Gwen before she gets herself hurt." He turned to Cesar. "I assume since you have started the Maddening, you'll want to go after Gwen."

All of Cesar's Warrior instincts told him to go after his mate. But he knew he couldn't. He needed to protect his kingdom from this threat. If he was lucky, he could channel the Maddening into killing whatever beings were preparing for war. "No, I will chase down the being."

The other three men looked like they wanted to contradict him, but as king none of them would.

Viking broke the silence. "All right then, let's go round up the newbies and plan this out."

Cesar took a moment to close his eyes and take some deep breaths before following the other men out. This was going to be hell. He only wished he was more prepared for it.

Chapter 7

Well, that hadn't quite worked the way Gwen hoped. When she finally used one of the spells Oracle had taught her, she ended up on her balcony. That's what she got for casting a spell while angry. Gwen knew she was lucky she hadn't been hurt. She heard the entire conversation from inside.

She was pissed about August actually being the warrior king, and confused about whatever the Maddening was, she never heard the term before. Gwen always sensed there was something more to Poet. He had a different energy than the other Warriors, but she never mentioned it because he so obviously didn't want it mentioned.

Gwen waited patiently for the four of them to leave before going back inside. She was grateful the Warriors did not have the advanced hearing and sense of smell that Weres did, or they would have found her. Gwen quickly changed into dark jeans and a black hooded sweatshirt. She pulled her hair into a sloppy bun. She needed to blend in with the crowd and since she was going to be heading into Seattle, that meant looking like a college student. If she blended in and shielded tightly she could remain undetected by the Spirit World as well. Gwen packed a black shoulder bag with everything she could possibly need for a few days. She needed to find out what was going on in the Night World and it was easier to do that without a Warrior escort.

Once she had packed, Gwen locked her apartment and headed down the stairwell. She walked slowly and stroked Viking's amulet, the way Oracle taught her. "You will not see me. You will not see me," she chanted in her mind. Gwen couldn't afford to take chances with this one. She needed none of them to see her as she crossed the hall from the stairs to the back door. That was going to be the hardest part.

As she reached the bottom, Gwen took a deep breath and felt her somewhat muted power pull over her like a blanket. She had never tried this on so many people, let alone Night World people. Gwen pressed the door lightly so she could hear down the hall. There were no voices, so she opened the door enough to slip out, then slid it shut. Exhaling some of her stress at getting through the first step, Gwen ran across the L-shaped hallway to the back door.

She had just about reached it when the door to the lounge opened behind her.

Gwen froze, pinning herself to the wall as August and Raider stepped out. Neither saw her and she relaxed. How they couldn't hear her pounding heart, Gwen didn't know. It sounded deafeningly loud to her. All she had to do was wait for them to go down the hall so she could open the back door without suspicion.

"Where does she usually go?" August asked roughly.

Raider shrugged. "There's no real consistency to where we used to find her. It depends on what she is looking for."

"Do you think she is headed to the same place we are?"

Raider shook his head. "I don't know. I'd like to think she's not stupid enough to go alone, but you never know."

Both men were silent as they turned the corner and Gwen's knees just about gave out. She hadn't expected the spell to work, but it had. The relief was overwhelming. Not wanting to waste any more time, Gwen slowly opened the back door and shut it softly behind her. She would have to walk past the staff parking next, but at least there would be cars to hide behind. Careful to be fast and quiet, Gwen turned the corner that would take her to the nearest bus stop.

A voice wafted from behind her and she jumped. "I'd go north."

Gwen swore her heart stopped mid-beat. It was Poet. She turned to see who he was talking to. He was looking right at her. Poet leaned against the building, arms folded with a sad smirk on his face. He had obviously been waiting for her.

When she continued to blink at him in shock, Poet actually laughed. "Don't worry, I won't give you away, but the plan is to go south first. So you should go north."

Gwen finally found her voice, but it only came out a whisper. "How can you see me?"

Poet pushed off the wall and came to stand about a foot away from her. "Suffice it to say, I made some deals with some very nasty beings centuries ago for powers other than my own. But that's our little secret." He smiled at her.

Gwen trusted Poet, more so than Raider and Viking did. She knew at his core Poet was striving to become better, and she respected that. But her curiosity was getting the better of her.

"I thought you said you weren't going to help me run away this time?"

He had helped her do it multiple times.

"I changed my mind." His mouth twitched.

Gwen smiled, quickly leaned in and gave him a peck on the cheek. He actually looked surprised. "Thank you, Poet. I owe you one." Then she took off running north. If she hurried she could catch the next bus.

———————

Venture's only slow night of the week was Sundays. So, true to form, the place was full when Gwen arrived. Which was a relief because it meant no one would be paying extra attention to her. At first glance she would pass as a lower level MP, maybe even a young Immortal. With the Immortal compound about an hour away, Seattle's Immortal population was extremely high. It would only be with a very thorough magical look that anyone would sense the Spirit World on her. That was the beauty of Venture. No one cared that much.

Venture was the first 'Night World Only' club in the world. It welcomed all Night Worlders, as long as they didn't cause problems. There were so many spells, incantations, and wards on the place it practically hummed. There were jokes the building could survive World War Three without a scratch. Venture was owned by the largest local Wereleopard Pride with twenty Leopards, most of whom worked at the club. Strangely, not all of Venture's staff members were Leopards, but they were still taken in by the Pride, making the Pride huge. They ruled it with iron fists. There was even a spell on the building to repel non-Night Worlders, which kept unnecessary accidents to a minimum.

Gwen came for help and information. For one reason or another, the source she sought used this place as her usual haunt. Gwen ignored the attention from the random male Weres-- they were such horny little buggers—and hunted down Sin. She could have asked any of the staff; they would all know if Sin were there. Sin had that effect on people. After a moment of adjustment, Gwen scanned Sin's usual tall corner table, furthest from the dance floor. There she was. Gwen made her way across the large crowded club.

Sin was a Shapeshifter. Sin wasn't even her real name, but since she scared the crap out of just about everyone, no one asked her about it. She worked for the Shapeshifter bounty hunting agency and she was damn good. Gwen counted the woman as a friend. Sin hated people, but she actually showed affection for Gwen, in her own way. She was tall for a woman, at five-ten, and she always wore two inch, knee-high, buckled, black leather boots. She sat in her usual outfit of slightly loose black leather pants, a black v-neck corset top with her black fitted leather trench coat slung over the back of her chair. Her waist length black hair was slicked back in a tight French braid. Sin was a bit monochromatic.

Gwen slowed down as she neared Sin. The tables around the other woman were, not surprisingly, empty despite people looking for tables. No one was daring enough to take a seat near Sin. Gwen needed to know what type of mood Sin was in before she approached the other woman. If Sin was in a bad mood, or working, Gwen would have to look elsewhere for help.

She quickly got her answer. A waiter, probably new from the lack of fear, walked up to Sin's table with a pint glass of brown liquid. Gwen knew if there was whiskey in that glass Sin was safe to approach. If there wasn't then Sin was working. As she watched from yards away the waiter set the glass down and turned away. Definitely new, wait staff always asked if the customer needed anything else. Sin didn't even take a sip; within seconds she had the young waiter pressed against the wall with a long knife at his throat and a snarl on her face.

People moved away from the wall but no one paid any more attention to it. That was Sin's normal behavior and they all expected management to take care of it. Gwen cursed and started pushing her way over there. She knew she had a good chance of talking Sin down, but it would mean blowing her cover.

Vincent, Venture's Pride Leader, beat Gwen there. She wasn't surprised; you couldn't beat a Were for speed. As Gwen made it to Sin's right, opposite the calm-faced Vincent, he was already talking.

"Now why in the world would you put whiskey shots in the lady's drink?"

Gwen tried not to smile. Only Vincent would ever call Sin a lady and not get his balls cut off. The young waiter had put unwanted alcohol in Sin's drink. Damn, Sin was working.

The young guy sputtered a little before getting an answer out. "I heard some of the other staff mention that no alcohol was a bad sign. I-I just thought it would ease tensions."

Sin latched on to that idea. "Who? Who was talking about me?"

Oh, that was not good.

Vincent put his hand on Sin's shoulder and she visibly tightened. Sin hated being touched. Vincent removed the hand once he gained her attention. "Sin, leave it alone. Everyone knows you're easier for the staff to deal with when you're drinking."

Sin just snarled at him before turning back to the frightened waiter.

Vincent switched his attention as well. "Apologize to the lady, Archer."

With a name like that Gwen was betting the boy was a Were.

"S-S-Sor-r-r-ry." The young man's voice shook.

"Now Sin, would you please do me the favor of letting the boy go? I promise you he will be properly reprimanded."

Gwen heard the authority in his voice. He was definitely not happy with the boy. It was always odd to hear that much authority coming from a man who couldn't be older than thirty-five, but somehow Vincent could be pretty intimidating.

Sin held the boy there a moment as if contemplating Vincent's words. Gwen held her breath. With Sin it really could go either way. Suddenly she stepped back, her knife disappeared, and the boy slumped to the ground.

Both Gwen and Vincent exhaled, and Vincent smiled his relief.

"Thank you, Sin. I'll be back with a new drink for you myself."

Sin nodded. "Bring two."

Vincent nodded in return and stood waiting for Archer to stand up, apparently he wasn't going to help the young Were. After a minute or so both men walked away.

Sin turned to Gwen. "What brings you west of the lake, Gwen? And unescorted?"

Gwen motioned to Sin's table. "Can we sit down first?"

Sin headed back to her table. A few moments later Vincent returned, setting a pint glass in front of each of them and grabbing the alcoholic drink. He downed it before turning to Gwen. She stared in surprise; she had never seen him drink before.

"You come to my club without your escort, Gwen, I cannot reasonably protect you."

"I do not ask for Venture's protection, only its silence."

Vincent seemed to gain interest and tilted his head. "Silence from whom?"

"My guards when they come looking for me later tonight. I only ask that no one saw me."

Vincent watched her for a moment before glancing at Sin, then back. "Done." Turning, he made his way through the crowd.

Sin leaned in with her hand around her glass. Her unsettling gaze bored into Gwen. "What happened?"

Gwen quickly told an abridged version of events, leaving out the Maddening and Poet's extra abilities. Sin did not appear to blink the entire time.

"You want me to tell you what I know? And help you find more information?" Sin asked.

Gwen nodded.

Sin took a long drink from her Coke and stared out into the crowd for several minutes. Gwen didn't interrupt her. Sin was a fountain of information, if you had the patience to get it from her. She possessed all three kinds of Were in her a Wolf, a Bird, and a Cat. She was not exactly a stable person.

"There have been more Warrior sanctions than usual. More non-Night World being sanctions than usual actually. Over the past few months both Assas and I have been sanctioned to kill regular people. But they were never really regular, always something wrong with them, if you know what I mean."

Gwen didn't, but she knew better than to mention it. Assas was Sin's Midwest counterpart. They spoke to each other more often than anyone else.

"I haven't heard anything about a war, though. I've heard about that group of rogue Warriors. I came across a few in B.C. last month. They're strange creatures, convinced they had to drink blood to survive. I killed one while he was getting it on with some crazy chick. The rest of them ran back across the border. But then I killed another rogue Warrior in the same situation the next week, just without the whole blood thing. That's about it." Sin looked at Gwen. "You know who might know? Sivia. That girl seems to talk to everyone."

Sin stood and finished her pint. Gwen took a large sip of hers, barely halfway through.

"Come on, let's pay her and Karin a visit." Sin grinned as she slammed her empty glass on the table.

Gwen was confused. "Don't you have a job to complete?"

"Sure, but this sounds much more fun." She headed toward the exit.

Gwen took one more gulp before scurrying after her. It was hard to keep up with the taller woman's stride. She hadn't thought to go to Sivia. The Immortal princess did know a lot about supernatural healing, but would she and her Werepanther roommate really be able to help her find information? Gwen found herself wondering about the Maddening thing and what it had to do with war.

"Sin, have you ever heard of something called the Maddening?"

Sin didn't even break stride as they headed toward her bike, parked illegally at a storefront down from the bar, but of course, no one would tow Sin's Harley.

"Of course."

When there was no more to that answer, Gwen prodded. "What is it?"

Sin threw Gwen the extra helmet. "No clue. Makes a Warrior go crazy. Assas killed one once."

Gwen knew she wouldn't get any more of an answer. Neither said another word as they got on the bike and headed north.

Chapter 8

Nearly two hours had passed since Gwen disappeared, and to Cesar's knowledge, there was still no sign of her. For what seemed like the hundredth time Cesar shook himself to keep his mind on the present.

Cesar, Viking, Kegan, and Rochester stood in the shadows a few houses down from where the police stormed a blue house exactly as Gwen described.

"Get yourselves ready, whatever it is might come out kicking and screaming," Viking said as he slid the Warrior pendant around his neck.

Warriors had been making deals with MPs and Immortals for thousands of years for those pendants. Since the Warriors took it upon themselves to protect the Night World, they had bartered for magical items. It helped the wearer see the larger goings on in the Spirit World. Nowhere near the level of Gwen, but enough for them to find the beast in front of them. Some Warriors Cesar knew never took theirs' off. He put that thought aside as he used the activating words. Cesar's undivided attention went to the house. He could feel the being moving closer to them.

"Whoa, do you feel that?" Rochester whispered.

Whatever this thing was, it was strong and not on its own. Cesar could feel other power backing it. This thing was bloated with power that did not belong to it. It appeared to delight in the hatred seeping from its host.

When the police brought the kidnapper outside, they held their breath. An impossibly large black shadow followed the man and seemed to be wrapped around his middle. It reached seven feet above the man's head. Cesar could sense the being's anger at being captured. It lashed out with its giant clawed hand at Carter and two other cops. They ignored it. Carter must have taken Gwen's advice and protected himself against harm.

"Look at the boy." Kegan began to panic.

Cesar began scanning for the child, but he didn't see him. "Where? Where is the child?"

Kegan cursed. "No, sorry. I meant the young officer. He's by the vehicle. See how he glows?"

Gretchen S. B.

All of them turned to look at the barricade of cop cars. It took a moment, but Cesar saw him. The young cop couldn't have been twenty. He glowed in their pendant-enhanced sight. He was probably a sensitive, a human psychic with no knowledge of his own abilities.

The being noticed the boy a second later, and swinging out, it slammed him against the nearest car. All four Warriors sprinted toward the chaos, Viking chanting something in his native tongue. But Carter reached the boy before them and checked the young man's pulse. Cops were everywhere trying to figure out where the hit came from.

Cesar watched the being prepare for another hit and shouted. "Carter, to the left."

Without responding, Carter was up and facing left, guarding the young officer with his body. When the blow came it bounced off of whatever Carter used as protection. The being let loose an angry howl that had all the Night Worlders, and the kidnapper, flinching. Then it turned on the Warriors with all the hatred it possessed.

All four of them began to back up as it stretched. They needed to get as far from civilians as possible. They automatically spread out, to prevent accidentally hitting each other.

The being surrounded the Warriors on all sides. It wasn't attacking, but slowly closing in, which Cesar was pretty sure would kill them.

Cesar emptied half his magazines into the mass in front of him. The black did not even pause, just absorbed the bullets as they hit. He looked around him to see the others blowing through their ammunition. Viking was swinging a small, ancient battle axe. The blades cut through the black as if it were mist, but Cesar watched Viking tug the axe out again. The being was trying to take the axe. That gave Cesar an idea.

"Viking! Can you swing it like a fan?"

Viking obliged, turning the blades to the side and waving up and down. The being stopped moving in as the black in front of Viking thinned slightly.

Cesar knew Viking's axe was heavily enchanted. This being was not knowledgeable enough to fully wield its gifted power. Any magic items the Warriors had on them might be able to overpower it.

Adrenaline flowed through him as Cesar pulled the short sword a powerful MP had given him when he became King. Pulling it from under his jacket, he swirled his wrist into the blackness on his left as fast as he could. The blackness began to thin. Cesar moved toward it, baring his teeth and swiped at the black in a large arc. The blackness retreated a few inches.

"Swipe at it with any enchanted objects you have. It is not strong enough to deal with all of them at once."

Cesar hoped whatever the other men had on them would work as well as Viking's axe.

"I don't carry magic objects!" Rochester shouted.

"Be resourceful, damn it! Here I have matching blades," Kegan growled.

"We can't exactly do this forever," Viking commented between blows with his battle axe. "Sooner or later someone's going to hit a solid object."

"Isn't this why we have the Lady of the Dead?"

"Oh shut up, Roch."

Cesar couldn't think of another way out. Viking was right, they would run out of room, or energy. It might be thinning, but it was only several inches at a time. Warriors could outfight just about anyone in the Night World, but they possessed no talent for magic. This was definitely a case for magic.

Suddenly the walls stopped thinning, followed by a deafening roar as the blackness was sucked away from them. Cesar felt about as shocked as the cops looking at them. For the cops, the four Warriors must have appeared out of nowhere and they were maybe thirty feet away. That would take some explaining. Cesar deactivated his pendant and out of the corner of his eye he saw Viking remove his altogether.

Carter maneuvered through the wall of cars and stood a few feet from them. He looked at them appraisingly before speaking to the cell phone he held out in front of him.

"Thank you, Lucia. They appear unharmed and that thing seems to have left them alone."

A female voice came through the speaker. "Good. I will be there in the morning to bind it in person. Now, what about my payment?"

Gretchen S. B.

Cesar knew then Carter had enlisted an MP to save them. He hoped the Wolf hadn't paid too much.

Carter rolled his eyes. "I'll take care of Barrett's speeding tickets. What about my officers?"

"What will you give me for them?"

Yup, definitely an MP.

"Really, you would bargain over keeping the secrecy of our world?" Carter didn't even fake surprise.

"Practitioner cardinal rule, get payment for everything."

Carter sighed. "What do you want for it, Lucia?"

Cesar could practically hear the woman grinning.

"You agree to join the auction."

That caught Carter by surprise. Cesar didn't know what it meant, but it obviously wasn't expected.

"You want to bid on me, Lucia? Isn't your dance card a little full?" Carter raised his eyebrow at the phone, as if the woman on the other end could see it.

For all Cesar knew, she could.

"It is not for me. Call it Karma. Take it or leave it, Lieutenant."

Carter went silent. Cesar could tell the other man was struggling to figure out the MP's angle. After a moment, he sighed again in defeat.

"Deal."

A creepy girlish giggle emanated from the receiver. "Oh, excellent. Take me over to the officers, then."

Carter lifted his hand to Cesar before moving back toward the majority of the cops.

Cesar exchanged glances with Viking, and they moved several yards back. It was a habit; never get caught up in MP magic if you can help it. The other two men followed after them and they stood in a huddle. Cesar made his question plain on his face.

Viking folded his arms. "Lucia is an MP, obviously. She's very strong for her age and holds a position on the MP's council. She's the second strongest MP in the Tristate area. She lives with two male MPs, so that obviously amps all three of them up."

Cesar whistled. MPs tended to live in Strata. A Strata could be spread over fifty miles, or it could be one household. MPs fed off each other. Three MPs living together could be very strong or very crazy. Viking didn't seem worried, so Cesar left it alone.

"That's not much of a payment for magic like that. I've seem MPs ask thousands for less." Kegan seemed amused by Lucia's asking price.

Viking snorted. "You don't know Barrett. The guy drives a black sports car and gets at least three tickets a month. I don't know how he still has insurance. I think last year he picked up seventy. No clue how many are actually on his record. Plus it's a sliding scale with MPs. Price all depends on what they think they can get and how easy the magic is for them specifically."

Cesar tried not to laugh at the two younger men's expressions. They were dying to know how Viking knew all that. It was an age thing. If a Night Worlder kept their ears open long enough, they could learn all kinds of things.

Carter walked back to them but now the phone was to his ear. The MP must have wiped the officers' memories because everybody else seemed to be leaving.

Carter turned to Cesar. "Lucia wants to know if you would like her help retrieving your lost lady." He lifted an eyebrow.

They hadn't told the Wolf about the missing Lady of the Dead.

Cesar gave a questioning look to Viking, who only shrugged. Neither of them knew how the MP would have that information.

Cesar turned back to Carter. "What makes her think the Lady is missing?"

There was a pause. She must have heard Cesar without the Were's assistance.

"She says if the Lady of the Dead were present you would not need to call her."

Cesar cursed. Now it would get out that the Lady of the Dead was missing and there would be a free-for-all after Gwen.

Carter pulled the phone from his ear. "Sorry, she's cackling in my ear." After several seconds he brought the phone back and listened. "She says her silence will cost you."

Cesar rolled his eyes. "Of course it will."

The Wolf's face scrunched into a frown. "What have you been smoking lately, Lucia?"

Another pause, he looked at Viking. "She says it will cost Viking's bodyguard services two months hence." Carter sounded as confused as Cesar felt.

Viking didn't hide his suspicion. "What am I guarding exactly?"

Carter listened but only seemed more confused and surprised. "What the hell, Lucia?" Another pause. "She says it's a women's retreat for her church, and I mean church, not her Strata."

Viking blinked several times. "Lucia goes to church?"

"Apparently."

Cesar didn't know the woman so he couldn't commiserate with the shock on the other two men's faces.

"Does her silence mean she will silence others?" Viking asked cautiously.

"She will not go out of her way, but should the subject come up, yes."

Potentially a lot of work. MPs were usually about the quick fix. Cesar wanted to meet this MP.

"All right, she has a deal."

Viking didn't seem entirely sure about his decision. He sounded like he was waiting for the catch.

After a few more beats, Carter hung up the phone. "She's been really weird lately. Ever since Narcina died, Lucia's been a bit off."

Viking nodded. "No kidding."

Cesar knew who Narcina was. She had been the most powerful MP in North America. She had died two months ago and no one knew exactly how. All the MPs were spooked.

Carter shook his head. "She's coming over tomorrow first thing in the morning to check this out. Maybe she'll be able to tell us exactly who we are dealing with. I'm assuming you guys will want to come?"

Viking nodded. "Yeah, depending on a few factors, someone will be there."

The Were watched for several beats. "Do you need help finding Gwen?"

Cesar couldn't quite hold back the growl, but both Carter and Viking ignored him. The two young guys' faces were full of surprise.

Viking sighed. "No, she'll turn up. We don't want too many people looking for her. It would gain notice."

Carter inclined his head to Cesar. "Very well then. I'll see you tomorrow."

Viking turned to Cesar. "What next?"

Cesar took a deep breath. The effects from the fight had begun to wear off and the Maddening was flowing back to the forefront. Viking was trying to help him think of something else.

"Where can we go to gather information about an influx of new power?"

Viking didn't even hesitate. "Venture."

"Then we go there."

Cesar knew of the club, but never went there. He prepared himself to be surrounded by Night Worlders. The Maddening made crowds a whole new kind of torture.

Chapter 9

Gwen sat on the pale brown couch beside Sin in Karin and Sivia's living room. The other two women were perched in matching chairs.

"Let me get this straight." Karin almost seemed to laugh. "There's a big baddie that somehow latched onto a human but is maintaining ties to something else and they want to start a war in North America, which is home to a hell of a lot of truly scary people. But we don't know who, but it's big enough three dead MPs and the Warrior King of North America are involved. Oh, and our local King is also in the Maddening."

Gwen had never been entirely comfortable with Karin's sense of humor.

"Yes."

Karin burst out laughing, her blond curls falling around her face.

Gwen looked at Sivia. The other woman's mouth twitched, but she fought it.

"Forgive her. She loves a good fight and this is ironic timing for the Maddening to take root in Cesar. I've met him, and the idea is actually quite hilarious."

Now Gwen was confused. "Cesar?"

Sivia stopped smiling. "Yes, that's what the old ones call him. It was his name before he was King."

"That's not the name he gave me." Gwen tried to ignore the hurt that shot through her chest.

Sivia cocked her head. "What name did he tell you?"

"He said people would know him as Roman, but to call him August."

Karin stopped laughing and stared at Gwen. "That's really sweet."

Before Gwen could ask what she meant, Sin did it for her.

"Okay, what the hell are we talking about? Being out of the loop makes me agitated."

Sivia and Karin exchanged glances before Sivia spoke.

"The Maddening is what happens to Warriors when they meet their mate. It's very hush-hush. I only know because my brother, Orion, told me. Who knows where he got it. When a

Warrior touches his mate's skin for the first time there is a biological reaction. He has less than a week to bed her before the Maddening takes over completely. If that happens, usually they are killed. Can you imagine the damage a crazed Warrior could do? Our King, it seems, has met his mate." She motioned to Gwen.

Gwen's mouth couldn't have dropped any farther. She was to mate the King of North America? How had that happened?

She looked at Sin, who seemed absolutely appalled.

Sivia waited until Gwen turned back to her before continuing. "He gave you the name of his right hand man to keep his Kinghood a secret. But the name he gave you to call him, I would put my next three months' salary on it being his birth name. It's sweet. He wanted his mate to use his birth name, even before he knew who you were."

"That's disgusting."

Everyone ignored Sin.

"You have to decide what you're going to do about him. I mean, you ran away. He's going to consider that as giving chase. He'll be absolutely bonkers by the weekend. If you really intend to hide out for a few days you might want to hire an MP to take you off every radar."

Gwen thought about it. She knew how to keep herself well hidden; the only ones she worried about were Weres and their sense of smell. "I think I'll be okay for now. But can we concentrate on the war part? The Maddening part is a little too much right now."

Sivia nodded. "Fair enough. I heard about a group of rogue Warriors in Canada a few months back. They were nosing around some MPs, hinting about making pacts. As far as I know no one was biting. I mean, come on, after the mayhem the King and his crew cut through to bring stability? The Night World has a long memory. That was like six months ago. I haven't heard anything since. But if there is a war of some kind coming, we should nose around and nip it in the bud. I can call my Canadian contacts in the morning. Maybe a few around here."

"I killed one last month."

Everyone looked at Sin, but Gwen seemed to be the only one that understood.

"She killed a rogue Warrior last month."

"What was his crime?" Sivia asked.

Sin shrugged. "No clue, just supposed to kill him."

Sivia, Karin, and Gwen exchanged glances. They wanted to know who would sanction Sin to kill a rogue.

"I'll ask my Pack Leader. We're small, but every little bit helps right?" Karin gave a lopsided smile before walking out of the room.

"You two are welcome to sleep here, the couch pulls out."

Sin launched herself off the couch, startling both Sivia and Gwen. "If it's all the same, I'll come back in the morning. I have people to kill." She didn't wait for an answer, just left.

Gwen and Sivia sat in silence for a few moments, until it seemed Sivia couldn't hold her tongue any longer. "It's hard, I know that. I've been unofficially promised to the Immortal High King."

The entire Night World had buzzed with that rumor, but Sivia never confirmed it. The admission surprised Gwen.

"But at least I can hide. You, I'm afraid, don't have that option. You either screw him and leave him, screw him and stay with him, or screw him over. Fate's a twisted mistress like that."

Gwen grabbed on to her thought like a life preserver. "You mean I could sleep with him once and he would be fine? Life could go back to semi-normal?"

Sivia frowned. "Not exactly. It would definitely be more than once. They have to get the Maddening out of their system. You probably haven't seen a Warrior with his mate. They don't leave them. They are like puppies. Their mates become the cornerstone for their existence. I do not think King would let you leave. Best case scenario, he would negotiate regular visits."

Gwen didn't like that idea. But she didn't have it in her to let August go insane and be killed. She would need to talk to him about it, but she couldn't. There were more important things to do and he wouldn't be exactly rational.

Karin came back in the room, effectively halting the discussion.

"Marnie answered and told me Minnie would get back to me tomorrow. I guess at the moment she is entertaining a Wolf." Karin crinkled her nose at the thought. "I asked Marnie if she heard anything and she told me that the Pride in the Northern peninsula has been surprisingly quiet for the last month or so."

She turned to Gwen. "There is a Pride of Tigers, seven, all male, all young. So as you can imagine, they get a bit rowdy. A month is a long time for no news of them."

Gwen knew the other two women thought the same thing she did. Someone was quietly drawing a line in the sand and no one else had caught it. In the Night World, that was very dangerous.

Gretchen S. B.

Chapter 10

The man standing guard at the inner door to Venture had to be into lifting weights, as his muscles were huge. Usually in the Night World that bulk would mean a Warrior, but Cesar didn't know him, so he was betting Wolf. Werewolves put bulky muscles on better than the other Weres.

The guy took one sniff of them and blocked the doorway. "You're kidding right? You really think I'm gonna let a Warrior in Maddening into a club full of Night Worlders?"

Cesar gave the man his full undivided attention. "You will because I am King of North America and I demand entry."

The man snorted and touched his ear piece, but didn't move. "Hey boss, I got a guy out here you're gonna wanna set straight."

After a few seconds, he turned to Cesar. "Vincent's coming to meet you. See if you are who you say you are. Still not letting you in, though." Then he stared past them as if they didn't exist.

Cesar felt himself shake with anger. The Maddening kept him on edge and he wanted to rip the bouncer's throat out. The images going through his head calmed him down, they were just crazy enough to make him think straight. Cesar didn't kill people for doing their job.

After a few more minutes, Vincent appeared behind the bouncer and the man moved out of the way. Cesar knew Vincent from when the Leopard had approached him about starting Venture. When Vincent started the club, he had visited every major leader to get their backing, and to better keep the peace. A brilliant idea that was catching in other parts of the country.

Vincent looked at the group, frowning, then his eyes widened and he started laughing. "Oh that's priceless. Absolutely priceless."

Cesar was quickly getting sick of reactions to the Maddening.

"I'm sorry, King. What did you come here for? Understandably I can't let you into the club."

Cesar sighed, trying to control his anger. "I need information."

Vincent raised one thin eyebrow. "On?"

Cesar glanced at the bouncer. "I'd rather not say in public."

Vincent nodded and waved them out the front door. "All right, let's step outside then."

Vincent ushered them into an alley on the far side of the club. Then he folded his arms and looked at Cesar expectantly.

"We ran into a being today, tied to a human. As well as an outside source. It was able to slap a sensitive into a car. Then it surrounded us. Our regular weapons didn't work and an MP finally had to rescue us.

Alarmed surprise slid across Vincent's face before he went calm. "I see, and you want to know what could do such a thing? Or who could control it." He stood quiet for a moment. "You know the Immortal court would know better than I. But of course they are never big on sharing. We've had some rowdy ones lately. The strong MPs haven't come around much, but that's understandable, you know how suspicious they are. I've heard a rumor about rogues, but I assume you know about that."

When Cesar didn't give Vincent a response he continued. "I've also heard that Sin has been sanctioned to kill humans lately."

That took Cesar completely by surprise. By the others' expressions, no one knew about that.

"Yes, that was my thought when she told me. Even she thought it smelled a little funny. Killed them anyway, as it turned out they were bad people. But I'm afraid that's all I have. I can put feelers out. But as neutral ground I can't exactly be direct."

Cesar knew what that was like. He did most things indirectly. "Thank you, Vincent. Let us know if you hear anything."

Vincent gave him a tight smile before heading to the back of the building.

"That wasn't terribly helpful," Rochester mumbled.

Cesar disagreed. He now knew the rogues where making a move. He had left them alone too long and they were probably in Seattle. He would put money on them targeting Gwen. She was a valuable ally to have and if they were starting a rebellion, she would be the perfect bargaining chip.

"Let's go back and see how the others are doing," Viking suggested.

Cesar nodded again.

There was silence the entire way back, too many thoughts swirling around to hold a conversation. Cesar had to get on the phone with his other generals. Those rogues needed to be found and taught a lesson.

"What do you mean, nobody's seen her?"

How could the Lady of the Dead fall off the face of the Night World?

Poet shrugged. "No one's seen her. I mean, we couldn't outright ask. We can't have people knowing she's missing. That would be a disaster. Not to mention, Viking, you know as well as I do how loved Gwen is. People will lie for her easily."

Viking mumbled something.

That surprised Cesar. *People here would actually lie to hide the Lady of the Dead from her protector? Why?*

"What makes them lie for her?" He wasn't asking anyone in particular.

Raider answered him, shoving his hands in his pockets. "The Night World dynamic is different here than in the rest of the country. There's so damn many of us crammed on this coast. There are a few, for one reason or another, everybody knows. Gwen, being one of a kind, is one of them. Another is the Immortal Princess, Sivia. Then there is the Shapeshifter, Sin. Venture's owner, Vincent. Since Narcina died, Lucia is working her way up there. There's obviously Buccaneer and Bandit. Also pretty much anyone from Yukon Animal Pack. Say any of those names to any west coast Night Worlder and they will know who you're talking about. There are a few others that are well known here and there, but not to the same extent.

"Both Gwen and Sivia are known for their respectfulness and authority. They treat everyone equally. Most of the local Night Worlders feel they have a personal connection to one or both of them. They are well loved, King. If Gwen asks them to keep her presence a secret, there are not many who wouldn't. No one sees lying to Warriors as a big deal."

Cesar was astonished at the way things worked out here. Everywhere else in the country, people bent over backwards to stay out of the Warrior's path. Here they would stand in the way. Part of him was proud to have such a beloved mate. Even if she did hide from him.

Viking folded his arms and looked at the other men. "Who did you question in the three hours you were out?"

Poet smiled and began counting on his fingers. "Well, we searched her haunts first. The south bus station. The north bus station. Deane's That Occult store south of Bothell. None of them saw her. We tried Chelsea and Bentley's, no luck. We stopped in at Beth's Café, and they hadn't seen anyone with her description. We tried Sivia, and Karin yelled at us for calling so late. Went to Venture, no go. We actually wandered around Seattle after that, checking in various parts of town, hotels and that kind of thing. We found Sin in Pioneer Square. When Raider asked her if she had run into Gwen today she said, 'Why the hell would I do that, someone's insides are their own business.' Then she started sneaking around a building as though stalking something. We figured it was probably best to move it along, fast."

Viking nodded. "Probably a good idea. Did you get the impression anyone lied to you?"

Poet seemed to think about it. "Not really, but I would put money on her showing up at Venture if she hasn't already. There are only two hot spots and we are the other one."

Cesar didn't like not knowing where his mate was. "If the rogue Warriors truly are in Seattle, then they are looking for Gwen. She needs to be somewhere I…WE can protect her from them."

The expressions on the other three men's faces said they heard the slip but wouldn't say anything…yet.

Raider cleared his throat. "We will make the same rounds tomorrow, but tensions are high. Since Narcina's death, we have to be careful not to step on other species' toes. Plus, should Gwen find herself in danger, the pendant will let us know. I think after tomorrow's round we should put our concentration into finding these rogues, before they have a chance to find our girl."

"Agreed." Viking's voice held the authority of a man with centuries of experience to back it.

Cesar didn't like the idea of giving up on the search for Gwen. It went against all his Warrior instincts. Yet he knew the others were right. Finding the rogues was best, and if what Raider had said about the community loving Gwen was true she was probably protected, wherever she was.

Gretchen S. B.

"All right. I will call Roman and get the location of their last known whereabouts and we can track them from there. They are likely to hit Seattle. We need the area's Warriors on alert. I can get the sanctioned Warriors, however, since they are not officially under my authority, I cannot contact Buccaneer or Bandit."

Poet pulled out his cell phone. "Don't worry about them, just let me know what you want me to say."

"I will call Roman and see what he has come up with."

Cesar walked out of the lounge and ran up the stairs to the top floor. He didn't stop moving until his back was propped up against her front door. He took several deep breaths to calm himself. It helped to be in her space. The Maddening heightened and tuned his senses so he could feel her energy through the door, the life force a place developed from being lived in. Being in her space calmed his nerves. It would be better if he was inside but he refused to break into her home just to make himself more comfortable. Pulling out his phone, Cesar speed-dialed Roman.

The other man answered after one ring. "Are you alone?"

Cesar smiled at the concern in his friend's voice. "Yes, Octavian. I am alone."

It was one of the inside jokes the two men shared. They were both named after the same man and neither were like him.

Roman exhaled. "How are you fairing, truly, Augustus?"

"I could be better. Between you and me I think I can last the three days, maybe even five. But no more than that. I will need you to come kill me after that. I do not want any other to do it."

There was silence for a moment; he wasn't sure Roman would answer. "You have my word, Augustus, that I will be the one to kill you. I will be there in a day's time. Considering the late hour, that will be tonight."

Cesar spoke over his friend. "I do not think that is wise."

Roman snorted. "You are not thinking at all. Command me not to come, it does not matter, I have already bought my ticket. Apollo can keep things in check for a few days. He may be Greek, but the man is not completely incompetent."

They laughed at the old joke. Even a thousand years later it still riled the Greek.

"How are things going with the woman?" Curiosity filled Roman's voice.

Cesar stopped laughing and was unintentionally silent long enough for Roman to pick up on it.

"My friend, I realize it has been a very long time, but wooing a woman is not that difficult. I hear she has a love of coffee. Can you not bribe her with that?"

Cesar chose his words carefully. "It is not that easy…"

Roman snorted again. "You always did make things more difficult than they needed to be."

Cesar pricked at that, even if they both knew it was true. "We do not know where she is. There was a fight and she disappeared, literally, no one knows where she has gone. Apparently she does this from time to time, then reappears when she is ready. I am told it has been years since they have been able to find her when she runs away. She has become too good at hiding herself."

There was a beat of silence then Roman's laughter filled Cesar's ear. It went on longer than Cesar found decent.

"Your mate ran away from you. Oh, that is priceless. I must meet this woman. Let me guess, she sensed something wrong and you made people promise not to tell her."

Their friendship was too strong for Cesar to be surprised by Roman's guess. "Something like that."

There was more laughing. Cesar couldn't quite work up the energy to be annoyed.

"I would not worry about her. From the official and unofficial reports I receive, Gwen can take care of herself, or will know where to go if she can't. Apollo is always saying women demand the truth or a pound of flesh. You should have listened to him. When you see her next you should tell her. Before you say it, I know why you wouldn't but this is not exactly the time to be a gentleman. Now that I have said my piece, I know you will be wanting information on those rogues."

He paused to let Cesar jump in. When he didn't, Roman took it as a sign to continue.

"It would appear the intelligence we received late last year was more accurate than we originally thought. The count was twelve rogues working together. All but four had dropped off the map by the next report we received. So we thought it was a fluke, an overestimation of numbers. I believe it was us who got it wrong.

Gretchen S. B.

Those four made their way west. They headed to Alaska, but disappeared, then reappeared much farther south.

"Three individuals matching the descriptions we have were detained by border patrol early last week. When officers came to question them all three were gone. They had been locked in a room for maybe half an hour. There was no car, they were walking across the border. I do not know where the fourth has gone. I would guess the rogues are most definitely in town. There are many heavy hitters from Vancouver, B.C. down to Portland. Rogues could be trying to recruit any of them."

Cesar agreed there was no reason to lean toward one target or another, but his gut told him Gwen might not be their only target, but she was definitely one of them.

Cesar dreaded the thought that came next. "They have to be getting outside help to completely disappear like that."

"I was thinking the same thing. This truly could turn into a war, and unlike the last one, we can't exactly hide it."

The last thing Cesar wanted was the Night World becoming public knowledge because of a war he could have prevented.

"Send me a debrief with all the information we have on this."

"Already done. I sent them to Viking's email, since you still refuse to use a computer. I sent word out to our Warriors in B.C., Washington, Oregon, northern California, Idaho, and Montana to look for these guys. I'm also sending out extra people to those states. We will find them and root them out before they do any more damage."

"Why do I feel as if you have been doing my job?" Cesar tried to sound upset, but he wasn't. It was good to see the world would still run in his absence.

Roman laughed. "Because I am. Since you're mating now, I'll probably be doing it for the next several months."

Part of Roman's report kept tugging at Cesar's attention. "What do you mean by more damage? I was unaware they had done anything worth noting."

Roman was silent for a moment. "The time period right before they reappeared in B.C. was when Narcina mysteriously died."

Cesar cursed. That was bad—very, very, bad. Narcina had lived in B.C. She was one of the oldest and most powerful MPs in the world. Younger MPs were known to make pilgrimages to meet her. If rogue Warriors were in some way responsible for her death, every MP in his kingdom would hunt them down without mercy. Then they would go after him. A war between MPs and Warriors would be the quickest way to anarchy in the North American Night World, but maybe that was what these rogues wanted.

"How big of a leap is that, Roman?"

"About three hundred miles difference."

Cesar cursed again, a very strong possibility. "I'm going to have to meet with the local MPs. Try to smooth things over now, before this gets out."

Roman only grunted.

"All right, keep me informed if anything else happens. Look for those other nine rogues. There has to be a sign of them somewhere."

"Will do. Take care of yourself, Augustus." Roman sounded worried.

It was a rare enough occurrence to catch Cesar off guard. "You too."

There was another grunt, then Roman hung up the phone.

Cesar sat there a moment. It was about an hour until dawn. They needed a plan of attack. Waiting for the rogues to make a move did not sit well with him. Cesar had always been one to start on the offensive when there was a problem. He should have gone with his instincts and brought the rogues in months ago. He needed a plan to smoke them out, but his brain wasn't working properly.

Cesar had greatly exaggerated when claiming he could last five days. At this rate he would be lucky to make three. He needed Gwen. He needed her nearby, and was absolutely sure his resolve would win out if he could just touch her, take in her scent.

Growling, Cesar stood up. His Warriors needed his full attention. How to smoke out the rogues? The MPs were key. Maybe he could get the MPs to act as bait to locate the rogues? That was it. He would have Viking take him to this Lucia today, and they would strike a bargain before meeting the Alpha. Set in his plan, Cesar headed back downstairs to have Viking read Roman's email.

Gretchen S. B.

Chapter 11

Gwen hated mornings. As a general rule, she thought they were evil. Sivia and Karin, it seemed, were morning people. If Gwen didn't like them so much she would stab them. She had given up the pretense of sleeping on their couch when their phone rang at seven o'clock. Now Karin was on the phone with her Pride Leader.

Gwen sat up and rubbed her face. Sivia loaned her some pjs but the Princess's style was definitely different from her own. The night dress hit Gwen mid-thigh.

"Really? What did he look like?" Karin's voice couldn't have held more interest.

Gwen exchanged looks with Sivia. The other woman shrugged and set a cup of coffee on the counter for her. Gwen mouthed her thanks as she moved into the kitchen.

"Well that is definitely good to know. I'll give her a call." She paused and smiled. "Absolutely, Minnie, I would never keep you from a good fight." Then she hung up the phone.

Before either Gwen or Sivia could speak, Karin held up one finger to silence them and dialed another number. It went for several rings before someone picked up.

"Good morning, Lucia. I hear you have an appointment with our hunky Alpha and some Warriors on Lady of the Dead detail." Karin smirked at Lucia's response. "We want to know what you heard." Karin had a split-second of surprise but she recovered fast. "Yes, that does include Gwen."

Both Gwen and Sivia stiffened. Neither wanted Warriors banging down the door.

Karin was silent for several moments. "If you agree to play on our team, I'll tell you a secret." She gave both Sivia and Gwen a thumbs-up.

Gwen had to smile. Gossip and secrets were a huge weakness for Lucia. She loved gaining new information; somehow very few people understood this and even less used it to their advantage.

She knew Karin's huge grin meant Lucia had agreed. "The King of North America is in town because of this." There was silence for a moment. "And I would put money on him being at your meeting this morning." Another pause, and Karin frowned. "Well,

I'm not done yet so hold your horses. He's in Maddening." She paused again, this time she put her hand over the received and mouthed 'she's laughing'. "Yes, there is more, don't worry you'll get your effort's worth. Gwen is his mate." Again Karin told them Lucia was laughing. "Here's the kicker; he thinks she doesn't know any of it. He's keeping the Kinghood, the Maddening and a possible war all a secret." She paused again and had no facial expressions as she listened. Then she smirked and gave another thumbs-up.

Karin was on the phone with Lucia for a few more minutes, but Gwen didn't listen. She knew Karin would tell her anything important. Now they would wait until Lucia could do some probing and Sivia would call her contacts. Gwen had been up half the night going through people she could call that wouldn't get back to the Warriors. Most would be better in person and she wasn't entirely sure she could risk being out and about that much. She hated having to rely on other people's contacts but if it got things done, that was all that was important.

Karin hung up the phone, grinning. "Lucia wished to extend her congratulations and condolences on your mating a Warrior King. She also is very excited to play 'boys versus girls' as she put it, since we all know the boys wouldn't let us play on their team with the King in town. She'll swing by after she leaves the precinct, she's thinking between ten and eleven. She said we could let Barrett and Marco play, that it's up to us. Which by the way I say 'yes' to. The more MPs in this, the better.

"But the reason I called Lucia in the first place was apparently the Wolf Minnie was bouncing around with last night is a cop. I guess some of the Warriors went to watch the kidnapper get arrested and the thing ended up trapping the four Warriors in a solid black mist, after it threw a deputy into a car. He's going to be fine, by the way. Some broken bones and a concussion. Minnie told me the Warriors couldn't get themselves out. That the Alpha called Lucia and bartered with her to get them out. Also, her bedfellow had to skip out early because Lucia is coming down to the precinct first thing in the morning to bind the vicious sucker, whatever it is, and see if she can identify whoever else it is connected to. So I skipped a few steps and just called Lucia." When she finished, Karin was giving the room a wide grin.

Sivia smiled. "Excellent, now let's see what else we can find out about this war that may or may not come."

Gwen pulled out her phone and all three of them started making calls.

Chapter 12

Cesar didn't understand Lucia. Raider called her to make an appointment for seven a.m., before she met Carter at eight. She then called back ten minutes later and canceled. So here he, Viking, Raider, and Carter sat waiting for Lucia to show up.

Cesar wanted nothing more than to bring order to this part of his kingdom. When this was over he would take Gwen away from these bad influences to the structure of the Warrior estate in Montana. She would see how the rest of the Night World worked. That thought caught him off guard. He assumed Gwen would choose to be with him and he wouldn't be dead or crazy by the time this was all over. Cesar gave himself a mental shake. He needed to concentrate on the problem at hand. Once these rogues were dealt with, he would hunt down Gwen himself, since no one else could seem to find her. Cesar would find her. There wasn't a doubt in his mind.

A woman walked toward them with a small smile on her face. This had to be Lucia. She didn't look like Cesar expected. She was tall for a woman, five-ten without the two-inch heels. Her thin body seemed ruthlessly toned from hours at a gym, her tiny waist made her hips look curvier in her pinstriped suit. Pale brown hair hung like a cape just short of her elbows. Large violet eyes dominated her tan face.

Cesar could feel power rolling off of her. He wasn't entirely sure if it was natural, or if she did it on purpose for effect. She looked straight at him and didn't stop walking until she was across the table from him.

"You, I don't know you."

Her eyes narrowed and her power rolled over his skin. It wasn't unpleasant, just not as nice as when Gwen did the same thing. Lucia had better control of her power and she was using it to get the answers she wanted.

"You feel like power." Her eyes flashed a shade darker, a common effect when MPs used their magic. "A lot of power. Tell me who you are. If you are truthful, we can all march in and poke at that being in harmony. Answer wrong and I'll take myself out for coffee instead."

She was a more powerful MP than Cesar was used to dealing with. He didn't think she was bluffing. Just how many powerful Night Worlders were in this state? Usually he could go anywhere undetected, but every damn being in Washington seemed to know who he was, except Gwen, the one who counted. Cesar felt a pang of guilt.

"I am King of North America."

Lucia smiled brightly. "Well then, shall we go meet the beast?" She didn't wait for an answer, just headed to the interrogation room where the kidnapper waited.

Cesar turned to Viking as the four of them stood. "Is she always like that?"

Viking blinked at him, confused for a beat. "Cocky? Yes. Why shouldn't she be? Remember, this coast has more powerful women than the rest of the Kingdom. The dynamic is different here." His mouth twitched. "Now let's watch the lady work."

Cursing himself for not having a better grasp on this part of his kingdom, Cesar put all his concentration into following Viking, Raider, and Lucia into the tiny room attached by the two-way mirror in the kidnapper's interrogation room.

The overweight man looked very worse for wear. Cesar said the activating words for his pendant and quickly saw the black form, slightly diminished, hovering around the man, feeding off him while it still could.

Cesar glanced to his left and blinked. He hadn't expected to see Lucia's magic, but there it was, a grey halo that matched her eyes, stretched about a foot out from her body. She was concentrating on the man in the other room.

Cesar turned back in time to see Carter close the door to the interrogation room behind him. The being swatted at him, but Carter didn't appear to feel it. He just sat down across the table, folding his arms over his chest.

"Ask him who he feeds off of."

Cesar actually jumped when he heard Lucia speak. She must have an earpiece because Carter touched his right ear and repeated the question.

At once the being seemed to be sucked into the man's body, the man's face went dead as if he were a puppet, but his mouth still moved and his voice rang out. "I feed off of filth, for now. Soon I will be strong enough to feed from anyone." There was a pause. "Who are you, sorceress?"

Lucia didn't answer, she mumbled under her breath. "He's not a smart one. That's for sure." Then she began drawing symbols against the glass. "Ask him who his master is?"

When Carter repeated the question, an inhuman roar came from the kidnapper's mouth. "I have no master."

Lucia snorted but continued drawing. "Well, that's certainly not true, but fine, have it your way. Ask him who his collaborators are, because they sold him out. His ride is dying of cancer."

Cesar wasn't the only one to turn to Lucia in shock. Carter actually turned in his chair before repeating her question.

There was another roar, louder this time. Carter's ears must have been screaming in pain, but he didn't show it.

"That sorcerer would not dare lie to me. I can crush him like an ant."

Lucia made an interested noise. "A male MP, huh? That is interesting. Tell him I will free him from his ride if he shows me all of his collaborators."

There were several sounds of disapproval as Carter repeated her proposal. No one wanted that thing free.

Lucia waved her left hand at them, since her right was still drawing. "Relax. I said I would free from his ride, not free him. I'm sending him back to where he came from, regardless."

Cesar was surprised she would do that without negotiating a price first.

"You will free me if I show you him. Will you punish him?"

Lucia's mouth twitched. "Are you familiar with the name Sin?"

The kidnapper's body actually shuddered; the effect was creepy.

"Yes, she will do."

Lucia pressed her hand to the glass, closed her eyes and murmured something. The glass glowed gray for a moment then became glass again. She walked past Cesar and then out of the room. A few seconds later she was in the interrogation room and reaching out to touch the kidnapper's bare hand.

"Show me," she said softly, like most people would to a small child.

Her eyes closed for a minute or two. When she opened them again, she removed her hand and walked over to the glass. She tapped it three times and the glass glowed gray. She put the palm that touched the kidnapper up to the glass and murmured something. A second later the gray shot off the glass and hit the kidnapper between the eyes. The momentum shot his neck back. Then the black being seemed to ooze from the same spot. It built itself into a solid ball the size of a fist. It pulsed and began to squirm as if starting to realize what Lucia was doing, but not fast enough, because ten seconds later it faded back to wherever it had come from.

Lucia continued to murmur for a few more beats, then she opened her eyes and turned to the glass. "Excuse me, but I have the overwhelming urge to wash my hands." Then she disappeared from the room.

Cesar deactivated his pendant. He never actually watched magic performed like that before. Was that how MPs saw the world? Was that how Gwen saw the world? Cesar quickly dismissed that thought. No, Gwen saw the Spirit World. That was different.

About five minutes later they sat around the same table as before. It was as if none of them really wanted whatever information Lucia could give them, and she was not in any particular hurry to give it.

Lucia looked up from the table, her eyes going from Cesar to Carter. Cesar knew something was up; she only looked at the leaders, which meant a power play was coming.

"I ask for sovereignty over punishment since this is a Magical Practitioner matter." Lucia's voice was flat, as if she hoped that would make them not want to call her on her absurd request.

Carter leaned in. His eyes narrowed and his jaw clenched. "He injured one of my men, Lucia!" He was quiet but the threat was there.

Lucia did not appear fazed. "With all due respect. It was one of your officers, not one of your wolves therefore your claim has no standing here."

Cesar couldn't believe it. Only Narcina and maybe two MPs in the old world would have challenged an Alpha like that. What was she thinking?

Lucia continued before any of them could speak. "Besides, I'm sure if we take a good look at the officer injured he will turn out to be a human psychic and we all know, for better or worse, they fall into the Magical Practitioner category. So that makes it a crime of MP on MP. My giving you any information is simply a courtesy." Then she stood, straightening her skirt.

"Lucia!"

Cesar turned at the threat in Carter's growl. The other man was furious and looming over the table.

Lucia simply turned, head high, giving Carter an unamused, almost bored stare. "Lieutenant. It would be unwise to challenge me in an open forum."

There was a rhythmic clicking to her heels as she walked back to the table. She stood across from Carter and looked him directly in the eyes. Her voice was only loud enough for those at the table to hear it. "You think I am unaware of the video cameras in this precinct. You can't touch me, there are too many non-cop witnesses. I, on the other hand, could give you a heart attack even a coroner wouldn't question." Then she leaned back to encompass the whole table. "And if you think I'm stupid enough to send a pissy Wolf and a Maddening Warrior after one of my own, then you have another thing coming. Don't worry, I'm not charging you for banishing that thing." Her hair swirled around her. This time she did leave the building.

"Damn it!" Carter hissed as he slid back into his chair.

Viking patted the other man's shoulder. "She has a point. It's an MP matter, and they prefer to police themselves. As one of the strongest known MPs on this coast, she had the right to demand sovereignty."

Cesar couldn't believe what he was hearing. In any other part of the country, Warriors were the top of the Night World food chain, period. Then came whatever Were was most predominant to the area. This every group for themselves didn't happen, outside of Immortals. Warriors were the dispensers of justice for the Night World. He couldn't wait to get back home.

"I need this social structure explained to me, now." It came out harsher than Cesar intended, but he didn't try to fix it.

Raider sighed and scrubbed his face. "Okay, first." He held up one finger, then turned to Carter, who appeared confused.

"Anywhere else in the world, an MP wouldn't dare refuse you information. In most of the northern world, Wolves are top of the food chain, second only to Warriors. There is a reason our leader is called King."

Carter snorted. "Must be nice."

Raider ignored him and turned back to Cesar. "In the Pacific Northwest, most of us settled here because it was as far west as we could get. It was to escape the structure you love so much. We are more of the 'to each their own' type. The Night World is like that once you get past the initial social hierarchy. You just don't know it because even amongst thieves you're a top dog. For those of us without a title, we pretty much intermingle, or don't. We don't fight for power over others the way you top dogs do. It just so happens there are so many of us regular Joes here that the entire social structure fits the majority. Get it?"

Cesar nodded slowly. "You don't interfere in other species' business because initially no one was truly powerful enough to do so and you were all trying too hard to escape mankind anyway."

Raider waved his hand. "Close enough. So are we walking Seattle in search of rogues yet?"

Cesar cursed. He had meant to ask the MP if she could track them. Somehow he didn't think she would.

"Let us go check in with the others and then we will divide up the territory."

With that they headed back to the east side of the lake.

Chapter 13

Sin picked the lock, instead of knocking, at about nine-thirty. She was whistling and her irises had been red, so no one said anything. Red eyes are when a Shapeshifter was most dangerous. Red eyes meant Sin was still in Blood Lust from killing whomever she had been sanctioned to kill. So Gwen and the others tiptoed around her for the twenty minutes it took for her eyes to clear. Then they filled her in on the information they'd gathered. She giggled disconcertingly at the idea of getting to kill people.

It was ten-fifteen when Lucia came knocking at the door.

Karin turned to Sin. "You see how she knocks instead of breaking in?"

Sin shrugged. "Then how does she practice?"

Karin shut her mouth and opened the door. Sin's logic was never something any of them wanted to encourage.

Lucia gave them all a tight-lipped smile. "Before I begin." She turned to Sin. "I need to hire you for a job."

Sin narrowed her eyes. "I'm not allowed unsanctioned jobs. You know this. Are you trying to get me killed?" Most people would have been joking with that question, but Sin meant it.

Lucia didn't take her eyes from the Shapeshifter; it was a generally accepted rule that if Sin was in the room, anyone without a death wish kept one eye on her. "Of course not. Then you couldn't kill Marvin for me."

Sin seemed to relax and nodded. That made perfect sense to her.

"I called the headquarters in Illinois and registered my complaint and requested you. I thought they would have called you by now." Lucia gave her phone a puzzled glance.

Sin leaned back on the couch and stretched out her legs. "Nope, takes at least two days. Seven if it's not dire. Lots of paperwork, and Shapeshifters hate paperwork. That's why I never do mine." She smiled.

Lucia folded her arms. "You mean if I want somebody dangerous killed I have to wait two days?"

Sin's focus became eerily clear. It happened sometimes, but it still made Gwen uneasy. To see just how sharp a mind Sin had under all the Shapeshifter instabilities was always unsettling. "Or do

Gretchen S. B.

it yourself. We are trying to survive here. If our sources say that the kill won't start a feud or a war, or that we won't be killing a decent person then I'll get the go ahead call. We are not in the business of giving others a reason to start killing off Shapeshifters again." There was a beat, then the clarity faded and Sin was back to looking mildly crazy. "If not, the call will come through that you set me up and I'll get to kill you." Then she started whistling again.

The rest of them exchanged glances. No one seemed sure what to do with Sin's moment of clarity. So they unanimously ignored it. Gwen was grateful.

Lucia cleared her throat. "Okay, well it looks like there might be trouble in our world after all."

She waved her hand at Karin before the other woman could do more than open her mouth.

"Let me get all the way through this first."

Karin shut her mouth and folded her arms.

"So I skimmed Carter and the Warriors' thoughts as I approached the building. I know, I know, it's against all sorts of treaties, so let's pretend I got the information a different way."

Gwen really didn't like the idea of Lucia poking around in other people's heads. It was unethical, but she kept her mouth shut. Depending on what information Lucia got, Gwen might be showing the Warriors how to better guard their thoughts.

When no one spoke, Lucia continued. "I have to say, I'd heard rumors and Narcina's description, but this was the first time I've ever encountered a Warrior in Maddening." She looked at Gwen. "His mind was hotter than hell. Every other thought was about you. He was trying quite valiantly to keep his mind on the problem at hand. It was quite noble. I mean, he was failing miserably, but it was a good effort. I had to call Barrett on my way over here and make him promise me a quickie. I'm almost envious of you, almost, and that's saying something, since I'm never envious of anyone.

"Once I was able to get past the Maddening, and before they saw me and put up their guards, I was able to get that there are rogue Warriors in the area and the general consensus is that they are after Gwen. I don't know how they came to these conclusions or what facts there were, as I didn't have the time to delve before they noticed my intrusion. As for the being; he was interesting.

"He called himself Sufix. I don't know where he got it from; he wasn't very bright. Had Gwen been at full power—by the way Gwen I can see big gaping holes in your shielding and your power is shining pitifully and that needs to be fixed soon—if Gwen had been at full Lady of the Dead status she could have handled this thing. He was of the Spirit World. Since that is not my forte, I don't know what Sufix was beyond that. He wasn't ever human, that much I gathered.

"He wasn't strong on his own, more of a tool for the use of beings more powerful than he. An MP snagged him in a trap, the likes of which I have never seen before, but as I said, I try to stay out of the Spirit World. It's just so messy. The MP trapped him and bartered with him. If Sufix would pledge allegiance to him then the MP would find a good ride for Sufix to feed off of. Unfortunately for the MP, Sufix is a moron and unused to that level of power, so he drew a lot of attention and the MP abandoned him. But once an MP makes a bond like that, it takes time for it to completely clear, so I was able to see the trail. Instead of tracking it, I made a deal with Sufix, who showed me the MP and the trap. On the downside, I know the MP."

Gwen began to panic. Lucia lived with her two lovers, Barrett and Marco. She might be the strongest MP in several states, but they were both known for being damn strong themselves. The three of them would never betray one another. If one of her guys was to blame, Lucia would move heaven and Earth to save them. Gwen couldn't bring herself to ask.

Sin, on the other hand, had no such qualms. She was stroking her outer thigh, and Gwen knew Sin carried a wicked looking blade under her leather pants. "So, who is he?"

Lucia frowned. "That's the weird part. His name is Marvin. He lives in the US, but that little bit of land is surrounded by Canada, I can never remember the name. Marvin can barely be called an MP, I mean he has powers and all, but could not do this kind of spell. Even stranger is that Marvin is a red MP. This trap of his is black magic, and it's too complicated for someone who's newly black to do. Plus Marvin isn't on the watch list. Every white and gray MP has a black list in their home, just as a precaution. I check that thing every morning. Marvin isn't registered as black. That's damn scary. That means someone stronger is working with him. MPs don't just gain power, we are born with it, and no one should be able to hide from the black and red lists."

There was silence for a few moments. MPs were very secretive. Gwen hadn't known most of what Lucia had just told them. She had no idea what those lists were and she was afraid to ask. She hadn't known MPs were color-coded.

Karin broke the silence. "Okay, now what?"

They all looked at her.

"I'm sorry, but Were culture isn't as secretive as all of you guys. We are all fairly out in the open. So I'm sure I'm not the only one wondering what the hell Lucia is talking about with the rainbow and magical lists. So either enlighten us or don't mention it at all, because I want any and all information that will help me hunt down the bad guys."

Sin's fist shot straight up in the air. "Here, here."

Gwen fought her smile. That was why she had so many Were friends. They might have the least in common with her but they hated secrets. Weres were all about having everything in the open. It was refreshing after her quiet Warriors.

Lucia looked at the two of them with annoyance. "There are four categories of MPs: White, Grey, Red, and Black. White is the rarest, and incidentally, the most powerful. White MPs are pure in one way or another, as they have never done magic for personal gain, or to harm others. They are just all around goody-two-shoes.

"The vast majority, I'd say about fifty percent of us, are gray. Sure, we occasionally slip up, or what have you. We aren't good or bad, but we lean more toward the white. We just aren't prissy.

"Then there are the Red. They have done something bad, not Black bad usually, but still bad. Red is usually a transitory color; people don't stay Red for more than a few years. There are exceptions of course. Red is a very fine line to walk, and they tend to keep a low profile or get banished from their Strata, or group. They either get killed or become Black.

"Black MPs are dangerous. They do all the really nasty magic: killing, summoning bad beings, removing free will, rigging it so the Red Sox become champions. They are devious and don't have anything to lose. That's why we have the Black and Red lists, so that we came protect ourselves from specific MPs.

"If this stuff gets too messy, I'll have to drop out. I'm too powerful to go Red. If I got Red, the Strata-Enforcers will put me down. They won't risk it and I won't either."

Gwen saw Sivia reach for a necklace under her shirt at the mention of the Strata-Enforcers. Her curiosity got the better of her.

"And they are?"

Lucia looked right at her and it was the first time Gwen ever saw real fear in the other woman's eyes. "They are like the police, except with less rules. Their entire job is to enforce MP council rules and to keep balance in the MP world. To make sure the Black is under control. They are the bogymen for us MPs, kill first maybe ask questions later." Lucia shuddered.

Gwen didn't like the sound of that. "Wouldn't they kill this Marvin guy, then?"

Lucia shook her head. "Not if he isn't on their radar. Most powerful MPs are on the east coast or in the old world, and the Strata-Enforcers are global instead of regional, Even if they heard about him, it would take them months to get here. That is why Strata banish Red MPs; none of us want the Strata-Enforcers at our doorsteps."

Sivia continued to finger the necklace under her shirt. "So, you think this Marvin guy is working with someone stronger?"

Lucia nodded. "Absolutely, but I don't know who. There are only a handful of Reds in the Pacific Northwest powerful enough to cause this level of trouble, less now that Narcina is dead."

She paused to draw in the air in front of her. Gwen saw MPs do this regularly; they were very superstitious, almost as if their drawings would protect them from their own words.

"And there is only one Black and he is in Idaho. Plus he hates Marvin's guts, something about an old girlfriend. So he would never work with Marvin. Perry, that's the Black's name, actually bound some of Marvin's powers to weaken him, so though he is powerful, Marvin can't really do much. The only reason Perry doesn't kill Marvin is to avoid the Strata-Enforcers. We need balance in the magic world, according to Perry, and as long as he doesn't kill, the Strata-Enforcers have told him they won't kill him. It's all very complicated."

"What about the other Reds? There must be one in the immediate area? Would they help Marvin?" This was from Karin.

Lucia shook her head. "No, never."

"How can you be sure?"

Lucia's face showed her nervousness a second before she blanked it. "Because Barrett only works with Marco and me."

The silence was so thick Gwen felt she could have swam on it. Barrett could become a bad guy. That was dangerous. Gwen had no doubt Marco and Lucia would stand with him no matter what. That alone would rip the Pacific Northwest Night World apart. At least for the moment they were the good guys, right? Gwen shook that line of thought from her head.

"I give you my word I won't share any of this."

Gwen knew she had said the right thing when she saw Lucia's shoulders lower.

Both Sivia and Karin said the same thing and Sin laughed.

"Not to worry, I'm phenomenal with secrets. No one can ever tell if I'm joking."

It was true. Even if Sin told someone, they wouldn't believe her. Well, Gwen would, but everyone else wouldn't.

Lucia inclined her head. "You have our gratitude."

Karin shook her head, as if clearing it. "Moving on. My cousin, Orlando, manages a hotel downtown, and he told me he saw more Warriors this morning than in the last month. I'm guessing that means the Warriors have tracked these rogues to Seattle, or they are desperate to find Gwen. We are going to have to tread very lightly so they don't realize we are hiding their future Queen." Her lip twitched with that last word.

Gwen rolled her eyes. "Could we not call me that please? In fact, let's ignore it entirely."

"Done!" Sin jumped in so fast it startled everyone.

Sivia blinked a few times at Sin before speaking. "Yes, um, I spoke to both Buccaneer and Bandit. Poet already spoke to them, but neither wants to work with the 'establishment' as they called it. They plan on teaming up and hunting the other rogues themselves. They claim that these other rogues give all rogues a bad name. I didn't really have to convince them to work with us instead. Buccaneer is docking his boat on Lake Union about now and Bandit's driving down from B.C. He should be here this afternoon. That's a plus. So we will see what they've gathered. But we need a place to meet. The Warriors will get suspicious if so many random

Night Worlders 'just happen' to be in Shoreline...at our apartment. Usually I'd say Venture or Gwen's store, but those are out of the question."

Gwen felt bad about that. If not for her, they could all go to Venture. She was becoming a hindrance.

Sin stood up. "I know a place."

They all looked at her, suspiciously.

"What? I do. And the Warriors won't look for us there because the owner is very anti-Night World. We can go in, but we have to behave." Sin sounded like she was repeating an order given to her before. "There is a club near the stadiums called The Swollen Bowel, and it is run by a family of Reoccurring Immortals. They keep to themselves and won't bother us as long as we don't become regulars."

Everyone looked as surprised as Gwen felt. Apparently none of them knew there was a group of Reoccurrers in Seattle. As long as they weren't too obvious, none of the Reoccurrers would know they were other Night Worlders. Since Reoccurring Immortals were some of the weakest beings in the Night World, they tended to stay away from everyone else, with Seattle's high concentration that was almost impossible. The only Reoccurrer Gwen had ever met was Lexa, the grad student who worked for her.

Sivia recovered first. "Okay then, Swollen Bowel it is. Let's say seven. Both Karin and I will be off work by then. I'll let Buccaneer and Bandit know. Karin, let Minnie and Marnie know. Lucia, do you want to have your guys there?"

Lucia nodded once. "Absolutely."

Sivia turned to Sin. "Does that work for you?"

Sin shrugged. "I'm currently without assignment."

When she didn't say anything else, Sivia seemed to take it as a yes and turned to Gwen.

"You're more than welcome to stay here. It'll be boring, but you'll be safe."

Gwen shook her head. She couldn't do nothing, it was against her nature. "No. I'm going to take a bus to Bothell. There is a store where they know me and will let me work in peace. I'm going to see if I can use the Spirit World to hunt down these rogues or this MP."

They watched her suspiciously. Gwen knew why. She was talking about powers that no one knew she had. No one would question her ability to do it, though, because Lady of the Dead powers were so rare and, unlike the Warriors, these women would trust her to take care of herself. If she said she could do something, they would believe her.

Lucia folded her arms. "What store? Should we need to find you, we need the name. I could scry for you but knowing the name would save so much time."

Gwen nodded. "It's called That Occult. It's in Bothell. It is run by married witches."

Lucia raised an eyebrow. "What type of witches?" MPs were not particularly fond of human witches. Gwen could never figure out why.

"The man, Morris, actually is an architect and doesn't spend too much time in the shop. I have a sneaking suspicion that he is a lower level MP. He was orphaned very young so I don't think he knows what he truly is, and it isn't our place to tell him. Deanna is your run-of-the-mill human witch. They are good friends of mine and they know I like to escape from time to time, so they'll find nothing strange about me just showing up."

Sin shoved her hands in her pockets while staring at the front door. "I'm coming with you, so we'll take the bike. No arguments, I don't like the idea of you by yourself with all these crazy people about."

Gwen knew the irony of Sin's statement was not lost on any of them, but no one would point it out. No death wishes in this room. With everything settled, they went their separate ways. Gwen tried to think of a way to explain Sin's eccentricities to Deanna without spilling the beans about the Night World. She walked a fine line but she also knew Sin couldn't be convinced to go somewhere else. Reasoning with Sin was like reasoning with an oncoming train: you just get out of the way.

Chapter 14

Getting Lucia on the phone proved harder than Cesar would have thought. She didn't answer Viking's calls until after one. She then told Viking she only answered because she was beginning to find her ringtone irritating. After ten minutes of negotiating, Viking finally convinced Lucia to meet him and Cesar in Seattle. Both of them now waited for her in one of the hundreds of Starbucks stores Cesar had noticed since he'd arrived.

He couldn't figure out this obsession with coffee these people harbored, and Viking couldn't explain it to him. Despite the time of day there was a steady stream of customers for the twenty minutes they waited. There were all manner of people, from college kids to business people. Some of the drink orders contained so many words, said at such a speed, that to Cesar, it seemed one five-second burst of gibberish after another.

Lucia finally sauntered through the door at a quarter to two. She glanced at Cesar and Viking, and holding up one finger, she passed them and stepped up to the counter. She gave the dumbfounded guy at the register a dazzling smile.

"Hi there, can I get a grande, extra hot, half-caf, no foam, soy, three pump, sugar-free vanilla latte, please."

The guy blinked at her a moment before nodding and scribbling on a cup and rattling the order back at her before naming what Cesar thought was an exurbanite amount of money for a cup of coffee. Lucia just continued to smile before handing him a gold card. She continued to ignore Cesar and Viking as she waited for her drink.

Cesar ground his teeth. His patience was worn thin and this MP only made matters worse. It didn't help that the Maddening kept him on edge at all times. He needed Gwen. Cesar let out a rough exhalation; he was becoming disgusted with himself.

Lucia finally sat down at their little black table and watched him as she crossed her legs. "You're still early in, aren't you? If you were two days farther along you couldn't just sit here." She took a sip from her cup.

Cesar clenched his jaw. How was it that she knew about the Maddening?

"We are not here to talk about me. I wish to ask for your services."

Lucia's left eyebrow quirked up but she didn't say a word.

"We have reason to believe some rogue Warriors are looking to recruit an MP to work with them. What would it take to get you to either track them or to bait them into wanting you?"

Lucia gave him a speculative look. "That depends on how dangerous they are."

Cesar sighed. He had hoped she wouldn't ask that. "We have reason to believe they may have been involved with Narcina's death, though we have no proof to back it, especially since they seem to be in hiding."

Lucia's eyes flashed darker, but that was the only reaction to his statement. "I will do the former for you, but if what you say is true, they will be after me soon anyway, therefore I will not do the latter."

Cesar figured as much, but he hadn't expected such a calm reaction to his news. "Fair enough. What will it cost me?"

Lucia set down her cup. "How many are we talking?"

"Three, maybe four."

She seemed to think about it a moment before answering. "I have no immediate need of anything, but I will take a rain check and some information as my payment."

That was dangerous, but Cesar wasn't sure he had much choice. He needed the location of the rogues, but a rain check held by a MP was a bad idea. She could collect at any time. He needed her help, and Viking, Poet, and Raider had assured him she was their best hope. He couldn't risk the rogues getting to Gwen first.

Growling he nodded. "Fine, I agree to your terms." He stuck out his hand. A handshake with a MP was more binding than any paper contract.

Lucia raised her eyebrow again and smiled as she shook his hand. Cesar's hand received a jolt, like static electricity. He had made enough deals with MPs to recognize the feeling. She just bound him to her terms. Whether he liked it or not.

As she let go of his hand, she grabbed her cup and leaned back in her chair, smiling at him. Cesar didn't like it.

"Now for my information. What are you planning to do with Gwen?"

Cesar's temper flashed on the tail of his surprise. What exactly did Lucia know? Cesar didn't want to give her more information than necessary.

"What do you mean?" It took every ounce of strength he possessed to keep his voice quiet and his tone even.

Her lips twitched. "We are very protective of her. Won't let her mate just anybody and the Warriors that protect her sure won't contest you. We, on the other hand, have it in our power to keep her hidden from you until you're past redemption."

Lucia knew where Gwen was. She was helping hide his mate. Cesar's heart speed up and with it came a new spike of lust-induced madness.

His voice was all growl. "Where is she?"

Lucia didn't appear intimidated at all. "I actually do not know her exact location at the moment. Answer my question."

Cesar took several deep breaths, trying to clear the heavy fog from his mind. Ripping the MP's throat out would not help anyone. His answer to Lucia would affect his future, and he needed a clear head.

"If she will accept me, I will take her back to Montana with me."

That didn't go over well with anyone at the table. Lucia frowned and Viking straightened.

"We can't have that, King," Lucia responded, shaking her head.

Cesar felt his head begin to cloud again but Lucia held up her hand before he could speak.

"She means too much to the community here. She has created a safe place for people in our world to go. But setting that aside, we can't allow that because it would kill her. Take it from someone who actually knows her, maybe not well, but better than you. She would wither in that Warrior fortress you have in Montana. She needs a lot of freedom to flourish, and you would be taking that and her home away from her." Lucia stood up and looked down at Cesar. "If she loses her mind and accepts you as her mate, saving you from madness and death, maybe you shouldn't punish her for that."

She looked at Cesar as if they were the only two people in the café. For the first time, Cesar started to worry about what might

Gretchen S. B.

happen when this was all over and if Gwen said yes. Would things be worse for her then?

Lucia blinked and looked from Cesar to Viking. "Be at my house at six tonight and bring all the information you have on these rogues, the more the better." Without another word, she left and crossed the street to a forest green SUV.

There was silence for several minutes as thoughts chased each other through Cesar's clouding mind. He saw Viking shift to face him out of the corner of his eye. The other man waited until Cesar looked at him to speak.

"I will follow her. Wherever you see fit to take her I will follow her, even if you command me not to. She is my family now and that is more important to me than my allegiance to you and the kingdom."

There it was, a glaring line in the sand. In that moment, Cesar knew he and his mate were doomed because no matter her decision, one of them would be screwed. Cesar growled in frustration. After a lifetime of fighting, the cosmos had finally rewarded him with a mate, but as fate would have it, he wouldn't be able to keep her. Cesar resigned himself to the fact that if Gwen did accept him he would only be able to keep her through the first stage of mating. After that it would be back to the solitary existence he no longer wanted.

Cesar stood up quickly and tried to concentrate on the problem at hand. The last thing his people needed was him distracted. Viking followed suit as Cesar strode out the door.

"We'll cross that bridge when we come to it," Cesar said more to himself than Viking. He wasn't even sure if the other man heard him.

The two of them were to meet Raider and Kegan outside Venture. The four of them could probably get one more sweep of the city before heading back to Gwen's to grab copies of the information they had on the rogues.

Chapter 15

It was five-thirty and Gwen hadn't gotten any pertinent information from any being in the Spirit World. She had gained all kinds of semi-useless information. Gwen had been told Warriors were hunting around downtown for four men she assumed were the rogues. Apparently they didn't know Sin already killed one.

Sighing, Gwen unfolded her legs and stepped off the yoga mat she had sat on for the last hour and a half. Her legs ached, and that was what ended her search. Her screaming leg muscles. Gwen had just started stretching when the door to the small meditation room opened. Deanna stood in the doorway with Sin right on her heels. Deanna smiled apologetically.

Gwen met Deanna's husband Morris four years ago, at the annual convention for holistic healing. Since her bookstore held similar subjects Gwen and Poet attended yearly. Originally she couldn't get anyone else to go, it became her and Poet's tradition. Morris's lecture on ways to create and encourage balance within one's home spoke to Gwen. Morris was a fantastic public speaker and Gwen went out of her way to tell him so. He blushed and humbly thanked her. Then introduced her to his wife. Gwen and Deanna hit it off immediately and were close ever since.

Deanna was twig thin, like most vegans Gwen knew. She kept her fine pale hair waist length and almost never wore it up. Deanna and Morris were both five-ten. Deanna had this air about her that breathed a calm, loving presence into whatever room she entered. She seemed wiser than her forty years.

At the moment Deanna seemed to be struggling between apology and amusement. "Sin wishes to speak to you. She is not exactly happy with me for making her wait. I told her you would be undisturbed until you came back to yourself. When I informed her you re-entered the building, I barely beat her back here. Where you able to find anything pertinent?"

Deanna respected people's space. She would never outright ask what Gwen was looking for, but she was too maternal not to ask if the search had been a success.

Gwen smiled. "No, but I'm going to give it one more try before we head out."

Gretchen S. B.

Deanna nodded. "I am sorry to hear that. Morris and I will send well wishes for you when we meditate tonight. Will you be eating when you leave here?"

Gwen held in her chuckle. Deanna was always the mother. "Yes Deanna, we are going to a place that serves food. I promise I'll eat something."

Deanna left Sin and Gwen in the room, shutting the door behind her.

Sin inhaled deeply. Gwen knew she was trying to scent something. Finally she just wrinkled her nose. "I don't get it. She smells of ginger, lavender, and sage, but there's something I can't put a finger on. I can't smell it but I know it's there."

Gwen bit her lip. Sin had a good sixth sense, she just didn't believe in it. She always attributed the feelings she got to one of her five senses. Gwen didn't think it was worth arguing over.

"It's her power. You can sense her power."

Sin tilted her head. "I can smell power? That's cool. I like that."

Gwen shook her head. "You wanted to talk to me?"

Sin gave her that blank eerie stare for a few moments. "Did I?"

Gwen wasn't entirely sure if Sin was going to remember whatever had been so important in the first place.

After another moment, Sin tapped her chin with one of her long black nails. "Was it the creepy thin man...No, that's a movie...that it will rain next Tuesday...OH!" Sin's eyes snapped back to Gwen. "Lucia called while you were out. She has a meeting with Wally at six."

Gwen held up her hand and waved it to stop Sin. As expected the sudden movement gained all of Sin's attention and she stopped talking. Gwen quickly ended the movement.

"Who's Wally?"

Sin blinked down at her. "Wally, the Warrior's Leading Laddy. Wa-l-ly."

It was Gwen's turn to blink. "Did Lucia call him that?"

Sin tilted her head. "Call him what?"

Gwen shook her head. "Never mind. Lucia told you she had a meeting at six."

The other woman scratched her head absently. "Yes...Wally wants to hire her to find the rogues. Also that she asked him what he plans to do with you if you accept him. He said he would take you to Montana. Lucia told him that made him stupid. Then she said not to tell you that part because it might upset you." Sin smiled at her perceived success at relaying the message. Then she left.

Gwen just stared after her. It didn't matter how long she knew Sin, the woman still threw her off half the time. So August had hired Lucia to find the rogues. She would no doubt tell the rest of their group what she found. Lucia was right, however. The idea of Montana was not something Gwen wanted. Western Washington was her home. It had everything she could ever want. The community here knew her, and to some extent cared about her. Gwen couldn't live in the isolated Warrior fortress. She needed to be able to run to a sports game, or a play, or a concert on a whim. Gwen was a city girl, period. She wouldn't accept a man who would hold her hostage, no matter how hot he was.

Gwen shook her head. She needed clear thoughts to search the Spirit World for information especially since she hadn't fully recovered from last night. Her powers weren't anywhere near one hundred percent, making her doubt her efforts to make any progress at all.

She did a few more stretches but thought better of trying another search. She and Sin were pretty far north and they were going to hit rush hour driving through the cities. Gwen rolled up the borrowed mat and placed it on the rack before leaving to find Sin.

Chapter 16

Cesar didn't know much about Seattle's outlying cities. He knew Seattle, Bellevue, and Olympia, and that was it. When Viking said they were going to a city called Lynnwood, Cesar hadn't the slightest clue where they were going. On top of that, they hit rush hour traffic, which was horrendous. Cesar never thought rush hour could get this bad in Seattle. He was glad to not be driving, but the stop and go traffic rubbed his already raw nerves. Every time they came to a dead stop, Cesar wanted to punch someone.

He was not even a third of the way through the Maddening, yet Cesar already had a constant erection, and his temper spiked at the slightest provocation. He was becoming a tyrant and there wasn't a thing he could do to stop it. He needed to find Gwen, badly.

It was increasingly hard to clear his head. As Raider pulled the SUV up to a townhouse in a half-built development, Cesar felt as if his mind was surrounded by a red fog.

Before the four of them reached the porch, the front door opened and a bald man of about thirty stood in the doorway. Something about him reminded Cesar of the South American Warrior King, who in his first life had been an Aztec warrior. This man's skin was a shade or two lighter and he was an inch or two taller. He was all lean muscle just like the Aztec. From what Viking told Cesar on the way here, this man must be Marco. Marco didn't step aside as they reached the door. He merely eyed them, suspiciously.

Raider folded his arms as he addressed the other man. "Are you going to let us in, Marco, or leave us to freeze our butts off?"

Marco snorted as his eyes settled on Cesar. "You are Warriors, you would not freeze. But Lucia did not tell us one of you was in Maddening. Barrett and I wouldn't have agreed to letting you in our home had we known. I'll be having words with her." A beat after he finished his sentence, Marco moved to the side so the four of them could go in.

Cesar was sure had he been clear-headed he could have appreciated the wide front room but he couldn't keep his attention on the room long enough to get a good look at it.

He did see Lucia standing over a table in the middle of the room with a large man, who could have passed as the poster boy for

WASPs everywhere. The man, Barrett, was looking at Cesar and frowning. Cesar had to fight not to let that piss him off.

Lucia held out her hand. "May I have that file please." It sounded like a question, even though it wasn't.

Kegan moved from where he stood on Cesar's left to hand Lucia the photos and descriptions of the rogues. Then he backed up.

Lucia actually smiled. "Who's afraid of the big bad MP?" She sang it.

It must have been a reference to something because Viking snorted from behind Cesar.

Lucia flipped through the file, skimming each page. She stopped at the first photograph and caressed the image. In one quick move she dropped the file, ripped up the picture, and tossed the pieces into a large bowl filled with blue liquid on the table in front of her. Then she started mumbling and drawing symbols over the bowl.

Barrett turned to the blank wall on Cesar's left. It was a half wall since it was technically the side of the staircase. He began mumbling and tracing.

After a minute or so, blue light began to emanate from the bowl. Then images in the same blue appeared on the wall, as if there was a projector in the room. Cesar watched as three of the rogues walked down some street he didn't know.

"Does anyone recognize where they are?"

Raider's voice came from behind Kegan's shoulder. "Give it a second, I might."

They stood in silence as the three rogues turned a corner in whatever city they were in and entered a grocery store.

Raider cursed. "Yeah, they're in Burien. There's a rather large nest of Werehawks in Burien; there are seven adults."

The image snapped off and Lucia sat down on a nearby dark green couch. "There's also a new Strata a little south of there. Their territory is Burien to SeaTac, and there's maybe thirty of them, all young."

Cesar cursed. Whether the rogues were after the Hawks or the MPs, it was his problem and either way it would start a war. Cesar turned to the men behind him. "How long will it take us to get there?"

Gretchen S. B.

Viking shook his head. "If we hit no traffic, forty-five minutes. Rochester and Kincaid are still downtown. Trapper, Native, and Deuce should be around somewhere."

Cesar nodded. "Call them. Tell them we are en route but if anyone is closer they should tail them but not move in until we get there. Hopefully someone can keep an eye on them." He then inclined his head to Lucia. "Thank you for your services. You will understand why we will be leaving without further price negotiations."

Lucia mirrored his movement. "Of course. Please let me know if they get one of my people. I will be calling them as soon as you leave."

Cesar nodded as he and the other Warriors all but ran out the door. If they were lucky they could stop these rogues before they did anything else stupid. If he didn't have to kill them right away, maybe they could get some information out of them.

Chapter 17

The Swollen Bowel was almost as gross looking as the name. Inside the club the walls and ceiling were black and splattered with glowing red paint. Gwen knew it was the effects of the black lights, which was the only lighting inside the club, but it was still eerie.

She and Sin waited in line for ten minutes before getting in. It took another ten to hunt down Sivia and the three Werepanthers. They sat at three square tables pushed together in the far right corner of the room. Gwen and Sin waded through the other tables, about three-fourths of which were full. Gwen couldn't understand how they could be this full so early on a weeknight.

Gwen ordered a chicken burger and Sin a steak from their young waitress when Buccaneer and Bandit came through the doors. Buccaneer and Bandit, known to the local Night World as the Pirates, were one of the two sets of Warrior twins in the world.

Their father had literally been a Caribbean pirate, and their mom had been the daughter of a wealthy merchant. Who, according to legend, had been furious to find out his only daughter had taken up with a criminal. He killed said daughter and lay in wait for when the pirate came to take her away with him. The legend went one of two ways at that point. Either the pirate killed the father and everyone related, or the more popular version, the merchant only claimed to kill her but really sent her away to raise the babies in a convent and the pirate never did come back for her.

Neither of the brothers would say what really happened or how they settled so far north. Gwen was pretty sure they enjoyed all the speculation. Both men were six two and sandy blond. They both kept their hair back with the tail reaching their shoulder blades, except for one very thin braid that hung loose from each of their left temples. Bandit, however, dyed his hair black, and it was the only way to tell them apart. They had identical lean builds and Gwen never saw them wear anything but leather pants. Currently Bandit wore a black fitted tee and a black leather duster. Buccaneer wore a Misfits shirt. As the two of them made their way toward the group, they turned quite a number of female heads.

Gwen knew they were both very attractive but she had been friends with them so long she didn't really think of either man that way. Both of them helped her run away on several occasions. She wasn't as close to them as she was to Viking, but they were closer than most other Warriors, even if she did have to sneak around to see them.

"I've always wanted to bed one of them." Minnie sighed.

"Which one?" Karin asked her Pride Leader.

"Doesn't matter."

Gwen wasn't the only one laughing when the pirates reached the table. Both raised an eyebrow as they sat but neither said a word.

The young waitress came back and the pirates each ordered two beers with fish and chips. Once she left again they turned and looked directly at Gwen but it was Bandit who spoke.

"So who's the lucky sod?"

Gwen blinked. "I'm sorry?"

Buccaneer laughed. "You're fated for a Warrior. Any Warrior over a certain age will be able to feel it, but it's so light I'm guessing you've left the poor fool in Maddening."

Gwen didn't particularly like that half the Night World knew her personal business. "How can you tell?"

Bandit waved his hand. "It's hard to explain. It's a survival instinct, really. While the Warrior hasn't fully bonded with his mate, the mate is protected from other Warriors' advances. To us there is an air about you that makes us want to unconsciously avoid you. Buck and I have seen it enough over the centuries to recognize the cause. So who is he? Your detail did just change. Please tell me it wasn't one of the young guys. That would just be such a waste."

Both twins grinned at her and Gwen wasn't entirely sure what to say to Bandit's last comment so she ignored it. "It's the King of North America."

Both their mouths dropped and there were several creatively explicit curses.

Bandit recovered first. "That's hilarious. Cesar has a bloody stick up his arse. You'll be good for him."

Again Gwen wasn't sure how to take that, but she was saved any further conversation by the arrival of the MPs. There was some small talk until the MPs placed their orders, and then the table went silent. No one seemed to want to be the first one to broach the subject they'd gathered for.

Lucia cracked first. "The rogues were tracked to Burien. The King and nine others are probably there now hunting them down."

Buccaneer drained his first bottle. "We're ten minutes from there. Should we be tracking them ourselves?"

Lucia shook her head. "No, leave them to the King. I have a sneaking suspicion that those three rogues aren't working alone. My vote goes for tracking down whoever's helping them. I looked at the file the Warriors gave me on the way down here and there is no way these rogues could be here without outside help. They escaped border patrol with magic, not brute force."

Bandit began swirling his bottle. "You're probably right. How do we go about tracking them, though? If they can hide the rogues they can certainly hide themselves."

There was silence as their food appeared and everyone but Sin picked at their plate. Barrett cleared his throat to get the group's attention. It was rare for either male MPs to speak, when they did, everyone paid attention.

"Gwen could ask. Couldn't you? Correct me if I'm wrong but wouldn't the Spirit World notice that kind of thing?"

Gwen shook her head. "Not necessarily. I would have to find something pretty powerful. Most beings over there are too weak to notice or care what happens over here."

It wasn't exactly a lie. The beings in a specific area would know what was going on in the immediate vicinity, but since none of them knew where the rogues' partners were operating from she couldn't guarantee a helpful answer. She would have to scan for something with a great deal of power, and most things in the Spirit World with that much power were not friendly.

There was a longer silence this time as everybody ate. Gwen began to feel bad; if she was their best chance she didn't want to hold out, especially since it was her fault they were all here anyway.

Buccaneer pointed a French fry at her several minutes later. "What if I could give you an approximate location?"

Gwen felt a sliver of hope form. "How approximate?"

He shoved the fry into his mouth and swallowed. "I was approached by some men a few weeks ago while I was getting supplies up in Everett. They asked me how I would feel about bringing back the original North America. I told them the only man I worked with was my brother and that level of distrust was very

Gretchen S. B.

original in North America. I told Bandit, but since the guys were young and not all Warriors, we decided it was someone else's problem."

Sivia chimed in. "How young?"

Buccaneer shrugged. "I don't know, college maybe."

Gwen rolled the idea around in her head. Bothell was really as far north as she ever went. She knew where Everett was but she wasn't one hundred percent sure she could get there, though she wanted to try. They needed to prevent this war.

"It's worth a shot. Let me finish eating, I need the extra energy and then I'll give it a try. You guys have to cover for me, though. You can't touch me or move my body while I'm gone or I'll be yanked back, or worse, stuck."

The pirates exchanged glances. Gwen knew what they were thinking. That wasn't a Lady of the Dead skill, but she knew the two of them well enough to know neither of them would say anything.

When Gwen finished eating, she closed her eyes, and leaned back in her chair. She felt every person at the table go on guard. Gwen almost laughed; they were so protective of her, even when it wasn't something they could protect against. Taking deep breaths, Gwen lowered her head and slowly rolled out her power into the Spirit World around her. She was trying a technique Oracle showed her, exiting her physical body to reach farther away. Since it was a new skill, Gwen struggled with it. It had taken four tries this morning to finally get it right. This time she headed north. She didn't know the area too well so Gwen concentrated on the directions she took. The last thing she needed was to get lost outside her own body, where she couldn't defend herself.

After several minutes, Gwen passed over a school playground in a residential area. A huge shadow creature hunkered down on all fours watched a group of teenagers who stood on the opposite side of the fence. Gwen could feel the malice vibrating from the creature. He was strong but bound to the schoolyard. He seemed to be weaker in the waning sunlight that still illuminated his surroundings.

Gwen landed on the far end of the fence, away from the teens but careful to keep the fence between her and the creature. Once she began hovering near the fence, the thing slowly turned its head to look at her. Gwen gasped and fear flooded her system.

Its head was twice the size of hers and round. Its jaw protruded slightly and when it smiled evilly at her, she could see every single one of his teeth were razor sharp. His eyes were narrow and the irises black. The body was bulky and almost disproportioned. Gwen knew if this thing stood on its hind legs it would be somewhere around eleven feet tall. She couldn't stop the fear coursing through her.

It moved much faster than Gwen expected it to, crossing the yard in under ten seconds. He moved like a gorilla, putting weight on his knuckles and swinging his back legs forward. He didn't stop until his face was up against the fence. He straightened slightly so his face and Gwen's were only feet apart. His breathing was ragged with excitement. Gwen knew her fear rolled off her and this creature could feel it, but she stood her ground. She could feel the spells put on him and the playground. He couldn't get to her as long as she was on this side of the fence. But he was still damn scary.

"What brings the Lady of the Dead to my corner of the world?" His voice was inhumanly low and high at the same time.

Gwen's fear spiked, he knew who she was.

That voice laughed at her.

It was one of the scariest things Gwen ever heard, and she automatically shuddered. "I'm looking for information about some men."

It gave her an unblinking stare. "You are not yet strong enough to force answers from me. I can smell your fear and weakness." It sat down on its haunches. "I also smell your determination, and that interests me. I may or may not answer your questions."

Gwen wasn't quite sure how to take that. This thing was clearly evil, but it might help her. She knew she needed to tread lightly because without a doubt he had an ulterior motive.

"There are three rogue Warriors that may be in the area. They may be trying to start a war."

The thing's pointed ears twitched and he interrupted her. "What kind of war?"

Gwen fought to keep her voice steady. She knew the effort was pointless since he knew she was terrified, but she needed to try for her own sake. "We believe an all out one in this kingdom."

Its breathing slowed and he closed his mouth, staring at her for several beats. "No, they will fail."

The answer was so abrupt Gwen actually blinked. "What?"

It smiled at her again and Gwen's fear rose. "The Warriors you speak of, I know of them. Though they are not stupid enough to try recruiting me, they may have recruited Basilix, an enemy of mine. He is too strong for them to handle. Eventually he will eat them, or use them. It is hard to tell with Basilix. These Warriors you seek have been making alliances will all manner of Night Worlders. Now run along back to your body, little girl."

One giant clawed paw contorted through the chain link fence and slashed across Gwen's stomach. She screamed as pain shot through her and the shock from it broke her concentration, sending her shooting through the Spirit World back to her body.

The crash back in was jarring and made her feel like she had been hit by a bus. Her stomach burned so bad she screamed. She was only dimly aware of a hand over her mouth. The pain was stealing her consciousness. She barely heard Sivia's muffled voice from far away.

"Lucia, quick, mask her and clean the blood. We need to get her out of here."

Pain consumed her and the world appeared to go a dull red. Gwen swore she could hear that creature's voice laughing. Then there was silence.

Chapter 18

Viking shouted and grabbed his stomach, doubling over. "NO!"

All the Warriors froze. None of them seemed to know where the danger came from.

Cesar felt his pendant heat up. His blood ran cold and the world turned red. Gwen was injured. He turned to the other Warriors. Cesar had no doubt they all knew what was happening. He looked directly at Raider.

"You're in charge. Get any information you can."

Then Cesar was off, running at top Warrior speed, not caring if anyone saw him. He barely registered that Viking was in step with him. The only thoughts going through Cesar's head were of Gwen. She wasn't far away; he could feel the proximity.

"CESAR!" He barely heard Viking's voice in blur of his anger. His general was opening the door of the car they came in. Cesar skidded to a halt and jumped into the passenger seat. He knew the car was their best bet, but every bone in his body was convinced running would get them there faster.

Cesar felt a tug. How he knew he wasn't sure but Gwen was moving farther away from them. "She's moving," he growled.

"I know!" Viking growled back.

They were silent for ten minutes until Viking pointed to a SUV two vehicles ahead of them. "There! She's there, in that car. Sivia's with her, working on her. I can feel her magic mixing with Gwen's. She's barely keeping her alive."

Cesar's anger spiked, as did his panic. He could lose her to death.

It was another ten minutes of illegal driving before the SUV parked in front of an older apartment building. As Viking swung to a stop, Cesar leapt from the car. He got to the back passenger door of the other vehicle as it was opening and Sivia looked up at him, startled. Cesar looked past her to see Gwen lying across her and another woman's laps. Barrett was in the front chanting, and a Warrior Cesar wasn't acquainted with was in the driver's seat.

Gwen's torso had four large slashes, each about the width of half his palm. Blood soaked her shirt but somehow was nowhere else.

"KING! KING!"

Cesar finally heard Sivia through his blind rage. He looked down at her.

"I need to get her inside the apartment."

"Mine!" Cesar grunted and reached across Sivia to grab Gwen.

He slowly lifted her free of the car and cradled her to his chest. Touching her made the haze in his brain clear, but that only made the fear center stage. Everyone had gotten out of the cars, and no one tried to take Gwen from Cesar, but Viking was hovering, clearly needing to touch her.

A few silent moments later, Sivia unlocked a fifth floor apartment and moved aside so Cesar could enter first.

"I need her on the couch."

Cesar nodded absently. As much as his body was screaming to hold her, he knew Sivia could take better care of her. Cesar laid his mate down as gently as he could. A few seconds later Sivia was there lifting Gwen's shirt. The gashes were clearly scratches from something very big.

"GO OVER THERE!"

Sivia's hand was waving in Cesar's face. He registered the loud growl coming from his chest. He turned his full attention to Sivia, who was looking at him in frustration.

"I need more room than either of you are giving me. Both of you need to go stand with Buccaneer."

Cesar looked over to see Viking hovering at the back of the couch. Buccaneer was pacing across the open room by the front door. The effort was painful but Cesar made his body stand up and slowly move toward the front door, grabbing Viking along the way. Cesar's legs ached with the effort to go against his instincts. Every step sent a shot of pained rage through him. He needed to be holding her, or brutally kill any being that would dare harm her. Cesar knew his body was visibly shaking.

Trying to distract himself from his mate's potentially fatal injuries, Cesar turned to Buccaneer, who stopped pacing but couldn't seem to take his eyes off the back of the couch. It was obvious how deeply the other man wanted Gwen to be okay.

"What happened?" Cesar put all the authority and sanity he could into his voice.

Buccaneer snarled at him. "You are not my King. I don't answer to you."

Cesar felt his anger shift and direct toward the man in front of him.

"That may be, but I am still King here and someone attacked my mate. You do not want to challenge me on this."

The two of them stared each other down for several long minutes. Cesar was debating putting his fist through the other man's face when Buccaneer let out an anatomically impossible curse.

"I don't actually know. She was not in her body at the time. I don't even know how she did that. Hell, she shouldn't be able to do that. The last Lady of the Dead and I had relations for a while. I know Gwen shouldn't be able to leave her body like that."

"What do you mean by leave her body?" Viking sounded suspicious.

Cesar glanced at his general. The other man looked concerned.

Buccaneer shrugged as if struggling to find the right words. "She said she was searching outside her body. That we couldn't touch her or move her while she was gone. Then about fifteen minutes later her body jerked. Sin covered her mouth half a second before Gwen screamed and blood began seeping through her shirt. If Sin hadn't covered her mouth when she did, the entire club would have been looking at us. Her body slammed against the back of her chair so hard that if Bandit hadn't grabbed it she would have toppled over. She screamed again and her breathing picked up. Sivia told Lucia to cover and clean up the blood. I guess Lucia and her boys made it look like we all just walked out of there. The four of us piled into my Rover. Barrett trying to keep as much blood in her as possible and Sivia trying to heal her. Sin just wouldn't leave."

When he said the last part, Buccaneer looked over Cesar's shoulder. Cesar turned to see the other woman from the backseat sitting on a bar stool spinning herself. She didn't seem the least bit aware of what was going on.

Cesar turned back to the other Warriors. "What is she doing?"

Viking shrugged. "It's best not to ask."

Sivia's chanting started to grow more frantic, as did Barrett's. Cesar looked over at the couch to see the two of them kneeling over Gwen. Both their expressions full of concern. Beads of sweat popped up on their faces. Cesar's head whipped around when he heard Viking curse.

The other man's gaze locked on the air above the couch. Cesar's heart fell to his stomach. Looking back to the couch, Cesar knew he wouldn't see what Viking saw, but he instinctively knew what Viking was looking at. Gwen was leaving them.

"No, it's not time to leave yet."

Cesar heard Sin's seemingly distracted voice and turned to look at her. He was startled to see she was looking at the same place Viking was. Shapeshifters couldn't see the Spirit World, so how could she see Gwen?

"Oh all right. Sivia." Her voice gained a far away quality. "SIVIA!"

Sivia continued chanting but looked up at Sin, her expression aggravated.

"They say to get Bensia's Bane and a compress." Sin began spinning again.

Sivia barely waited a beat before shooting up and running down the hall. She returned a moment later with a squeeze bottle about the size of her hand. She knelt down and began squeezing green ooze into Gwen's wounds. No sooner had she finished did she drop the bottle and begin a different chant.

"She did it. How did Sin know that?" Viking's tone was full of awe.

Cesar glanced at his general before turning back to watch the couch. "What? What happened?"

"Gwen was hovering there. She was struggling to keep hold of her body. Not in the dying way but as if something was dragging her away. I think we all assumed she was dying, so Sivia preformed the wrong magic. When she used that goo and the new chant, whatever had hold of Gwen let go and she fell back into herself."

Cesar didn't like the idea of someone trying to steal his mate. He wouldn't know anything for sure until Gwen woke up and told them what happened. Sivia and Barrett seemed to calm. Cesar took that as a good sign.

They watched in silence for about five minutes before both Sivia and Barrett sat back. Then Sivia stood up and walked back

down the hallway. Barrett took a deep breath before looking up
wearily at the waiting Warriors.

"We have some big problems here, but for the time being
Gwen should be okay. Something pretty strong wants her but I've
put some wards in place that will hold until Sivia can clear its
presence from her system. If that stuff Sivia used is what I think it
is, Gwen is going to be really sick for about a week." Barrett made
direct eye contact with Cesar, his expression grave. "I mean
vomiting, dizziness, cramps. There is no way she could help you
with the Maddening in this condition."

The room was so silent a pin could have dropped in the next
apartment and it would have rang clear. Cesar tried to steady his
mind as Sivia came back with a bowl of towels covered in some
kind of cream. She knelt down and carefully placed one over each of
the four slashes.

Gwen wouldn't be able to help him with the Maddening.
That thought wasn't as horrible as it should have been. Cesar
thought she was going to die, and that he couldn't handle. He would
last as long as he could and trusted Roman to kill him should he
become beyond redemption. Gwen's life was his priority.

A loud knocking startled all three Warriors; they should have
heard people coming down the hallway. They exchanged glances
before Buccaneer checked the peephole and opened the door.

Six incredibly worried people stepped into the apartment.
Cesar recognized both Lucia and Marco. He figured the Warrior was
Bandit, as he and Buccaneer were practically identical. The last
three women Cesar could tell were Weres, but he didn't know which
kind.

The shortest woman held the power of authority of a Were
Leader. She wasn't a Wolf, because Carter was unmated and all of
his officers were men. All three women turned to him as one after
glancing at the couch. It would have been eerie if Cesar hadn't been
so used to behavior like that.

The tallest, a lean muscular honey blond, spoke first. "I'm
guessing she's relatively okay or his highness would be out of his
mind right now."

Cesar didn't know why he was still surprised every time
people knew who he was. He should be used to it from these crazy
Northwest Night Worlders. Cesar just watched the newcomers with

Gretchen S. B.

a blank face. This was the perfect moment to see how this corner of his Kingdom worked.

Barrett walked over to the MPs and the three began whispering to each other. It must not have been too big of a secret because Cesar held no doubts the Weres could hear every word they said.

Viking cleared his throat from were he stood over Cesar's right shoulder. "King, this is Minnie, the Pride Leader of the North Seattle Panthers. Her second Marnie, and Sivia's roommate Karin, one of their Pride Mates."

The smaller one inclined her head first, then her taller counterpart. Cesar was sure the two women were related, their looks were too similar not to be

Cesar knew Viking didn't introduce Bandit on purpose, and there was no way he could be anyone else. Standing next to his brother made that painfully obvious.

The room seemed much smaller now with eleven of them crammed into half of it. Suddenly the theme from the original Star Trek began to play and they all went quiet. The music came from a phone Sin pulled out of some pocket.

"Y'ello." There was a pause as whoever was on the other end spoke. "No, really…Oh snap, then what happened…It wasn't his baby…She's in a coma, again."

Cesar had no idea what Sin was talking about until he heard Marnie mumble under her breath. "I have no idea how she can watch that crap. Days of Our Lives is so much better."

Cesar just blinked and stared for a minute. His mate had been barely brought back from death and the Weres were discussing soap operas. What was wrong with these people?

Sin finally stopped spinning and stood up. "And they're where? …Missoula? …Where the hell is Beta? …Tell Vander I'm going to hack off his balls with a rusty wooden spoon and mail them to him from middle of nowhere Montana mixed with the balls of these Mega men so he won't know whose is whose…Yeah, gimme four days." Then she hit a few buttons and jammed the phone back in her pocket.

Sin strode over to the couch and leaned down so she was looking directly at Gwen's face, as if his unconscious mate could see her.

"I gotta go kill some guys raising zombies, but I'll be back next week. I'm sure you'll have this business all sorted out by the time I get back." Then she pivoted on the heels of her boots and shoved aside anyone standing between her and the door.

After Sin left, the silence remained. Cesar could tell the room had mixed reactions to her departure, but it seemed they were all at least somewhat relieved.

Viking jumped and a split second later his phone started to ring. His general gave him a meaningful look before stepping out of the apartment. Cesar knew what the other man was doing. Most likely it was Raider checking in. Neither Cesar nor Viking wanted to risk the others hearing how the hunt was going.

Most of the room watched curiously, but no one said a thing. Sivia seemed to have finally finished with Gwen because she stood up and came to stand next to Cesar. She was paying him the respect of his title as well as Gwen's mate by speaking to him directly instead of to the group.

"Gwen has been marked by something pretty strong and unpleasant. It is trying to call her to it, since Gwen isn't exactly at one hundred percent, or at full Lady of the Dead power, and she can't really fight back on her own. I've given her something that should clear it from her system within twenty-four hours, but since the gel is made for Immortal chemistry and not human, Gwen's body is going to have a very adverse reaction for probably a week. We got very lucky that I'm an Immortal, as no one else would have anything remotely like that gel. Barrett seems to have whatever that thing is at bay until Gwen's body expels it.

"We could track this thing down and kill it but that would mean having to expose Gwen again in order to track it. Or we could wait and hope wherever this thing is it stays put until Gwen is healthy enough to show us. I'm leaving that up to you. As her mate, you make those decisions.

"We can't move her for several hours, literally she needs to stay exactly where she is. I had Barrett put a sleeping spell on her so she'll be out for the next day anyway. Now all that aside. I think we should probably start working as one big group because I'm pretty sure you're not much better off than we are at tracking down these rogues and their cohorts." As she finished, Sivia laid her hands on her hips.

Gretchen S. B.

Cesar was not happy that all of these people were hunting the rogues behind his back, it pissed him off. It was not their job, it was his. Cesar hid those thoughts, maintaining a blank face.

"Why would I share with you? It is the Warriors' job to find these rogues. You have endangered my mate and I'm sure you've withheld information from me and my men. I see no reason to work with people who so obviously can not be trusted."

He had angered them, Cesar could tell. Every person in that room with the exception of Sivia was giving him an angry look. He didn't care, really he wanted to rip all of their heads off for harming his mate.

They were saved the argument by Viking coming back and rapping at the door. Cesar bypassed all of them and opened the door enough to slide through it. He motioned for Viking to follow him down the hall and out of hearing range.

Once they were down the hall, Viking began his report. "Raider tells me they caught up with one of the rogues outside of the apartment building the Werehawks reside in. They were able to take him down easily and are transporting him back to Bellevue, that way if the other rogues go after him we will have the home court advantage. Trapper, Native, and Kegan are still hunting in Burien. Raider informed me Rochester and Stylus are en route down there as we speak.

"If they are after the Werehawks, Cesar, odds are they will be after MPs as well. Five Warriors cannot watch out for thirty MPs scattered around several cities. We should have Lucia warn them to band together to easily fight off the last three rogues."

Cesar nodded. "Agreed. Call her and tell her to join us out here."

Viking gave him a look that said he didn't quite agree with Cesar's word choice but didn't comment as he pulled out his phone.

Cesar knew that if the rogue was in Bellevue, that was where he needed to be, but he wasn't entirely sure he could bring himself to leave Gwen. It went against everything in his Warrior nature to leave his wounded mate. Then he had a thought. Roman would be here soon. Roman was closer to him than a brother. If Cesar could get Roman to watch over his mate, then Cesar would not worry unnecessarily about Gwen's well-being. Roman would protect her with his life.

As Sivia's apartment door opened, Cesar pulled out his phone to check the time. It was almost nine, and Roman should have landed by now. Cesar turned to Viking.

"Get Lucia up to speed on her MPs down south. I will be right back."

Viking gave him a questioning look but didn't comment as Cesar headed down the stairwell to the floor below. Once he was sure he was out of earshot, Cesar made the call. Roman picked up on the first ring.

"Augustus, surely I need not kill you yet." Though Roman's tone was joking Cesar knew his friend was somewhat serious.

"No, not yet, Octavius. I have a favor to ask, though."

Cesar could hear Roman go still through the phone.

"And that would be?"

A friendship that lasted this long had its perks, and favors were done with no questions asked.

"We have captured a rogue. He is being brought to Gwen's as we speak. Gwen, however, has been found and she is too injured to be moved."

Cesar was interrupted by Roman's growl. "Who would dare harm our Lady of the Dead?"

Cesar sighed. "We don't know. That, I need you to find out. I need someone to guard her, someone I can trust implicitly." He left the statement about his lack of trust in everyone else unsaid. Roman would understand.

"Tell me where you are and I will tell the cabbie."

Cesar felt his shoulders slump in relief. His mate would be guarded by the second best Warrior possible. He jogged outside, rattled off the nearest street sign he saw and the address on the building and waited to see if that was enough for the cab driver.

"He's asking what city you're in. Is it a place called Shoreline?"

Cesar scanned his surroundings. There were decorative banners on several lamp posts a few blocks down that stated WELCOME TO SHORELINE.

"According to the banners, yes."

Cesar heard Roman mumbling to the driver for a few seconds before getting back on the phone. "He says we'll be there in twenty. Am I to meet you or someone else?"

Gretchen S. B.

Though it would waste precious time, Cesar knew he couldn't leave Gwen with anyone but Roman. "I will be here."

Moments later he headed back toward Viking. As Cesar emerged from the stairs, he saw Viking and Lucia standing a few feet apart with identical unhappy expressions. Once they saw Cesar, Viking motioned to him.

"Tell the King what you just told me."

Lucia's frown deepened but she turned to Cesar. He wasn't entirely sure he would like this news.

"There are only three rogues down here. Sin was sanctioned to kill one a while ago. That is why you have only been seeing three."

Cesar's sight flashed red. Temper rose in him and he knew his voice came out full of venom. "What else has been kept from me?"

Lucia actually looked away. It was about time she showed him the respect of his station.

"There are other Night Worlders involved helping the rogues. We know this for a fact. I guess a few weeks ago several approached Buccaneer and asked him to join them. He of course declined, they weren't just Warriors, King. We have some suspicions as to who they might be but nothing definite beyond one Canadian MP. I have already put in an order to have him killed. This is very big, King. Far beyond one lone group of rogue Warriors."

Cesar was sure if this was as big as Lucia thought, he might need to contact the other Warrior kings. He doubted this was just his Kingdom. Cesar made a mental note to call Aztec in a few days, if he was still alive.

"What is our next move, King?" Viking asked.

Cesar didn't answer right away, hoping Lucia would get the hint.

She did, turning on her heels she spoke over her shoulder. "I will let my people know what is going on in their territory. Do not block us out, King. All of us are involved now whether you like it or not." She didn't wait for a response, just turned the corner and seconds later a door opened and shut.

Cesar looked at his general, making sure his face made no room for argument. "Roman will be here within half an hour. He will watch over Gwen. Once he arrives you and I will head to Bellevue."

Cesar watched Viking fight his objections. The other man did not want to leave but knew better than to argue with Cesar. Finally Viking nodded and they both headed back to the apartment.

As they entered the front room, all eyes focused on Cesar. He fought his smile. That was as it should be.

"As I see it we need to gather as much information on this group as we possibly can. Lucia, if you and yours would go south and help your brethren and send out feelers to see who might not be on the right side of this little war it would be much appreciated."

Both Lucia's men looked at him curiously, but she answered. "Absolutely."

Cesar turned to both Warriors, who stiffened. This might be difficult. Technically they did not belong to him and therefore did not have to do what he said, but by the same token he could kill them both without recourse.

"Since it is very well known that you both despise me, I think it would be useful, if you are willing, to sniff around up north and see what kind of trail these rogues left. People will talk to you because you hate me and you are both strong enough to get yourselves out of trouble, should there be any."

The twins stared at each other for a full minute and Cesar filed that away. There was a rumor that both sets of Warrior twins could communicate telepathically.

As they both turned back to him Bandit answered on their behalf. "We agree, but we are doing this for Gwen, not you. We couldn't care less about your kingdom. But we don't want anything else happening to her."

Cesar filed that away as well. The Warriors cared for Gwen deeper than they hated him. What had she done to earn such devotion? Putting that aside for later, Cesar turned to the three Weres.

"Would you ladies please check in with the other Weres in the area? I know none of you tend to mingle outside of your own species, but anyone you can warn would be most helpful. I doubt no Weres are helping these men, I think we should know who they are."

All three women gave him predatory grins and Minnie folded her arms. "We have some suspicions about some Tigers on the peninsula. I could send a female up there to check things out."

Cesar wasn't sure he liked that idea but he didn't say anything. The Night World worked differently here and for the time being he would go with their terms.

"Viking and I will be in Bellevue. I want everyone in contact with at least one other group. I'm fully aware some of you don't care for me, so call someone else instead. I just want all of us up to speed if anything comes up. We can rendezvous tomorrow at the store at ten a.m. If you can't make it, call in, that way every group is represented."

There were mumbles and nods but no one left.

"What of Gwen?" Buccaneer asked and the room fell silent.

Cesar looked straight at the other man instead of the entire room. "Roman is on his way. He will watch over her."

There was silence again, with various looks exchanged.

Barrett appeared to be the only one who found his voice. "Are you sure that is wise? Both the king and his right hand here? What of your other two generals? Are they capable of looking after the kingdom between the two of them?"

Cesar stopped himself from laughing. If only they knew one of those other generals was in the room with them. "Yes, each of my generals could handle matters in my absence."

There were a few more exchanged looks before people left group by group. The pirates were the last to leave. Cesar watched the two men. He had plenty of information on them as he did all the more powerful rogue Warriors in his kingdom, but all the intel in the world would not tell him what these two men were thinking.

Buccaneer began fiddling with something in his pants pocket. Bandit did the same with his jacket.

Buccaneer looked up first. "I taught her to sail and play poker. Bandit took her on her first trip to Canada on his bike."

Viking snorted. "Why am I not surprised to hear this?"

Bandit's head shot up. "Well, think about it, if the little thing was going to rebel wouldn't you rather she was with us than on her own?"

Viking didn't answer. From Cesar's understanding, Gwen's childhood had been full of attacks. Bandit was right. At least she had been with those who could protect her.

Buccaneer kept his eyes on Cesar; he was not happy with what he was about to say. "She reminds us of our little sister."

That surprised Cesar. He had never heard anything about the pirates having family.

"We understand you'll be taking her away once you're mated. We'd appreciate seeing her from time to time, if that could be arranged. We know it wouldn't be as regular as it is now, but we'd still like to see her, off your fortress."

Viking cleared his throat. "Exactly how regularly is that?"

Both pirates grinned from ear to ear. "Wouldn't you like to know?" Bandit chimed.

Cesar knew there were more pressing issues to deal with but he also knew the twins needed an answer from him.

He sighed. "All I can promise you is that I will discuss it with her when we get the chance. The last thing I want is her sneaking out to meet people."

Buccaneer nodded. "Fair enough." Then they left.

While they waited for Roman, there was an uneasy silence. Cesar sat on the floor in front of the couch, running his fingers though Gwen's soft hair. Viking sat in the matching chair next to the couch, watching Gwen sleep. Sivia seemed to be busying herself with quiet, unimportant things.

Cesar wanted nothing more than for Gwen to wake up and tell him she was fine. He hardly knew her yet, he felt more connected to her than to anyone in the world. Apollo said something like that once while in the first stage of Mating with Arianna.

"You'll see, Cesar, it is as if the entire world has shrunk down to the size of one tiny female and you will want nothing more in your life." The Greek then took a large swig of Warrior alcohol.

Apollo was right, though. Cesar wanted nothing more than to sweep Gwen up and take her somewhere no one would ever find them and he could have her all to himself. But that could never happen. Neither of them could afford to disappear, but at least being near her, smelling her, touching her, cleared his head. That was a small blessing.

Gretchen S. B.

Cesar jumped when his phone rang. He had been so absorbed in his mate that the ring shot adrenaline through his system. He pulled out his phone, trying to calm himself. It was Roman. The man was probably here.

"Yes, Roman?" he answered. There was no need for more of a greeting.

"What number am I going to? I could hunt you down, but this is so much easier."

Cesar shook his head at his friend's humor. "Fifth floor, from the stairs it is the sixth door on the left."

Roman hung up. Sivia didn't seem to need anymore information than that. Without a word she got up from her stool and went to the door, propping it open with her foot. Several seconds later, Roman strode through the doorway, dropping his duffel bag on the floor. He nodded to Sivia, who closed the door behind him. Roman headed straight for the couch and stopped once he could see Gwen over the back.

Roman's voice filled with amusement. "Well, I hadn't counted on her being quite so much your type." He folded his arms over his chest and grinned at Cesar.

Cesar gave him a droll stare. "What exactly does that mean?"

Roman nodded toward Gwen. "Look at her—pale, petite, and delicate. That's your type."

Cesar chose to ignore his friend's observations and bent forward to kiss Gwen's forehead before standing up. "I want to know when she wakes up. We need to know who did this to her and why. When you get the okay from Sivia, move her home. I'm going to need her nearby if we are going to get through this."

Roman nodded slowly but gave Cesar a look that said he knew Cesar hid something, but he wouldn't push, not yet.

Cesar gave Gwen's prone form one more glance before motioning to Viking and putting all his effort into leaving the apartment building.

Chapter 19

"Don't go moving around just yet, young lady. You need to stay put to keep everything in place."

Gwen didn't recognize the voice speaking to her. It was gruff. She knew he was talking to her because of the hand she felt on her shoulder. She was so groggy, like she had taken a sleeping pill, but she knew better. It was a spell. She could feel a number of spells wrapped around her like blankets. Gwen hated other people's magic being used on her. It always felt weird, like ill-fitting clothes.

After some effort she was able to open her eyes. A man sat on a stool, leaning over the back of Sivia's couch. A book was propped open next to his elbow. By looking at him, Gwen could guess who he was. This had to be Roman, August's right hand man. He looked like a more aristocratic version of August. There were small differences here and there. Roman's hair was a dark brown and cropped short. His nose was blunt and Gwen could make out two dimples as he looked down at her.

"Roman," Gwen said, giving a small smile.

He inclined his head and withdrew his hand. "Yes, young lady, I am."

Gwen felt curiosity tug at her. "Are the two of you related?"

Roman laughed, it was more gravely than August's. "No, not at all."

Gwen liked this man, there was something safe about him, the same sort of feeling she got from Viking the first time she met him.

"You're not just a Warrior are you?"

She was satisfied by the look of surprise that passed across Roman's face before he went back to smiling again.

He reached down and tapped the tip of her nose with his pointer finger. "I suppose in the same way you are not just the Lady of the Dead. But that is a story for a different time. You need to sleep. You and I can play twenty questions later."

Gwen would have been irritated normally by the dismissal, but Roman was right she knew she needed rest. "Don't tell August I woke up, okay? It will distract him from whatever he's doing."

Roman gave her a calculating look. "I hadn't actually planned on it, but I find it fascinating that you requested it."

He simply watched her after that. Not wanting to be stared at, Gwen closed her eyes and drifted back into the sleep spell.

Chapter 20

When he and Viking returned to the shop at ten past ten Cesar's mind clouded red. He made the decision that he couldn't, in good conscience, be part of the interrogations of the rogue. Not only would it let the rogues know he was in town, but Cesar wouldn't keep hold of his temper long enough to get any answers. He would have been the monster some of the non-threatening rogues thought him to be.

The rogue, who went by Jake, was taken to an interrogation room that had been built into the back of the building. Cesar's surprise that Gwen's detail needed such a thing only fed his anger. He should have known about such a room.

Poet and Raider waited in the small observation room on the backside of the two-way glass for Viking and Cesar to arrive. Deuce followed them in.

At first Cesar was furious that Deuce wasn't still in Burien, but it didn't take him long to figure out why the other man was there. Deuce used to go by Talker before he had been exiled to America. Talker was the best interrogator any Warrior had ever seen. He could get information from anyone. His various methods included torture, which was why he was sent to America in the early 1700s. He had played for the losing team and the winners shipped him off. Cesar was relieved when Deuce pledged allegiance to the kingdom. Deuce would have been a hard enemy. Now he mostly played professional poker, but Cesar knew the blond wouldn't have forgotten anything from his old trade.

Cesar made it clear to Deuce he drew the line at physical torture. Deuce simply nodded and left the room, appearing on the other side of the glass moments later.

"Well, hello there, Jake." Deuce could ooze a southern gentleman's charm when he chose.

Jake glared up at Deuce from the chair he was tied to. The lack of response told Cesar the Warrior was young, post-exile. Anyone from Europe older than four hundred years would know Deuce on sight. He used to be a bit of a bogeyman.

Deuce must have come to the same conclusion because his smile widened. "Now you are young, aren't you?"

Jake stiffened as if offended. "I am in my Second Life."

Deuce laughed; there was a hint of insanity to it. For the first time Jake appeared nervous.

"The boy is either young or stupid not to be out of his mind with fear at that laugh," Raider mumbled from behind Viking and Cesar.

Poet made a noise in the back of his throat. "I always forget you have been on the receiving end of Talker's attentions."

Cesar hadn't known that. He turned and looked over his shoulders at the two men. Both wore calm and blank expressions.

Raider looked at Cesar. "I stole something valuable from some very nasty people. Nasty people can afford to hire other nasty people." Then he looked back through the glass.

Cesar knew better than to ask what happened. He turned back to see Deuce leaning across the table and whispering something in Jake's ear. It must have been graphic because the boy grew pale. Deuce swung in and snapped his jaw inches from Jake's face. The boy made a high pitched noise and jumped as far as he could while being tied to a chair.

Deuce chuckled and straightened back over the table. This time the southern charm was gone and Deuce's real expression leaked through. His eyes emptied with a touch of evil; the smile was predatory. Deuce could be truly frightening when he let his true self leak out.

"Now boy, tell me something. Does the Lady of the Dead factor into this plan of yours?"

Cesar couldn't hide his surprise. Raider and Poet must have mentioned their suspicions to Deuce. They needed the full plan, not just one part.

Jake actually looked confused. "Yeah, but she's at the bottom of the list. We need more backup to get her away from her detail. She's scheduled for two days from now."

Deuce sat on the table and folded his arms. "What do you plan to do with our Lady?"

"An MP knows how to tap into her power. We just have to get her to the MP and get her tied down. Then all her power is ours."

Cesar's mind fogged red so fast he barely made out the growl rumbling from his own throat. All he wanted to do was to punch through the glass and rip the boy's head off. He was out the door and into the hallway before he regained control of himself.

Instead of returning to the small observation room, Cesar bee-lined for the back door, figuring the night air could only help. He knew Viking would update him if Jake said anything of importance.

Cesar began pacing. He needed Gwen nearby and safe. He needed to think clearly. After a few seconds he heard the back door open and slowly shut. A glance over his shoulder showed Poet leaning up against the building, hands in his pockets, watching Cesar pace.

"What?" Cesar snarled.

Poet continued to watch him with a peaceful expression. "I have more experience with the Maddening than the others. I know your behavior is nothing to worry about. That makes me the best candidate to keep you company while you dig a rut in the cement."

Cesar stopped pacing and stood inches from Poet's face. "I am King. I do not need a babysitter."

Poet actually laughed. Cesar was so caught off guard that he took a step back.

"I didn't say I was a babysitter. I simply waved at the room and followed you out. Remember, you don't scare me. I am older than you by a significant amount. I just have no wish for more power."

Cesar took a deep breath and went back to pacing. A part of him had always wanted to try Poet, see who was truly stronger, but he was never actually stupid enough to try. Cesar had not given in to violent outbursts in centuries. Now he was stupidly threatening Poet, one of the first exiles to America. Doing things like that would get him killed, and fast.

"When Gwen turned twenty-one," Poet's voice slowed as he began his story.

Cesar actually felt his heartbeat and pace slow and his mind clear, marginally.

"All she wanted to do was go on a twenty-one run. As they call it in this time. Basically she wanted to go barhopping with some of her younger friends. Viking told her we could all head out to Venture for some drinks. Obviously he didn't get the point. I can't say I did either, but I knew his plan did not suit her needs. I called both the pirates and asked how they felt about breaking Gwen out for her birthday. Of course they both jumped on that idea.

"So I told Viking I was taking her out as I understand the younger scene a bit better than he, and the four of us went to six different bars, I believe. Young Gwen had several suitors, but when she showed no interest the pirates scared them off. She had so much fun that night she went six months without a disappearance."

Cesar's pacing slowed a bit and he turned to watch Poet. "Why are you telling me this?'

Poet continued to watch him. "You feel better, do you not?"

Cesar nodded.

Poet shrugged and pushed off the wall. "Then it doesn't matter, does it." He reached over and opened the back door.

Cesar filed the entire story away for later study and followed Poet back inside.

Roman irritatingly told Cesar to stop checking in. It was the fourth time this morning. Cesar couldn't help it. He wanted to know the moment Gwen woke up. Intellectually he knew Roman would tell him but that didn't make it any easier. Cesar was now halfway through the Maddening. He paced in Gwen's apartment most of the night and found it impossible to sleep. Every little thing made him angry.

Deuce did not gain as much information from Jake as they all hoped. It turned out that these three rogues were given specific tasks to complete without knowledge of the entire picture. The tasks that Jake knew of were to recruit, either by force or coercion, the Werehawks and the MP Strata. Then to kidnap Gwen and lastly lure Lucia and her boys.

Cesar already expected as much but now they knew for sure the Warriors in Burien were circling the Werehawk nest and several MPs' houses. Both groups were already informed of the situation and were angry.

The Werehawks wanted to abandon their nest but between Carter, Minnie, and Craig, the local Lion leader, they convinced the Hawks to stay.

The MPs banded together and stationed themselves in three places. That way they could outnumber any intruders.

Cesar began to feel as if everything was falling into place too easily. Jake told Deuce there were a number of others involved. But he only knew the other two Warrior's names and the name of the MP who recruited them. That bothered Cesar. Why would Warriors take orders from an MP?

Lucia was correct in her guess at the MP's identity. Marvin was now on the Shapeshifters' sanctioned list and Cesar hoped Sin could kill him before he could do any more damage. He wanted to question the MP first, but Lucia assured him finding Marvin would be all but impossible for any of them. Cesar trusted Lucia was telling the truth. He wasn't entirely comfortable with the decision but at the moment there wasn't much else he could do.

Flicking his phone out of his pocket, Cesar checked the time yet again. Five to ten and no one had shown up yet. His pace increased and he saw Raider and Viking exchange glances. The three younger Warriors appeared agitated and nervous. Deuce leaned back in his chair with a cream cowboy hat covering his face. Poet read some women's magazine.

Cesar saw Poet glance at him over the pages before going back to the article. "There is a young group of Warriors in their first life that come hang out here regularly. Cedar, the giant mountain man you sent on the previous detail, took an instant dislike to these kids. He would grumble and curse at them, generally making them fear him."

"About two years ago Gwen disappeared, as she often does. Cedar was out looking for her when he ran into several of these kids. He snarled at them about finding Gwen. Of course they just saw her and were able to tell Cedar exactly where she was. It turned out she was simply sitting in a downtown youth hangout. Strangely enough, a place the young Warriors haunt. Cedar actually thanked them. In the years afterward, he even ended up teaching the young kids different skills, like throwing knives. Not a skill I am comfortable with those guys having, but that's neither here nor there."

The room fell quiet. Once again, as with the night before, Cesar felt his body calm down marginally. He was beginning to wonder how exactly Poet did that.

"Thank you so much for the mind-numbing trivia, Poet." Deuce sighed from under his hat.

Cesar actually understood this story, though. Gwen purposefully went to a place only the young Warriors would find her, forcing interaction between them and Cedar. How had she known that would work? He couldn't help the pride at knowing his queen was a good influence on his people.

As the door to the lounge opened, all heads except Deuce and Poet swiveled to the newcomers. The Weres were arriving together. Carter came in first, still in a suit, probably heading straight back to the precinct. Next came Minnie in a borderline inappropriate bright red tube dress.

Behind her were a tall man and woman holding hands looking about warily. Cesar knew this to be the reigning couple of Hawks from Burien. Were birds didn't have a single leader; there was a reigning couple, then several young or single birds underneath them. It was rare for the nests to have more than one couple and unheard of to have more than three. The Werebirds didn't trust anyone outside their nest.

Behind them was Craig, the Pride Leader for the lions in Washington. Craig was a huge man, known for a foul attitude and bad temper. With so few Lions in the kingdom, they tended to keep to themselves.

Lastly, Vincent trailed in with an air of disinterest. That is until he looked at Cesar. Then he began laughing, only stopping when he slid into a chair next to Poet. "And where is our little Gwen disappeared to now?"

Cesar's temper flashed and he barely noted several exchanged glances. It was all he could do not to walk over and rip Vincent's head off. When he spoke, Cesar knew his voice was a heavy growl. "She was badly injured by something in the Spirit World last night and now lays unconscious on Sivia's couch."

The total shock and disbelief on Vincent's face brought Cesar's temper down.

"What? What could do that?" Craig's gruff voice came from somewhere to Cesar's right.

Viking answered for him, which was good, as Cesar wasn't sure he could hold more of this conversation.

"We don't know yet. When she wakes up she can tell us. Then we will kill it." Viking's tone was absolutely lethal. There were several sounds of agreement.

In the silence that followed, Poet's phone rang and Barrett walked into the lounge alone, but with a Bluetooth in his ear.

"I got the Pirates on my phone," Poet told no one in particular.

Barrett nodded to Cesar. "I have Marco down in Tacoma."

Cesar took a deep breath in an effort to calm himself. Sivia was the only one missing, but then she really hadn't been given anything to do and Immortals would not have any information. Sivia was different than the rest of her people. Not only had she saved Gwen's life, but she took an active interest in those around her. It was a very un-Immortal like trait. Immortals barely seemed to care about their own.

As that cleared his head, an exhausted looking Sivia slid into the lounge. She tried desperately not to look worn down, but though no one in that room would be fooled, no one would say anything either.

"All right. Since they got here first, let's start with the Weres." Cesar put all of his authority into his tone. They needed to know he was in charge here.

Carter automatically took the lead. As the most prominent Night World presence in the area, Werewolves were used to being the top of the food chain.

"We can't really track down the other bird nests to warn them. They're all so damn finicky, and none of them are answering their phones. I spoke with my Canadian counterpart and he says that he has seven Wolves unaccounted for. Minnie sent Karin and Marnie to go check out those boisterous Tigers up north, so don't expect to hear back from them in the next few hours. Between the four of us we've reached all the feline and canine leaders in the Tri-state area. As Venture's leader, Vincent is able to blur the lines a bit more than the rest of us so he did most the work contacting other Prides in the area."

Vincent filled the pause before Carter could continue. "I was able to get a hold of several nests as well. We have a surprising amount of Eagle young and birds are damn protective. I also let the head of the local Reoccurring Family know what was going on. They won't get involved but I figured he would want to know what could go on in his house."

Cesar exchanged a look with Viking. He hadn't known there was a Reoccurring Family in any areas this densely populated. Viking shrugged. Apparently the other man hadn't known either.

Gretchen S. B.

Vincent seemed to read Cesar's mind. "He only let me know out of courtesy. I believe I am one of maybe a dozen people that know they are here and they would like to keep it that way."

Cesar nodded. "So we have a possible seven Canadian Wolves and some Tigers might be missing. Other than that, since we have the Werehawks' nest covered, are the Weres mostly untouched?"

There were several nods from the Were leaders, except the two Hawks. Cesar could tell they couldn't get out of there soon enough. He was curious why they agreed to show up in the first place.

Cesar turned to Sivia; he needed news of Gwen like he needed air. "How is my mate?"

All attention in the room switched to Sivia. She straightened her shoulders and looked at Cesar straight on. "Do you wish to discuss that in front of everyone?" Her tone was perfectly blank.

The real answer was no. He didn't think Gwen was anyone else's business, but he knew the others didn't see it that way.

Cesar gave his answer to the room but kept his eyes on Sivia. "Until she accepts me, but after that it will be no one else's business."

He swore he saw Sivia's lip twitch in amusement, but there was no other response to confirm it for him.

Sivia took a deep breath but didn't speak to the room. "She is stable, so the quicker she can heal herself the better. Whatever is on the other side is not giving me enough time to recharge between attacks. However, it weakened once the Sun came up. She is fine until nightfall, and depending on how healed she is by then I might need to be around to fend it off another night. I do not foresee her being her usual self and level of power until the middle of next week."

Cesar heard all the mumbles that came with that last sentence. Just about every person in the room thought their king was lost. He would be lying if he didn't admit to agreeing with them.

Barrett stepped forward so he was only two yards from Cesar. Cesar turned to look at the MP. Once he had Cesar's attention, Barrett bowed at the waist. It was the usual way a Night Worlder addressed the king. Cesar almost laughed, it felt like it had been weeks since anyone addressed him properly.

"I wish to offer my services to help protect your queen tonight, should the need arise."

Cesar raised an eyebrow questioningly. It was a good offer, but what was the catch?

Barrett's mouth curved up on one side. "Consider it a wedding gift from your local Strata. It beats shopping off a registry with Marco."

Cesar could tell from Barrett's expression that Marco had some very choice words for his friend.

Cesar smiled and inclined his head to the MP. "I accept your offer."

Barrett almost seemed relieved. "Moving on then. Between Lucia, Marco, and I we located most of the southern Strata. They have fifty-two members and thus far we have twenty-seven…sorry I'm being told it is thirty-four now, accounted for. I don't think it's viable to say that sixteen have joined the rogues. We just haven't had enough time to track them all down.

"We also spoke to several MPs in the area that are without Strata and, strangely enough, they are all accounted for. As are the two dozen or so Strata in BC and Western Washington. We have not had the time or means to search beyond that." That appeared to be all Barrett had to report because he stepped back until he leaned against the wall.

Cesar exchanged looks with Viking. The other man shook his head, the movement barely noticeable. They both knew an MP without a Strata was someone who had been kicked out, usually a Red or Black MP. It was uncommon for MPs in a Strata to have contact with those who had been cast out. Cesar noted it as something to watch. He was glad he and Viking were the only ones who seemed to know what Barrett truly said.

Cesar turned his attention to Poet. "What say the twins?"

"The king wants to know what say you."

Poet smiled at what Cesar assumed were several explicit comments directed through the phone. After a minute or so Poet looked over at Cesar, with a slight look of disgust.

"They've just finished speaking to Fairy."

The majority of the room groaned. Cesar had no idea who they were talking about.

Poet seemed to guess as much. "Hold on Buck, King doesn't know who Fairy is."

Then he looked at Cesar, his expression both amused and mildly repulsed. "Fairy lives just outside Blaine, Washington. He is basically on the Canadian border. His mother is a Canadian MP and his father was a Shapeshifter. So basically he's completely nuts. However, he isn't violent, so no one has a reasonable excuse to kill the loon. For some reason only known to the cosmos, Fairy knows every single bit of gossip circulating the local Night World. But to get anything from him you have to sit down and chat for an allotted amount of time only he knows. Buck says they just finished a three hour stint."

Cesar found himself glad he didn't know this individual. "What's with the name?"

Deuce answered him from under his hat. "The dude collects sets of Fairy wings, you know those things humans wear on Halloween and such. Has a spare bedroom full of framed wings. Makes you go in and see what's new in his collection every time you visit. Damn creepy."

Cesar wasn't entirely sure he could be comfortable with any information gained from a man Deuce considered creepy. He turned back to Poet.

"What did they get from this individual?" He couldn't bring himself to call a grown man Fairy.

Poet repeated the question and listened. "He says not all that much. They just wanted us to know they had been suffering."

Viking roll his eyes.

"They did get a list of people these rogues approached."

That gained Cesar's full attention.

"Buck will give it to me when we're through reporting. I'm also told Fairy informed them it was these rogues who killed Narcia after she refused to join them. Though he wouldn't tell them how he knew this. Also Fairy has a gift from Narcia for Lucia, but she has to come pick it up alone."

Out of the corner of his eye, Cesar saw Barrett stiffen. He didn't blame the MP. Bad news followed by that was not something anyone would want.

Poet's face filled with surprise. "Really? And he gave it to you?"

After another pause Poet's confused face looked up at Cesar. "Fairy gave them a present as they left and told them it was for Gwen."

Cesar couldn't even fake surprise. Of course Gwen would know the crazy man.

"The tag on it says 'Congratulations on your impending nuptials.' Buck says the small box was in the front hall when they first entered the house."

That did shock Cesar. How would he have known?

Poet paused again. "When they asked him about it, apparently he giggled and tapped his finger to his lips."

"Well that's not creepy," Minnie interjected.

There were murmurs of agreement.

"That's all they have at present. They were heading to talk to the Canadian Wolves, but since Carter has already done that they are going to stop by Scotia and CeCe's for the night on their way to see a member of the Yukon Animal Pack, though he won't say who."

Cesar nodded. He knew of Scotia, he was one of the Canadian Warriors who refused allegiance that he let live. Since the man was content with isolation in Northern B.C. with his half-Immortal Inuit mate, CeCe, Cesar saw no reason to hunt him down. Cesar was willing to bet if the rogues approached Buccaneer they probably paid a visit to Scotia and CeCe.

Poet pulled a small pad and pen out of nowhere. "If there is nothing else, I'm getting their list of names. Buck says not to worry about the missing Canadians. They will look into those while they are up there."

Cesar nodded before turning back to the room at large. It was his turn, and he could either share what they gained from questioning Jake or leave them all in the dark. He knew what he wanted to do, what he had every right as king to do. In doing so he might damage further lines of communication. How did Viking live in this backward environment so long?

"The rogue Warrior we have in our possession goes by the name of Jake."

He filled the group in on what little information they had gained. When he came to what the plan for Gwen was there were growling noises from the Weres.

Except the Hawks, who just became increasingly nervous. That gained Cesar's attention and he watched them out of the corner of his eye as he spoke. Werebirds didn't like groups, that was true, but these two were quite nervous, more than was normal. They might be birds, but they were still predators. They weren't acting like it.

Cesar went through a mental list of the room. Carter had the best nose. He could smell a lie. Vincent was a close second, but it would be less suspicious to talk with Carter alone.

So as he finished up, Cesar turned to Carter. "Before I continue my portion of the debriefing I need to confer some facts with Carter, to see if my hunch is or is not relevant."

Not even Carter's eyes gave away Cesar's lie. The other man simply nodded and made his way to the lounge door, opening it so Cesar could exit first. The angry looks in their direction were not lost on Cesar as he strode out the door.

Once Carter shut it behind them Cesar pointed to his lips then down the hall to the stairwell. Carter obligingly stayed silent until they stood on the landing for the third floor. The other man raised an eyebrow at Cesar.

Cesar wanted to be absolutely positive no one could hear them, he wanted to be better safe than sorry.

"So what is so dangerous you would risk pissing off the whole room?" Carter didn't bother hiding his curiosity.

Cesar cracked his neck and took a deep breath. "Correct me if I'm wrong. All Weres are predators."

Carter's silence confirmed Cesar's suspicions.

"If all Weres are predators, why are those Hawks just about shaking with fear?"

Carter raised an eyebrow again. "They do not smell of fear. But you are right. With their nest being threatened, they should be putting up a fight."

Cesar sighed. Not good news. "I believe their fear is being masked. I want to test that theory."

Carter's eyes flashed. "And I have the best nose in the room."

Cesar nodded. "I need to know what they are hiding. Honestly, we are lucky I caught this much in my current state."

Carter gave him a worried look. "I'll be your lie detector on this one."

Cesar gave him a thankful smile before heading back downstairs.

As the two of them walked back into the lounge they received either angry or curious looks. Cesar stood in the center of the room so all eyes would be on him. Carter leaned against the wall about a yard from Barrett, which put him just behind the Hawks. The Wolf pretended to look sullen, as if unhappy with what they discussed. Seeing his expression, the Hawks didn't appear as bothered with him being so close behind them. Cesar had to give it to Carter, it was a good cover.

Cesar cleared his throat. "As I'm sure you're all aware, for some reason out here everyone is in everyone else's business, Carter has four Wolves with border patrol. I wanted to get their input on the rogues' arrival. The three of them walked into the country last week. That means they have been in the States for at least eight days. Now even if they managed to convince those Tigers, which let's say took four days, it should not have taken them four days to get to Burien. That trip takes what, three hours?"

Cesar paused long enough to look at Carter for verification. Carter nodded. Only the two of them would know what Cesar was actually verifying. The Hawks were beginning to smell of fear.

"If they did not detour they should have reached their destination before even I was in town." Cesar looked directly at the Werehawks, putting all his authority into his voice. "What is it they did for four days, exactly?"

There it was. The male blinked twice in rapid succession. Cesar looked past them to Carter. Carter widened his eyes for emphasis as he nodded again.

There were several curses from a younger Warrior behind Cesar as the room at large grasped the situation.

"When exactly did the rogues approach you the first time?" Cesar aimed his question at the male Hawk.

The male straightened. "Five days ago."

More cursing from the young Warrior.

The Hawk glanced at the young man over Cesar's shoulder before returning to Cesar. "My mate and her sister went to pick up our nest's young from their school and were told they had been picked up at lunch by another in our nest. Since our entire nest is cleared with the school, my mate thought nothing of it until returning home. There was a message from the other in our nest stating the young were safe but to keep them that way we needed to cooperate with these rogues."

Minnie growled from where she stood several feet to the left of the couple. "Your nest thought as little about betraying you as you did the rest of us. Filthy birds!"

The female Hawk stiffened, slowly turning her head to glare menacingly at Minnie. "Flea-bitten cat! You clearly have no mate or offspring of your own to say such a thing." Then she turned back to Cesar with all of her anger in her eyes. "Soaren's mate is entirely human. She has no knowledge of our world. He wanted to keep it that way until he was sure she loved him enough to handle it. One of your rogues followed Soaren to her apartment and waited for him to leave. They took her to get to him. Then used him to get to us. It is not Soaren's fault that trying to be a gentleman backfired. We do not blame him for this and we trust he will protect our young with his life, but we do not wish to test that theory."

The room was utterly silent. Cesar couldn't blame anyone for not speaking. No one in that room could say they wouldn't have done the same thing if roles were reversed. More so because, to his knowledge, none of the others in the room were mated. Cesar stretched his hazy mind to think of a plan.

"How many young are we talking about?" Raider asked from somewhere behind Cesar.

"Six," the female answered. "My mate and I have three: two male, one female. My sister West and her mate Azure have one young son. Steam and her human husband, Derek, have two girls. Only one of Steam and Derek's daughters is a Were, and we are more worried about the other."

Silence again. That worried Cesar more. A human child could not withstand as much as the Were children could. They needed to get to those children.

He turned to the couple. "Do you know where they are keeping your young?"

They both shook their heads. "Even if our noses were as good as the other Weres, we are not entirely sure we could find them."

Cesar picked his words carefully. He did not want to kill a large Hawk nest over this, but he would if he wasn't given a choice. "I would like to save your young."

The male's face blanked and the female watched him suspiciously.

"I cannot, however, have you working with these rogues behind my back. I will win this little battle they are staging and anyone helping them will pay a very steep price."

Cesar made sure he looked at each of them. As he watched, he noted the female appeared to be the most dominant of the pair. It was a good fact to have. Unlike the other Were breeds, birds didn't have one dominant sex. It was very much a case by case basis.

The female straightened up and glanced briefly at her mate. "Skye would side with you in this without hesitation. But I wouldn't let him. We are trying to build a nest where mixed couples can thrive and not looking out for our young above all else would hinder that."

He could respect her reasoning. If the Hawks were giving a haven to Human-Hawk couples, then the young did have to be their first priority. That explained why their nest was so large. It was an interesting move from birds, who generally didn't like groups.

"I understand. I would like to reach a compromise of sorts. I will send out noses to hunt your young, in return you only give the rogues what I want you to give them."

Skye clearly liked that idea; Cesar saw the man squeeze his mate's hand. She turned to him and they held a silent conversation for several moments before turning back to Cesar. The female simply nodded her head.

Cesar exhaled his relief as Carter inclined his head; the couple were being truthful.

"I will pull Native, but I would appreciate two noses for him to work with."

It took all of the restraint Cesar had left not to command the Weres to hand over their people. Anywhere else in the kingdom, in the world for that matter, he could command without question, but not in the backwoods of the Pacific Northwest. Cesar needed to get back to Montana.

"I will loan you Ming. His is one of my best trackers and is itching for a good hunt." Craig's amusement threaded his offer.

Gretchen S. B.

Cesar turned to the Lion and inclined his head. The Lion barely smiled and bowed.

"My Orlando has a knight in shining amour complex and he's my best nose. He would love to help save the day." Minnie shrugged as if it didn't matter to her if Orlando was used or not.

It was an interesting response, and had Cesar been at the top of his game he would have read into it more. Instead he mouthed a thank you to the Cat.

"Walker is very young but he can be quite stealthy when he puts his mind to it."

Cesar raised an eyebrow at Carter, who shrugged. If this was the same young Wolf he'd met two days ago, Cesar found that hard to believe.

"Very well then. Have your representatives meet with Native in…" Cesar looked at Viking and Raider, they knew the area better than he did.

"An hour across the street from the Highline theater building," Raider supplied as he pulled out his phone.

It took about ten minutes before plans could be solidified with all parties involved. Cesar uses the time to clear his head. The world was hazy with all the fog in his mind. He needed Gwen nearby if he was going to maintain his position much longer. By the end of today, Cesar knew he wouldn't be able to lead his people. He would still be able to function without killing every person in sight, but he couldn't lead. He needed time with his generals to create a plan for once the Maddening progressed that far.

Once everyone settled again, Cesar turned to the Hawks. "We need to know what you are doing for these rogues."

Skye shrugged. "We were told to do nothing until your people contacted us. Then we are to report back everything. I got the impression they did not expect your arrival. They thought they could accomplish their goals and stay under the radar. They have no idea you are mated to the Lady of the Dead. I believe they would rethink their plan if they knew. They also seem to think you are Roman, not the King. They seem to be waiting on this meeting to decide on their move. They know you have Jake. We are to find his location if we get the chance."

There it was, loud and clear, the hole Cesar was looking for. He spoke up before Skye could continue. "Tell them I ordered the relocation of the Lady of the Dead because I did not want her in the same place where the rogue was being held."

Skye's eyes flashed as he caught on. "Only you and her three most trusted Warriors know her current location, so you left the rogue to the less experienced Warriors, because chained up in the Lady of the Dead's stronghold, he is no threat. They might fall for that, but they might also ask for the MP's help getting in here unnoticed."

Cesar felt the wicked smile curl his lips. "Let me worry about that."

In that moment, Cesar knew the Maddening had taken root and everyone in the room noticed. "I want everyone to go about business as normal, just appear more cautious. These two are not working alone and though they are the immediate threat, I believe we need to prepare for the long haul on this one. Once everyone leaves, I will go over the list Poet has. The list will be divided up depending on what flavor they are. I want everyone in contact with their groups as well as two others, that way we have back ups if something happens and I want all information filtering through here. If there is nothing else, you're free to go."

He was surprised when no one balked. There were no snarky comments or questions. Everyone but the Warriors simply left. There was a solemn tone Cesar had not seen in several hundred years, since the last time the entire kingdom was at war. The players were different but the attitude was the same.

Cesar looked around the room at the men he commanded, and with the exception of Poet and Deuce they all looked back at him. "Everyone except Viking and Poet needs to find somewhere else to be," he growled.

The younger ones practically leapt from the room. They feared their king.

Deuce slowly stood up and slid his hat back onto his head. He looked past Cesar and shook his head. "I wouldn't, Raider. You don't want to screw with a man in that condition. Best for all of us to do what the man says and leave."

Cesar turned to see Raider narrow his eyes at Deuce before looking back at Viking. Raider clearly wasn't used to being kept out of the loop. He stared at Viking's blank face a second before curling him lip and leaving.

Deuce followed him out but paused as he reached the door. He seemed to be debating something. Finally he turned to face Cesar, only he was looking at his shoulder instead of his eyes.

"I've only known two Warriors who lasted past three days. They were in hell. I made arrangements for one of them. If things come down to the wire, should I make arrangements for you? I would do it clean, quick."

Cesar stared at the other man in surprise. Deuce was asking him if when the time came Cesar wanted Deuce to kill him. He had not been the only person to offer, but then he was probably the only one crazy enough to follow through.

Cesar shook his head, part of him was grateful. "No, I've already made arrangements, but thank you."

Deuce bobbed his head then left without another word.

None of them said anything for a moment. It wasn't the easiest act to follow.

"That was…unexpected," Viking commented.

Poet tossed his magazine onto the coffee table in front of him. "Not really, it is a 'honor among thieves' thing. You just aren't used to it because neither of you spent much time with us bad guys before you were exiled. Deuce is a crazy masochistic prick, but believe it or not, he has his own code of ethics."

Cesar watched Poet after the other man stopped talking. It was a fact Cesar went out of his way not to forget. None of his generals were Warriors exiled for truly evil deeds, but his kingdom was full of sick, twisted individuals. Since he had stabilized the kingdom there were Warriors who willingly migrated to North America, but for the most part his was the kingdom of outlaws and he ruled them with his eyes open.

Sighing, he shook his head. "Enough, I do not have the energy for side conversations. Where's the list Buccaneer gave you?"

Both Cesar and Viking moved to the coffee table as they began narrowing down their list possible suspects.

Chapter 21

Gwen woke to a coughing fit, not her own but someone else's. She had a moment of panic until everything flooded back to her. She was safe, at Sivia's, and Roman was watching her. Gwen opened her eyes to see Roman still at his post at the back of the couch, drinking from a glass. She focused on him, trying to keep the nausea at bay.

He saw her looking at him and set the glass down next to him. There must have been another stool. "My apologies, young lady. I finished my book and borrowed one from the bookshelves. The cover and title fooled me, the content is not what I expected and it caught me by surprise." He closed the paperback so she could see the cover.

Gwen grinned. Karin had loaned her that book a few months ago as a joke. The first half was innocent enough but halfway through it became the dark side of erotic. She could see how a big bad Warrior would have a coughing fit.

"I've read it actually."

Roman blinked down at her in surprise, then set the book down entirely. "If I were to recommend this book to August would you warn him?"

Gwen giggled, this wasn't quite the type of conversation she expected. "No."

Roman leaned forward so his elbows and forearms crossed on the back of the couch. "Good, I approve of you for him."

She wasn't sure how to take that but it pulled a thought into her head and she struggled to sit up. Roman reached down immediately and helped her prop her back on the side of the couch before returning to his perch.

"How long have I been out?"

Roman looked at the clock on the far wall behind him. "It is almost four in the afternoon. I have been here more than fifteen hours." He paused, looking down at her.

He was testing her memory, Gwen knew it. "But I woke up and spoke to you."

She was rewarded with a smile. "That you did. It was shortly after August left, about ten p.m."

Gwen felt worry tug at her face. "How is he?"

Roman raised an eyebrow at her. "What do you mean?"

Frustration flooded over worry. "With the Maddening. He only has another day. How is his mind?"

She wasn't sure he would answer from the long pause he took.

"His temper is irrationally quick and he called twelve times since you last woke. Viking tells me he has not slept and has not been able to stand still longer than five. He also has your younger detail frightened of him." That last part Roman seemed to find funny.

"And how did you manage to be here?"

Roman's smile disappeared. "When you were injured, every pendant-carrying Warrior in this part of the kingdom felt it. Viking told me he spent a good part of the night fielding frantic calls. August and Viking tracked you down and then trusted me with your care.

"Now you need to answer one of mine. Who did this to you?"

Gwen thought about the best way to answer. She wasn't entirely sure what it was.

"It's a he and he is somewhere north, near Everett. He is this incredibly powerful being, only someone along the way trapped him with some heavy duty spells, in an old playground. I think he was there before the playground. He was telling me the rogues made a bargain with an enemy of his, than told me to leave and swatted at me.

"He actually clawed me I felt it. I flew into my body then everything was black and something big and bad began tugging at me. Once I heard Sivia and Barrett I struggled to stay near their voices. Then the struggle stopped and I crashed into my body again. Which feels like I've been hit by a car, by the way. I don't remember anything else until you."

Roman sat silently thinking about what she said for a moment. Gwen knew he would continue to do so for some time but she also knew she was going to puke and he would have to help her get to the bathroom.

She started struggling to get up. "I'm gonna puke, by the way."

Roman's eyes flashed and within a second he was around the couch and picking her up.

"I can walk," Gwen protested.

"I can walk faster."

Gwen swore she vomited for a full five minutes. That had to be a record of some kind. Afterward she just leaned against the side of the bathtub. Roman was clearly not used to illness because he leaned against the door frame looking at her, unsure.

"Getting you pregnant will kill August."

The comment was so out of the blue Gwen simply blinked up at Roman for several seconds. "I'm sorry, what?"

Roman's lips actually twitched. "You look so helpless and pathetic. It will kill him to see you like this every day, knowing it's his fault and he can't do anything about it."

She frowned at him. "I think I'm insulted by that."

He shrugged.

They stayed like that for several more minutes. Gwen was grateful both Sivia and Karin were in class. The less people who saw her in this condition the better. Then it occurred to her she wasn't wearing her own clothes, these were Sivia's. How much blood was on her clothes?

Her thoughts were interrupted by Roman clearing his throat. "You still with me over there?"

Gwen nodded.

"Doesn't really look like it but I'll take your word for it. I'm under orders to get you back home as soon as you are able. Normally I'd have you stay put, but you and I both know your presence is needed elsewhere. Are you in a position where you could travel that far?"

Gwen checked in with her body. She was definitely still queasy but she might have a half hour in her. She knew she couldn't walk any distances. Barrett may have put a pain spell on her but Gwen could still tell her body would not operate properly.

"Maybe. I won't be able to walk on my own. Unless traffic is horrendous, I should be able to make it without incident but I need to be in my apartment without visitors as soon as we get there."

Roman pushed off the door frame. "Done. Stay here, I'll call a cab, collect all our things and be back to carry you down to the lobby."

He was out of sight before she could argue. Gwen wasn't entirely sure she could have anyway so instead she sat there with her eyes closed and tried desperately to calm her stomach. She knew exactly how much effort this trip would to take and she really hoped she had enough energy to do it.

Chapter 22

Cesar felt her enter the building before Viking could do more than raise his head. The rest of the Warriors most likely knew what was happening when both men shot up and darted from the room.

They caught up with Roman and Gwen as they were entering the stairwell. Gwen looked only a step or two away from death warmed over. Growling loudly, Cesar swooped in and swept Gwen up before Roman could.

"Oh no, Oh no. Too fast, too fast!" she exclaimed.

Cesar stood stock still as only a Warrior could and waited until he saw Gwen's breathing even out and she opened her eyes to look up at him. It was a punch to his gut. He wanted to take her upstairs and claim her more than anything in the world, but he held every muscle still for her.

"Hello boys. August, I need to get into my apartment in the next few moments. Really I need to get to the bathroom."

All of Cesar's being focused on his mate's request. His arms locked in place so she wouldn't be even the littlest bit jarred. Then he took the stairs as swiftly as he could without making her sick.

Once he set her down in her black and white bathroom, Gwen smiled up at him then looked pleadingly at Roman. Cesar growled, he mate should be looking at no one else. Roman's hand gripped his shoulder and Cesar turned to look menacingly at the other man.

Roman's face was completely calm. "The young lady wished some privacy. An attempt at dignity."

Cesar only stopped growling long enough to look back at Gwen. She was giving him an apologetic smile.

"You will call when you need me?" Cesar cursed himself for the sheer need in his voice.

Gwen gave half a nod and began to pale.

All three Warriors walked out through the bedroom and into the hallway. Roman turned on the fan as they left to drown out the noise. They stood there helpless for what seemed to Cesar to be an eternity.

"I assume this means any meeting will now be run out of Gwen's living room." Viking kept his voice blank.

Gretchen S. B.

Cesar fought to stay on topic. "Yes...as much as I hate others in her home...I think it is the only way for the next two days."

Neither of the other men said anything. They both knew after two days they would have a whole new set of problems. "I...am going to need some time...it is taking the last of my reserves to stand out here knowing she is in the next room."

Roman looked him in the eye. "I will come report to you in three hours. Hopefully you will be rational enough to hear it and to let her brother here get near her."

The small, still functioning part of Cesar's brain felt bad about Viking, but both of them knew the Maddening would not let Viking touch Gwen.

"Agreed."

His generals left. Once they were gone and Cesar heard the lock slip into place he bee-lined for Gwen.

Warrior hearing was good enough that Cesar could hear Gwen vomiting through the closed sliding door, even with the fan on. He itched to go to her but knew it to be a bad move.

Instead he went to her closet. Cesar knew the clothes she wore were not hers and she would feel more comfortable in her own. He not so discreetly looked around until he found her night clothes and just about had a heart attack. She owned a plethora of immodest clothing for bed. If he was going to be able to keep his hands off her, he needed to find something that covered as much skin as possible. That proved easier said than done, as nothing was terribly modest. Cesar finally settled on a form-fitting bright green camisole and a matching set of loose cotton pants. The top was going to be hard for him but, considering his options, he would live with it.

As he walked out of her closet, Cesar heard Gwen's soft voice calling his name. His blood ran hotter and his lust spiked. Desperately he reined himself in. She might not know about the Maddening, and the last thing he needed was to scare her.

Cesar's heart dropped as he walked into the room and clicked the fan off. She looked broken. He wanted to hold her, protect her from the world and brutally kill whomever had done this to her.

Gwen looked up at him with slight amusement in her eyes. "You want me to change."

Cesar had actually forgotten he was holding her clothes. At her words he lifted the clothes and walked over to where she sat on the floor and squatted in front of her.

"Can you? Or will you need my help?"

She laughed at him. It was so startling Cesar blinked.

"I'm sorry. It's just you sounded so earnest. Look, I know what your body is going through and I know helping me dress would torture you. Let's split the difference, if you can help me up so I can lean against the counter I should be able to change myself."

Cesar didn't know why he was surprised to hear Gwen knew about the Maddening, but he was. She didn't appear frightened by it. Cesar squashed that flicker of hope. She couldn't sleep with him; there was no hope.

Without another word, Cesar slowly helped his mate to her feet and guided her to the counter before once again leaving the room so she could change. A part of him found it interesting that it wasn't for modesty's sake she turned his help away, but for his sanity. He wasn't sure he liked what that meant about her level of modesty. To distract himself, Cesar began pulling back the covers on her bed.

After standing on the other side of the sliding door for several minutes, Cesar heard Gwen's rustling move closer. He swung the door open to see her walking toward him. Without so much as a thought he swept her up and carried her over to the bed.

"I can walk, just slowly." She sounded indignant.

Cesar snorted at her as he tucked her in. "It has nothing to do with you being sick and everything to do with me needing to touch you."

That silenced her. She watched him finish tucking her in and continued to watch him shut her blinds and head out the door.

"Where are you going?"

The confusion in her voice made him turn.

"I will be in the living room should you need me." Cesar opened the door.

"NO!"

Her outrage surprised him so much he let go of the door and was standing next to the bed before he realized what he was doing.

Gwen glowered up at him. "You are not doing such a stupid thing. This time I'm vetoing you."

Cesar raised an eyebrow. If it was anyone else talking to him like that he wouldn't take it, but coming from her, it was a turn on.

"Why is that?"

"You only have a day left, if that. Roman told me on the way here about how you're planning to fight it. That's very sweet, but immensely stupid. We both know you need to be around me if we are to keep you sane. So darn it, strip down to whatever it is you're wearing under those jeans and get into bed. I might not be able to mate with you, but at least it would relieve your symptoms."

Cesar couldn't do anything but stare at her for a full minute. The gentleman in him warred with his lust. He hadn't thought he could get harder, he was wrong.

He needed two deep breaths before he could respond. "I am not sure that is the wisest idea, Gwen."

She glared up at him. "Deal with it or I am going to get out of this bed."

Cesar could tell she meant it. The last thing he wanted was her making herself sicker. He growled at her but there was no real threat behind it.

"Fine."

Then he shut the door again and stripped down to his boxers. Cesar was careful as he slid into the opposite side of the bed, trying not to move the mattress as he spooned her. Fighting every urge in his body, he draped his arm over her so his hand rested on the mattress. The position was awkward. Cesar had not laid with a woman in centuries.

"Oh for goodness sake, August." Gwen sounded exasperated.

She squirmed into him so almost every inch of their bodies touched. His cock nestled against her lower back. It actually jerked as she cuddled closer. Lastly, she grabbed his hand and slid it under her shirt. Cesar swore he stopped breathing as his hand slid along her skin. He heard her breathing hitch slightly as it passed along her waist. Cesar noted that for later. She finally guided his hand to lay under the curve of her breast, along her ribs. He stayed perfectly still as her arm retracted.

Female laughter floated to his ears. "Oh, will you relax, August? How am I supposed to get any rest with you vibrating with tension?"

Cesar took several deep breaths, slowly relaxing his muscles. When he got to his hand he flexed his fingers and heard Gwen's breath catch. That succeeded in relaxing him the rest of the way and he was glad she couldn't see his prideful smile.

———————————

Cesar may not have slept a wink during the three hours he lay with Gwen but his mind felt clearer. He was still the horniest he had ever been in his life, but at least the insane anger subsided. When he heard Viking unlocking the front door, Cesar really had to fight the urge to stay with the only peace he found in centuries.

By the time he slid his jeans back on and made it to the front room, everyone already made it inside. Roman watched him appraisingly and then gave him a curious look. Viking and Raider hung back by the door, along with Sivia and Barrett.

Cesar looked at Viking. "She's asleep and I would greatly appreciate her staying that way."

Viking blinked at him repeatedly in shock before bolting for the bedroom.

Raider looked at Cesar suspiciously. "You're okay with him being back there with her?"

"Yes, and I assume you want to see her too."

Raider's eyes widened before he nodded and followed Viking.

Roman continued to stare at him but Cesar ignored his friend. Instead, turned to the MP and the Immortal.

"Give them a few minutes before checking on her, please."

They both nodded at him. Cesar strode away down the hall to the spare bedroom he had been staying in, knowing full well that Roman wasn't far behind. Cesar began shoving items back into his duffel bag; he had made up his mind to take up residence in Gwen's room. He wasn't sure how long Roman would stand in the doorway watching him and he didn't particularly care.

"You didn't sleep with her, the Maddening is still there, yet you're being rational. What did you do? Or better yet what did she do?"

Cesar's anger did a quick spike but he maintained control.

"Nothing. I just lay with her while she slept."

He glanced over to see his friend lift an eyebrow in disbelief. "That was enough to soothe you this much? Damn Augustus, you have been too long without a woman."

Cesar glared at his friend as he zipped up his bag. "Don't you have a report to be giving, General?"

Roman smiled and saluted. "Yes, sir. We have set the stage for the rogues to come and break Jake out, if they so choose and with the rate they're going I'll bet they will. As for the troops, I've now heard back from all groups and everyone agrees no one will make a move until we get these rogues out of the way.

"Native called soon after you left, he's pretty sure they found where the Hawks are being kept. They are staking the place out as we speak to see if the rogues in question are there. He hasn't seen them yet and he doesn't expect to until the neighbors quiet down for the night."

"As for what attacked my queen…"

Cesar turned to look at his friend. He had forgotten asking Roman to look into that. Roman gave him a sad smile, as if part of him found Cesar amusing.

"She does not seem entirely sure. Gwen was speaking with something powerful in the Spirit World and it attacked her. When she described being dragged from her body, she did not make it sound like it was the same being. Perhaps whatever she talked to set a trap. I do not know its intent for sure and cannot communicate with it myself, unless Gwen takes me to it."

Cesar didn't like the idea of Gwen taking Roman to see what had attacked her. Or that she didn't know what was after her. Cesar would broach the subject with Gwen as soon as he got the chance. Hoisting his duffel over his shoulder Cesar headed back out to the main room, pausing as he passed his best friend.

"So you told her about the Maddening."

Roman's face filled with amusement. "Of course, what type of friend to the young lady would I be if I didn't warn her about what I was getting her into? You didn't forbid ME to talk about it with her."

Cesar shook his head, Roman always did make his life more interesting. "Thank you."

Roman shrugged. "Don't thank me. Gwen brought it up. She already possessed the basic information. How she gained it I don't know, and she knows you are the king too. I believe there is some kind of information leak out here on the coast. They all know so much about everything. Listening to your woman talk about other species was a shock. We used to prevent our Lady of the Dead from interacting with others. What is wrong with these people?"

Cesar snorted. "Tell me about it. While we wait for the others to finish, go look at the contents of her kitchen."

His general watched him with suspicious curiosity. "Why...Does Viking let her keep alcohol?"

He laughed, count on Roman to get it in one. "An appalling amount and she keeps Monk's Poison on hand too."

Roman's horrified shock was almost comical. "Why in heaven's name would they let her do that?"

Cesar shook his head. "I have no idea. She also has no meat."

Roman scoffed. "Now I know you must be lying." He turned and strode down the hall heading for the kitchen.

Grinning, Cesar followed after his friend. It was good to have someone here who thought this corner of the world was as topsy-turvy as he did.

Chapter 23

"Gwen, we need you awake for a moment. Do you think you can do that?"

Gwen heard Sivia's voice from where she floated between waking and sleep. Once the words registered, she fought to wake her body. It was more of a struggle than it should have been but when Gwen finally opened her eyes she saw the occupants in her room breathe a sigh of relief.

Once she saw who was in the room, or more to the point, who wasn't, she began to panic. "Where is August? How long have I been out?"

The room shuffled the same confused look from person to person. None of them knew what she was talking about. Viking's face lit up and he smiled down at her from where he sat at the foot of the bed, reaching to grab her right hand.

"It is okay, little one, the King is in the next room. He is being debriefed and giving us time to see you alone."

Tension washed out of Gwen's body and she squeezed Viking's hand in thanks. If they were going to put August down she made Roman promise to let her be there. So far he kept his word.

The others in the room were looking from her to Viking in confusion. Viking coughed to hide his laugh but didn't do it well.

"That would be a pet name for the King, derived from his birth name."

Both Raider and Barrett tried to hide their chuckles. Sivia did a better job; the only outward sign of her amusement was a twitching of her lips.

"Anyway Gwen, Barrett and I have to renew our spells. It would appear whatever attacked you before has moved on, because there is no chipping to the last protection spell I put on you. I also need to take a look at your stomach and see how you're healing."

Gwen tried to nod as Sivia spoke, but it brought the nausea to the forefront so she quit mid-motion. After taking several deep breaths to keep her stomach contents where they should be, Gwen put all her attention on Viking.

"Storebror."

He smiled down at her, relief so plain on his face Gwen ached for him. She wanted to give him a hug, but that was out of the question.

"Yes, little one?"

"I've really had my fill of public displays for the day. I would appreciate if you guys could wait outside while they check me out."

Gwen was careful to interject the right amount of embarrassment in her voice. She needed to talk to the healers alone, but she wanted Viking to believe what she said.

"Of course, little one. I understand." He bent forward to kiss her forehead before standing up, turning to Raider and motioning to the door.

Raider wasn't one to outwardly show affection. As he followed Viking out, he gave Gwen a relieved smile.

Sivia pulled back the blanket as the door shut and began examining the slashes.

Barrett waited to speak until the Warriors were no longer in earshot of the door. "You're good and if I didn't live with Lucia, I wouldn't have caught it either." He folded his arms over his chest.

Sivia frowned and looked up at Barrett from where she leaned over the bed. "What are you babbling about?"

Barrett's eyes didn't leave Gwen's. "She wanted to say something to us that she couldn't say in front of the parents."

Sivia's frown deepened before she turned her head to look at Gwen. "He's right. Are things about to get interesting, or worse?"

Gwen gave a small laugh. "Interesting, I hope."

Sivia's shoulder's slumped. "Oh, thank goodness." Then she went back to her examination.

Gwen looked at Barrett, who watched her in interest.

"I need your services."

If anything he became more interested. "Uh huh."

"August hasn't slept in I'm not sure how long. I think the lack of sleep is making the Maddening worse."

An eyebrow cocked up. "You're asking me to put a sleep spell on the king in the middle of a crisis?"

Gwen sucked on her lip, she knew August needed sleep, she needed Barrett's help. "Not exactly. I'm asking you to put a timed sleep spell on the bed. That way he'll get a full night's sleep without endangering anyone and your butt is covered because you had no way of knowing he would get into bed with me."

Sivia stood up and looked from one of them to the other. Barrett grinned down at Gwen.

"That is absolutely devious. I love it!"

"So you'll do it?" Gwen became wary. She and the MPs were friends but she still worried about payments.

"As a wedding present, should a wedding happen." His grin grew wider.

Sivia rolled he eyes. "Why am I not surprised you managed to get that in."

Barrett grinned at Sivia before turning back to Gwen. "We have a deal?"

Gwen sighed. "Deal. But you have to shake for me, I can't really lift my hand."

He leaned over and gave her hand one swift shake and Gwen felt the tell-tale tingle.

She waited until he let go before speaking to both of them. "No one can know, except Roman. If something happens he needs to know his king will be out of commission for a few hours."

This time they both grinned. "Deal."

Gwen took a deep breath. "Okay, do your checks and put me back to sleep before I need to puke again."

Gwen hoped her plan worked. She wasn't too hopeful considering it was a plan concocted in a fevered, be-spelled brain. She knew August only had maybe twelve hours before he lost his mind and less than twenty-four until they lost him. She had to do something. She was the only one who could. So here she stood in the training room Oracle always put her in, screaming for the woman every way she could think of.

"ORACLE!"

Gwen had been trying for ten minutes and there was no sign of the older woman yet. She was determined to keep trying, she never actually called the other woman before. Gwen hoped desperately she could.

"I assume you're calling me?"

Relief flooded Gwen as she spun around to the voice immediately behind her. She was so overwhelmed she hugged the other woman. Oracle was so shocked that she stood there several beats before hugging her back.

"Shh, It is all right, child. Everything is all right." Oracle began rubbing Gwen's back and making cooing sounds.

Gwen soaked up comfort from the stronger woman a moment before breaking away.

Oracle's arms fell gracefully to her sides and she tilted her head, face full of concern. "What is the matter? You have never tried to call me before. If I had not recognized your voice, I would never have come."

Gwen felt the first flames of anger whip around her belly. "Why not?"

The other woman actually chuckled. "Thessa, my name is Thessa. It is the only name when called, I will answer. Where did you get Oracle from, it is a little trite."

Gwen's surprise smothered her anger. Where had she gotten that name from? Did she just make it up when she was little? She must have.

Thessa rose her palm to silence Gwen's train of thought. "It does not really matter at the moment. You have need of me?"

Gwen took a shaky breath. "Yes, I've always suspected that you are real and not something concocted by my subconscious."

When Thessa didn't respond, Gwen continued. "I need to do something that I don't believe is within my abilities to do. I need to jump into someone else's dreams."

Thessa shook her head, folding her arms. "No, absolutely not. A person's dreams are their business, not yours."

Gwen began to panic, then her mind wrapped around the other woman's wording. Thessa inferred shouldn't, not couldn't. Gwen needed to convince her otherwise.

Words flew from her mouth, one on top of another. "Please, it's a long story. I've been chosen for a Warrior and he is about to enter the last day of the Maddening and I am far too injured to mate him. He's the king and we have rogue Warriors trying to start a war. The kingdom needs its king. I think if I can jump into his dreams and mate him there it might buy him some time."

Gretchen S. B.

Gwen's breathing and heartbeat were so fast she had a fleeting thought about whether or not she could have a heart attack in a dream. Thessa watched her with thoughts and emotions swirling around her face.

"If I do this for you, you must promise me you will show me who injured you." Thessa seemed to have settled on anger.

There was a moment's hesitation before Gwen nodded.

Thessa shook her head and anger was replaced by amusement. "Ironic, one of my children gifted to a Warrior." She shook her head again. "When his Maddening is over, you and I have some things to discuss. Call me, by my name, if you need me to do this again."

Gwen exhaled. "Okay."

Thessa raised her arms and it almost sounded like she was singing.

The sensation of falling was creepy, until Gwen realized she really was falling through a ceiling. She let out a yelp before she could stop herself and a moment later she landed with a bounce onto her own bed.

She blinked several times in confusion. She shouldn't be here. She should be in August's dream. Then she began to look around her. The blinds and window were open and there was a cool night breeze. No one would have left the window open.

The noise of someone clearing their throat behind her startled her enough to make her jump off the bed. She spun around to see August watching from the other side; he appeared to be in mid pace. He looked almost menacing, except for the shocked confusion on his face.

"Gwen?"

His voice so hesitant, her heart whimpered.

"Yeah."

"What are you doing here? How are you here? You shouldn't be standing." August was trying to sound authoritative but he wasn't pulling it off successfully.

"I'm fine. I made a few bargains to meet you in your sleep." She tried to keep her voice smooth, she didn't need him getting angry.

He seemed to be curious instead. "Are you saying you plotted against me to get me to sleep then made your way into my dream?"

Gwen wasn't sure which way he was going with that. "Y-Yes."

She was startled again when he burst out laughing. Gwen wasn't entirely sure what to do so she continued to stand across the bed.

The laughter died down after and minute or so. "Oh, fate has given me the perfect mate. If we get through this, I am going to have to keep an eye on you at all times."

Gwen frowned and swung her hands to her hips, she was sick of Warriors patronizing her. "I'm an adult, August. I don't need a babysitter."

He actually started laughing again. "No, that's not how I meant it. You will keep me on my toes. If I am not careful I could wake one morning and you'll have taken my kingdom from me."

He grinned at her. She really liked that grin. August was so much sexier when at ease like this. Gwen felt her indignation being replaced by lust.

"So tell me." August sat down on the bed. "Why? Why go to all this trouble?"

Gwen hesitantly slid on to the bed so she was about two feet from him and watched the lust spike in his eyes.

"You need sleep. If I'm right, rest will help your symptoms ease and before you ask I made sure someone let Roman know what happened so he won't waste time trying to wake you."

August appeared surprised and shook his head. "Of course you did. Why are you here then? Surely I can rest without the visitation."

He sounded like he was playing with her and Gwen found she really liked it.

"Obviously not. You're dreaming of my room and you were pacing. I'm putting your mind at ease."

August actually looked sheepish, like he was embarrassed to be caught in her bedroom. Gwen thought it was cute, she was flattered. Then there was a spark in his eyes and they narrowed. His gaze flicked back to her.

Gretchen S. B.

"You had no way of knowing what I would dream of. For all you knew I could have been on a battlefield centuries ago. You're in my dream for a different reason."

Gwen squirmed under the weight of his gaze. She should have known he was smart enough to see through her response. Taking a deep breath to steady herself, Gwen looked him straight in the eye.

"I came to have sex with you."

She was pretty sure August couldn't have been more shocked if she'd slapped him. He stared at her open-mouthed for several seconds before he seemed to realize how close they were and leapt off the bed,

"No, absolutely not!" He slashed both arms through the air.

It was Gwen's turn to be shocked. "Why the hell not?"

He frowned disapprovingly at her word choice. "Because you are a lady of status and as such should be wooed, not used like a street whore."

He was serious. Gwen couldn't believe he was serious. She burst out laughing and fell back onto the bed.

"This is not funny!"

August's outrage only made her laugh harder. It took her almost a minute to get herself under control. He glared at her.

"August, this isn't the same thing. It's sweet you think so, but you're wrong."

He curled his lip. "You're patronizing me."

Gwen let out a giggle. "Remember what it feels like next time you're doing it to me. Look, we're in a dream, not real life. Your Maddening is getting worse and if us having sex buys you more time then so be it. You can make it up to me after you're no longer off your rocker."

August continued to glare at her. He wasn't going to budge. Gwen sighed and an idea came to her. They were both under a sleep spell, and he couldn't escape her. Gwen watched August's eyes narrow further and the mischievous grin slid across her face.

"August, how long has it been since you were last with a woman?" She made her voice playful.

"A gentleman does not discuss such things with his mate." His voice was blank.

Gwen's grin slinked down to a smirk as she leaned forward and slowly crawled across the bed, giving her hips a little extra sway as she moved. Gwen knew she had hit a nerve when August's chest stopped moving as he held his breath.

When she reached the end of the bed she looked up at him with her eyes slightly widened and inhaled deeply. His eyes honed in on her breasts, or as much of them as he could see from down her top. Leaning back slowly Gwen sat and swung her legs off the edge. There was a small flicker of panic in August's eyes as she stood up an inch away from him.

Gwen knew he could feel her breath against his skin. She moved her gaze lazily from his gorgeous chest to his eyes. With one finger she began making slow circles around his left nipple. He breathed in a shudder. August wasn't looking at her anymore. His eyes stared straight ahead trying to ignore her.

She pushed out her lip and made sure he could hear the pout in her voice. "Don't you miss it?"

He was trying desperately to out will her. That wasn't going to happen.

Gwen smiled and her voice took on a purring quality. "Bodies sliding against one another. The panting. The moans. The little throaty voices."

She felt her breathing grow shallow as she thought about it and felt his breathing match hers. Her voice grew throaty. "August, August, yes, yes, oh please, yes."

There was a rumble in his chest seconds before he spoke through clenched teeth. "Stop that, Gwen!"

She was getting to him. She just had to tip him over the edge. Problem was, she was getting turned on herself. A light went on in her head.

"Are you telling me you would leave me breathy, wet, and needy? What kind of gentleman does that?"

August looked at her then. His expression was torn.

She almost had him. Gwen bit back her grin, instead making a face of shock and backed up several steps. "Oh, August I'm so sorry! I didn't realize."

Confusion covered his features.

Gwen had him. "It didn't occur to me." She couldn't hide her smile anymore so she turned away from him and started crawling on

Gretchen S. B.

the bed. "You don't remember how to finish a woman. Don't worry about it I'll take care of it myself."

There was a growl. A split second later she was being flipped and pinned to the bed.

"Can't finish a woman. I'll show you a finish only centuries of experience can bring a woman."

Then he was all over, his mouth on hers, his tongue demanding entrance. Her body jerked a moment before Gwen heard the tearing sound of her top being torn off. She gasped into August's mouth, which he took advantage of by sliding his tongue inside.

He trailed his hands up her sides. Gwen gasped and bucked. The masculine laugh told her it was intentional. How had August known that was a spot for her?

August's hands moved again, one to a breast and one moved south. Gwen's mind fogged over. He was right. August moved expertly. She was panting heavily in record time and he had yet to reach her panties. Gwen wasn't used to such ministrations. The guys up until now worked more for speed, get her wet and go. August stoked the fire.

His mouth broke from hers and Gwen let out a helpless sound in the back of her throat. There was a masculine chuckle in response.

"I can't be on top of you and remove the rest of our clothing, Gwen." The rest of his body heat disappeared.

She knew what he was doing but another sound escaped her throat anyway. When her eyes fluttered open, August was removing his gray sweatpants. Gwen was pretty sure he didn't mean for it to be a show, but it was. The man was breathtaking. Hard muscle Gwen really wanted to lick and bite. She began to sit up when August looked over at her. Gwen stopped mid motion at the playful hunger in his eyes. He let the sweats drop to the floor and leaned over her, so his arms were on either side of her chest.

"Did I say you could get up? You set the ground rules, little mate." August began slowly leaning in so he pushed Gwen back on the bed. "You wounded my big bad Warrior pride and now you must deal with the consequences."

Lust laced with anticipation shot through her body. His timing was perfect, and her head hit the comforter with his last word. August grinned down at her for a beat before his face disappeared again and Gwen felt his hands begin sliding her pants and panties off.

He touched her skin the entire way down. By the time his face appeared again, Gwen was back to panting. The triumphant smile on August's face would normally make Gwen angry but she couldn't seem to hold that thought long enough to stir up any negative emotions. August began kissing down her neck. One hand was back to her breast while the other lay on her inner thigh. He could flick a finger and have touched where Gwen so desperately needed him to touch her, but he didn't. He was torturing her. As long as he followed through, Gwen was sure she could handle it.

When his lips finally made it to her other breast, Gwen's back arched. He began flicking one finger in the right place and every thought shattered in the inferno that engulfed Gwen's head. A strangled cry escaped her throat, but August continued his pace. Every move, lick, and kiss threw Gwen higher but she didn't seem to be coming any closer to release. She could feel sweat beginning to form on her body. She needed to come soon.

"August, please." Gwen's words came out one at a time on the tail of a gasp.

She heard pride in his laugh and his hand finally moved from her thigh. Gwen had just enough time to be grateful before the world exploded. Her whole body bucked off the bed as if an electric current shot through her. The room seemed to tilt as waves of warmth hit her. The pleasure felt as if it coursed within her veins, simply making circles before returning at full force. Her body continued to buck and she felt her inner muscles squeezing at nothing.

Just as her body fell back on the bed, Gwen felt the verge of a second orgasm. She didn't even have time to be surprised before her body exploded with heat-laced pleasure. Gwen started seeing black spots and slammed her eyes shut. Her body was too weak to buck so it seemed to quiver instead. August hadn't so much as put a finger inside her. Gwen's inner muscles almost screamed in protest. As her breathing returned to panting, she felt him slid one thick finger inside. Gwen was pretty sure she screamed. It felt so good, she began milking his finger as August moved it in and out rubbing against just the right spot.

To Gwen's shock her body began to heat again, much faster than the first time.

"No way, no way I will come again." She wasn't sure if she was stating a fact or pleading.

August added a finger and within a few strokes her exhausted body peaked again. Her body was so hot she swore she was on fire. His fingers kept moving, bringing wave after wave crashing over her, and each seemed stronger than the last. This orgasm lasted longer than the other two, beating every orgasm that had ever come before it.

When her breathing finally slowed, Gwen could feel the blood starting to spread out to the rest of her body again. Her ears felt fuzzy, like she just changed altitudes. Without moving her head, Gwen knew she would be lightheaded. Her entire body was humming and she could feel August's fingers sliding in and out of her, but he was going out of his way not to rub her G-spot.

"You back with me yet?" August sounded soothed and quite pleased with himself.

"Just about." Gwen managed, her voice sounding a little hoarse.

His fingers stopped and Gwen felt the bed move as August laid next to her left side.

"Still think I can't finish a woman?"

Gwen couldn't sum up enough energy to open her eyes, let alone glare at him. "Yup."

There was a rumble of laughter. "Well, I'll try harder next time."

Gwen felt a small wave of panic. "Please don't."

More laughter, she felt his hand on her belly, fingers gliding back and forth. He seemed peaceful. Gwen was sure he had to be harder than rock. She turned her head and opened her eyes. She was dumbfounded. There he was watching his fingers with a look of complete contentment on his face. Gwen moved her head just enough to confirm he was fully erect.

Gwen looked back up at his face. "How can you just lay here like that?"

August sighed and laid his warm hand across her belly, but he still didn't look at her. "We have already been over this."

Gwen's eyes widened. "You have got to be kidding me!"

His eyes finally met hers. Gwen could see his determination. "Do not argue with me on this, I will win."

It went against Gwen's nature to keep her mouth shut. "Oh come on, you cannot tell me that doesn't hurt, especially after how many centuries of blue balls?!"

August frowned at her. "I do not like how colorful Viking has let your language become."

Gwen snorted and sat up. When the world didn't spin, she turned to look down at August. Though he was looking at her suspiciously, there was an underlying peace to his face.

"Look, either you let me take care of it or you do it yourself. Otherwise me being here has been nothing but counterproductive."

August scowled up at her. "No, it hasn't. Don't say that."

She was touched by his outrage on her behalf, but Gwen was not going to let it detour her. Before he knew what she was doing, Gwen wrapped one hand tightly around his cock and began stroking, though he was thick enough that her hand didn't quite fit all the way around.

He let out a loud hiss and his eyes fell shut before his hand slid from her leg to still her wrist. Gwen gave a light squeeze and continued to move her fingers as much as she could. Then she distributed her weight so her other hand could cup his balls.

August let out several words in another language before he sat up fast enough to dislodge her hands. He was faster than her and both his hands were around her wrists before Gwen could think of a new plan of attack. August was eyeing her warily as he scooted away, only staying close enough to hold her arms extended in front of her.

"Oh come on, August. Let me finish you." Gwen knew her voice was throaty.

He continued to watch her. "Why do you know to do that?"

The question caught Gwen completely off guard. "Are you kidding?"

"Viking should have kept you from men." August was actually growling.

Gwen's anger spiked and she twisted her wrists free then hopped off the bed. "Yeah, be a prick. There's a good plan."

When she faced him again, his face was angry but his eyes darted back and forth across the blanket in confusion, as he tried to figure out how he had angered her.

Gwen rolled her eyes and stormed over to him, leaning down in his face, which only seemed to confuse him more.

"I am a grown woman, your highness. I can see whom I want when I want. Viking does not control my life. He never did. A real gentleman lets a lady live her life the way she wishes.

"You are not the gentleman you claim to be. Life to you is about control and I get it as King it has to be, but if you want a mate, I mean a real mate not some plaything, you give me some respect and stop being an overpowering…prick!"

Gwen was too mad to stand still. She spun around and began pacing the end of the bed. "I can't believe this. What twisted universe promises me to a man that wants to keep me in a gilded cage. No booze, no sex, no thoughts of my own. Unbelievable!"

Chapter 24

Cesar had absolutely no idea what was going on. Not even five minutes ago he felt more at peace than any other time in his entire life. He wanted nothing more than to exist in that moment for the rest of eternity. Now his mate paced and ranted at him.

Currently she mumbled about being slapped for trying to help. Cesar didn't understand, no one would dare slap her. He had no idea what that gentleman comment was about. Cesar knew the right thing was to woo her first. A man didn't just screw the woman he cared for.

He demonstrated his prowess to her. She screamed for him after all. The look of bliss on her face was the most beautiful thing in the world. Then she touched him, expertly. That threw him. Cesar expected the hesitant touch of the inexperienced woman, not the sure grip he received. It felt amazing, but it meant she had knowledge of such things. No other man should be touching her. Gwen belonged to him.

His thoughts were interrupted by a magical tug. Someone was trying to wake him up. He struggled to stay with his mate.

"Gwen."

She ignored him.

"GWEN!"

This time she looked up, mid-step.

"Someone is waking me up."

Gwen didn't move. She looked worried. "Why would they do that? You need to sleep. That much magic will give you a killer headache."

Cesar relaxed when he heard the concern in her voice. She wasn't entirely mad at him anymore, which was more important to him than he realized.

"I'll ask. Thank you for the warning, my love."

He grinned as Gwen frowned at the endearment. As he let the spell pull him awake, Cesar knew that was his new name for his mate. She would hate it, and it was perfect.

"He's waking up."

"How can you tell?"

"His breathing changed."

Cesar couldn't make out who belonged to which voice but he wanted to kill them both for waking him.

"There better be a damn good reason for this or I am beheading you both and anyone else in the room who isn't my mate."

"Well, isn't that nice." Poet's voice came from some other part of the room.

Cesar inhaled Gwen's scent one more time before moving away from her and sitting up. Keeping his eyes closed, he rested his elbows on his bent knees and scrubbed at his scalp.

"How long did I sleep?"

"Five hours." Roman sounded close.

Cesar guessed the other man stood on the other side of the Gwen. Lifting his head, Cesar scanned the room. Barrett stood over him. Poet and Raider leaned against the far wall. Roman stood near Gwen's knees and Viking next to Gwen's head, running his fingers through her hair. It didn't bother Cesar nearly as much as it should have.

"Report! Someone before I become testy."

Poet opened his mouth, Raider elbowed him and he shut it.

"The two rogues are on their way here and they have backup. We don't know who the backup is yet. Skye called us fifteen minutes ago with the warning. Native called right before that to tell us to call off the hunt on those missing Tigers; four of them are holding the Hawks hostage. If I were to guess, the last three and the missing Canadian Wolves are who these guys have as backup."

Cesar nodded at his general. "Agreed. You're right, I want to be awake for this. Has anyone called Carter to send us backup? We have what, eight Warriors here?"

Barrett stepped aside as Cesar moved off the bed.

"Eight Warriors can take a legion," Raider stated blankly.

Cesar began rummaging through his duffel as he answered. "Very true, but not with civilians running around the store. We can't just close it, it would look suspicious. Plus we don't know who these rogues are bringing with them. They have who knows what on their side. The key to winning any battle in the Night World is to overwhelm your enemy and if you can't do that, then bluff."

There was silence a moment.

"I already have Conner and Hudson clearing non-Night Worlders from the store and keeping new ones out," Poet reported.

Cesar seemed to be the only one not surprised by Poet. Probably because he was the only one who knew anything about Poet.

"Good. Get hold of Carter and the cats see if anyone is itching for a fight. I want to fill the store with our people appearing like customers. I also want a ring of our people around the building. I want people on rooftops, posing as street people, anywhere we can put them and everyone communicates." Cesar stood up with clothing in hand, pointing at Viking, then at Poet and Raider. "We need to disappear. We are not supposed to be anywhere near here. So instead each of us will lead one of the outside teams." He turned to Roman. "You I'm leaving in charge of preparations inside."

Roman bowed; he knew what Cesar wasn't saying. Roman was in charge of his mate.

"I have called Lucia and Marco. They are on their way, free of charge."

Cesar inclined his head to Barrett. "My thanks to all of you. Ask them to park a street or two down if they can."

Barrett nodded.

Cesar turned to the rest of the room. "Then everybody out. I need a damn shower." Without waiting for a response Cesar strode into the bathroom.

The air was almost frigid on the rooftop east of the store, and Cesar was thankful for his trench coat. He and his team had been up here for over an hour now and there was no sign of an attack. Cesar wondered if they had been set up.

He sent Deuce and a handful of Weres to help Native free the Hawks down south. They waited for his go ahead to storm the place.

On the roof with him stood Craig and two wolves he hadn't met previously: Rain and Harley. Rain was third in Carter's Pack. Harley turned out to be mated to the pregnant Panther Sissy. None of them were talkers, which Cesar greatly appreciated because he didn't really have the brain power to hold a conversation.

The radio clicked to life and Carter's voice filled Cesar's ear.

Gretchen S. B.

"We have a visual on Floral Ave. They seem to be coming in force. I count twelve in all. There's only one Warrior in the group, keep your eyes peeled for others." The radio clicked off.

The other leaders checked in with no visual from their positions. Cesar turned to the other men. "We have a confirmed sighting of twelve heading in from the north. We will hold until they hit the building. Look out for others; we are missing a Warrior."

All three men braced themselves. They were on a three-story building; all of them could easily jump down without pause. It would take no time to reach the store.

The radio crackled and Viking's voice burst over the line. "Roman, someone needs to check on Gwen."

Cesar felt panic fill him. What did Viking know that he didn't?

"I just saw her myself fifteen minutes ago."

"Roman, just do it damn it. Something's wrong."

In the silence, Cesar held his breath. He stretched his senses, trying to feel what Viking felt. He knew it was useless, his general had a connection with Gwen that Cesar did not.

Blood ran cold as Roman's curses came over the line. "She's gone. How the hell can she be gone? She's under a sleep spell." More cursing. "We have a visual of the rogues."

Cesar saw red. His mate was gone. At the last sentence, he leapt off the roof, knowing the others would follow him as he sprinted toward the back of the building. Cesar arrived at the same moment as Viking. The two of them circled around and attacked from behind, their teams not far behind them. Four of their people burst from the back door seconds later.

Within minutes, the outnumbered rogues were all dead or unconscious. A small part of him knew they needed to question these beings but he couldn't bring himself to spare the two he fought.

Their only casualties were a Lion and a Panther, injured but still alive.

Cesar pointed to Craig. "You take care of our wounded." Then he turned to Viking. "You throw all their survivors together in with Jake. Make sure they are harmless and have someone dispose of the bodies."

Cesar didn't wait for a response from either man, he waded through the carnage, just about ripping the back door from its hinges. Before bolting up the stairs. "ROMAN!" he roared.

His friend wasn't in Gwen's apartment, but the front door was open. Cesar bee-lined for her bedroom. He didn't stop until he stood looking down at the empty bed. Grief and anger swirled through him. Cesar wanted to kill something; the two men he had killed were not enough. His breathing matched his racing heart. Cesar began turning the apartment upside down. As he slammed the balcony door behind him Cesar saw Roman standing at attention. Fury filled him as he faced his second in command. Cesar stood an inch from his general's face and growled.

"How dare you lose my mate!"

Roman didn't move, didn't even seem to breathe. His face was perfectly stoic.

Cesar railed. "You have no response for failing your king?"

Cesar shoved the other man hard enough for him to leave a dent in the wall. Roman simply got back up and stood stoically at attention. This only increased Cesar's rage.

"You don't even have the good sense to stay down." Then he lunged at Roman and began hitting the other man with everything he had.

Roman moved only to block Cesar's rage.

Cesar's mind was one large red cloud, he could see nothing but the violence he needed to cause. Every time a blow hit its intended target, satisfaction was quickly trailed by the need for more. Nothing in the world existed except the need for violence and pain. He didn't just want to kill, he wanted to cause as much pain as he could.

There was a loud blood curdling woman's scream. It cut through the fog like a knife and Cesar knelt perfectly still.

"August! What are you doing?" It was Gwen, she sounded muffled, far away.

Cesar shot up and searched the room frantically. She was standing in the hallway leading to her bedroom. She looked like a ghost. Gwen didn't appear more substantial than a thick fog.

Cesar didn't register moving, but suddenly he was right in front of his frightened mate. "Gwen, how? What has happened to you? Why can't I touch you?" He reached out to yank her to his chest, but his arms went through her.

Gwen wrapped her arms around herself and shook her head. "I don't know. One minute I was sleeping, the next Storebror was yelling at me that I had to get up if I wanted to save you. I ripped myself awake, followed him out here to see you beating Roman like a mad man."

She looked past Cesar. "Are you all right?"

Cesar turned to see blood flowing freely from one of Roman's eyes and an ear. His left arm hung awkwardly in two separate places. Remorse flooded Cesar. What had he done to his friend?

Roman nodded. "I will be. I've trained with him long enough to know his moves better than he does. All this will heal completely by tomorrow." Roman looked to Cesar and smiled through his cracked lip. "Do not worry about it, Augustus. I do not take it personally. I am just glad the young lady stopped me from having to kill you."

He knew Roman meant every word, but it still didn't sit well with Cesar. He did not like the fact that he so easily turned on his best friend. With Gwen safe, he felt the red fog thin and turned to find Viking.

The blond man was several feet from Roman, examining the damage to the wall.

"Viking, explain this." Cesar winced, it was harsher than he meant it to be.

Viking turned, unaffected by Cesar's tone. "I gave the body issue to Raider and followed you up. When I arrived you were beating the crap out of Roman, but he seemed to be holding his own for the moment so I went looking for Gwen. Imagine my surprise to see her sleeping in her bed, simply…non-corporeal"

Cesar's jaw tightened. "What do you mean non-corporeal. Why are we able to see her now and not earlier?"

Viking sighed. "When you assigned me to the Lady of the Dead, I read everything I could find on them through the centuries. One of the vast powers the stronger ones were rumored to exhibit was the ability to physically slip into the Spirit World to protect themselves from attack as they heal. I suspect Gwen's powers did this as a safeguard once she was left alone. She is healing faster while over there, I can feel it. As for seeing her, I put my pendant on you while you were preoccupied with Roman since you couldn't hear her otherwise."

Cesar looked down and sure enough, there was a Warrior pendant around his neck. Quickly he pulled out and activated his own. Once it was in place, he slid Viking's off and held it out for the other man.

Viking strode over and took it, slipping it into his pocket.

"How can you see her when we could not?" Roman asked. His own pendant hanging around his neck.

Viking shrugged. "Family trait." He shifted his attention to Cesar. "I bet she'll return once she finishes healing. She's actually using a good portion of her resources on you. I know you can't see it, but Gwen is practically throwing her calming influence at you."

Cesar turned so he could look down at Gwen. "We have a problem then. It seems I need you corporeal, but you'll heal faster if your not. You can affect me with your influence, but it drains your limited resources."

Gwen looked up at him with that beautiful, hazy face and Cesar felt a punch in his gut.

"I'll try to stay around you as much as I can. Not that I can guarantee that. I didn't even know I was doing this in the first place. I could probably shoot off somewhere without a moment's notice."

The gentleman in Cesar balked at the idea. Half his Warrior nature wanted her to heal the best way she could. But with Roman as proof, he knew that couldn't happen. He was in that last stage of the Maddening and there wasn't anything else they could do about it. He needed her around, corporeal or not.

Cesar turned to Viking and Roman. "We need to keep the pendants on at all times. I would feel better if Raider and Poet did as well. Viking, are you sure you don't need yours?"

Viking shook his head. "No, not for her. I am too familiar with her magic and too close for me to miss her."

Cesar wasn't completely comfortable with that but set it aside for later.

Taking a deep breath, he cracked his neck. "Let's head back downstairs and get updated." With no objections Cesar led the way downstairs.

Gretchen S. B.

Chapter 25

Gwen tried to find humor in the nervousness that filled the room as August explained to everyone where she had gone. It was a little unnerving when Poet smiled right at her in relief as she walked into the store. No one else seemed to catch it.

"Poet, why aren't you and Raider on the rooftops?" August snarled as he finished his story.

Gwen pushed a little harder to wrap her energy around August.

Poet didn't look at all fazed. "The Lady of the Dead was missing. We have made her our lives. You cannot expect us not to come running. It is ingrained in our nature. Our teams are still out there. We sent yours and Viking's teams back out. Carter came in as well, but that is because without Deuce he is the best interrogator we have. He and Barrett are interrogating the rogue Warrior as we speak."

Poet flipped his pendant over his head and waved at Gwen. She noted he didn't even move his mouth for the activating words. Gwen was willing to bet he only put it on for show.

"Fine, we will see what the rogue has to say then regroup, I want everyone on the lookout in the meantime." August's voice was gruff and full of authority. He left no room for questioning.

After some debating, August, Viking, Roman, Poet, and Lucia filed into the tiny room on the backside of the two-way mirror. Lucia argued that a non-Warrior needed to be involved for the good of everyone else. August argued against it, but finally gave in. Consequently, everyone in the tiny room could see her. Gwen found that disconcerting. The five of them made room for her near August when there was no need. Gwen could occupy the same space as them easily, but no one seemed comfortable with that.

Gwen could see things she wouldn't normally when outside the Spirit World, and some of those were creepy. Carter and Barrett stared at the rogue Warrior in silence. Gwen took the opportunity to raise her question. Lucia was standing to her right, so Gwen leaned over slightly.

"Lucia?"

Her tone drew the entire room's attention. Not her intent, but she wasn't surprised.

"Yeah?" Lucia questioned.

"I am seeing new…things…" Gwen didn't want the whole room to know what she was talking about. She had to keep it vague.

The men all stiffened. Gwen and Lucia both stared straight ahead into the interrogation room.

"What sort of things?"

Lucia's cautious tone made Gwen curious, but she knew to be careful with her answers. Some might not be things Lucia could see. A gray mist surrounded Lucia, and the way it swirled made Gwen think it might be other woman's power. A red, slightly less dense fog surrounded Barrett. Both were what she would have expected, but what was around the men unnerved her. An imprint of Carter's Wolf hovered around him, not quite an image, but a clear impression of a Wolf. Roman seemed to glow, simply appearing brighter than the others. Viking possessed the same mist as the MPs, but it was a pale blue, the exact shade of his eyes. Poet scared her. There was a large transparent snake wrapped around his torso, its giant head resting on Poet's right shoulder. Glowing green eyes had been watching her, but shut seconds before. Gwen had not seen it until she was this close.

"I see gray, red, blue, and a golden glow. A Wolf and something that slithers."

The men were silent, trying to decipher what she said. Poet's snake opened its eyes to look at her again and its tongue flicked out. Lucia nodded. She understood perfectly.

"Yes, I know, and before you ask, I could only explain the first two to you, the Wolf is self-explanatory. The other three I don't understand myself. Especially the last one, it comes and goes."

Gwen shivered, she did not like that thing around Poet, or that Lucia saw it regularly.

"Are you two speaking in code?" Roman asked on behalf of the men.

Lucia nodded again. "Yes, be thankful."

Then she touched the glass. Gwen watched some of the gray move out of Lucia's hand and the glass glowed momentarily. Gwen saw gray shoot through the glass and fly straight for Barrett's head. It hovered outside of the red mist before the red seemed to reach out and absorb it. Lucia seemed to understand Gwen's curiosity because she turned her head toward Gwen without moving her eyes.

"It is a request for communication. MPs within a strongly connected Strata can mentally communicate freely. This glass has spells in it. I must put in a request first so the glass will not take our exchange as a threat."

Gwen had not known any of that, except for the glass containing spells. They had hired Lucia to do that years ago.

"I asked Barrett what they have thus far. He tells me the rogue is not giving them anything, but one of the four Tigers called him Stanger. The rogue has not said a word."

Lucia leaned forward to look at August. "He is asking if you would like a coercion spell."

August frowned and his eyebrows slid together. "What will it cost me?"

Lucia didn't hesitate. "Magic done for this cause is gratis, within reason of course."

"Fine."

"You will want Carter out of the room."

August tapped his radio. "Carter, leave the room."

Carter gave the window a curious look before walking out of the room. Within seconds, the door to the tiny room opened and Gwen heard Carter swear.

"Am I going to fit in here?"

After some shuffling they fit him in. Everyone was shoulder to shoulder, except Gwen, who could not touch anyone.

"I'm guessing that empty space is Gwen?" Carter's voice held mild amusement.

"Yup, no one wants to smush her," Poet answered.

"I'm the only one in the room that can't see her, aren't I?" Carter didn't pause long enough to get an answer. "Scratch that, I don't really want to know. So why did I move?"

August made a gesture at the glass Carter probably couldn't see. "Barrett's using a spell on Stanger and we don't want you getting a backlash."

Carter snorted. "Appreciate it."

Everyone's attention went to Barrett, who stood behind the now nervous Stanger, moving his hands above the Rogue's head. Gwen could see red mist pooling in Barrett's hands. It wasn't going anywhere, just growing denser. Then Barrett splayed his fingers and the red mist shot through the room. Gwen jumped as it bounced off the glass.

August stiffened beside her. "Gwen, is everything all right?"

"Even I saw that one." Viking sounded astonished.

Lucia gave a chuckle. "You see why Carter shouldn't be in the room. Barrett's very powerful, but his targeting is crap."

Barrett came around the metal table and sat in the chair across from Stanger. "What is your name?"

Stanger's mouth opened and his eyes widened as he realized he couldn't stop himself from answering. "Stanger."

"Is that your birth name?"

"No." The rogue's eyes held a hint of fear.

"What is your birth name, place, and year?"

Gwen liked Barrett's approach, get information they could verify first.

"Thaddeus Brooke, upstate New York, eighteen-eighty-five."

Roman jumped in. "Have Barrett ask if he is related to Cecil Brooke."

A few seconds later Barrett repeated the question and Stanger flinched.

"He's my grandfather."

Roman swore. "He's Dubliner's grandson."

The other Warriors cursed.

August turned to Roman. "When we are finished here, make the call to Apollo. Dubliner should know what his kin has been up to."

Roman made a noise in the back of his throat. "That kid's in for a beating."

"Tell Barrett we need whatever we can get on the location of the other Warriors, the Hawks. As well as how he became involved and who else he knows," August said.

"See, aren't you glad I'm here?" Lucia answered smugly.

August's jaw twitched but he didn't respond.

After a few more seconds, Barrett nodded and spoke to Stanger.

"Three of you crossed into the US. Where is the blond one?"

There was a struggle on the rogue's face as he fought answering. "I don't know. He disappeared yesterday."

His face held so much anger and hatred that Gwen was sure Stanger was memorizing Barrett in the hope of killing him later.

"When exactly did he disappear and what is his name?"

"We secured the Hawks. Jake was going over there to rein in the rowdy Tigers. They were bickering with the Canadian Wolves. Jake didn't check in again but I received a call telling me he been picked up by you people. Ellis went to rendezvous with our contact while I get the kid and round up some MPs before getting out of Dodge."

"Who is your contact?"

Gwen could hear worry in Barrett's voice. He was hoping it wasn't an MP.

"A Warrior, goes by Stetson."

"WHAT?!" August growled so loud it hurt Gwen's ears.

Lucia must have conveyed the reaction to Barrett because the other man held his hand up toward the glass.

"What do you mean 'goes by'? Is his name not Stetson?"

The rogue snorted. "No, not with that accent he's not. He's French. Grandpa told me Stetson was born in Texas. This guy is using the name to give himself more authority in the North American Kingdom."

"Looks like Apollo will be calling Stetson as well." Roman sighed from where he stood on August's left.

Barrett lowered his hand before leaning in over the table. "Are you telling me rogues from other countries are involved in this little war of yours?"

Stanger gave a poisonous smile. "It's a new world order, MP. This kingdom is just the first."

The far corner of the interrogation room caught Gwen's eye. When she focused, panic flooded through her. A black figure similar to the one Gwen had seen in that playground was somehow seeping through the wall.

Without thinking Gwen appeared in the interrogation room. She was as startled as Barrett when she popped in on his right shoulder. She recovered fast and began shoving her hands through him as if she could push him out the door.

Her voice came out a scream. "BARRETT, GET THE HELL OUT OF HERE NOW! IT'S GOING TO KILL YOU!"

Barrett didn't second guess her. He shot up from his chair and bolted out the door. Gwen was on his heels. Once they both cleared the door, he slammed it shut and began chanting at it.

Lucia must have pushed through the men because when the other door burst open, she was the first to clear it. She bumped Barrett's shoulder as she skidded to a halt next to him, starting the same chant.

She paused long enough to get in some English. "Go see who in the other room called it and knock them out."

Barrett took off down the hall and ripped open the door where the rogues were being held. He ran in, arms moving.

Marco came running down the hall and didn't slow as he passed Lucia. He practically dove through the open door after Barrett.

Gwen was in the holding room before another thought crossed her mind. Shaking her head, Gwen focused on what was happening. She needed to get control of this flashing from place to place thing.

Barrett was battling to sever the connection between the rogue MP and the being on the other side of the wall. The mist surrounding this MP were black. Not as dense as Marco's or Barrett's, but they couldn't do his range of magic. Marco raised a sword Gwen hadn't seen before and brought the butt of it down on the Black MP's head with brutal force. Gwen watched as the MP crumpled and the connection snapped off. Both Barrett and Marco slumped their shoulders.

Gwen knew better. Even though the MP was unconscious, she knew the danger had not past. Her gaze slid to the wall behind Barrett's back. As if from some horror movie, the black began seeping back through the wall, this time faster because it was not tied to the MP.

Pure instinct drove her. She could not let this creature hurt her friends. She deliberately flashed herself to Barrett's back. Gwen felt more than saw him jump and stumble farther from the wall.

"Ouch, Gwen! You shocked me." Barrett exclaimed.

His words barely registered in Gwen's mind. All of her focus was on the three-fourths of the being on this side of the wall.

It looked down at her and gave the same bone-chilling chuckle as the being in the playground. "Step aside so that I can kill the MP, and I won't hurt you."

It was smiling at her, its gigantic fangs dripping, though the drips didn't land anywhere. She felt no fear as she looked up into the creature's glowing red eyes. Gwen felt her power pulsing stronger and stronger around her, adrenaline shooting through her veins. When she spoke, her voice was not quite her own. It was more.

"You will do no such thing."

The being's smile disappeared and it glared down at Gwen.

"You dare command me. You little wretch, you don't know who you're screwing with." Then it popped the rest of the way into the room.

Gwen's hands flew up in the air of their own accord and the being froze in mid-lunge. Its eyes widened with surprise.

Her own power whirled around her like a strong wind. That powerful voice flowed up from her throat again. "I know you, Insidious. I command you to stand down. You will not kill this MP. You will not help these beings in their war. You will return to where they recruited you and you will not become involved unless I command you to. You will warn the Spirit World that the Lady of the Dead is watching them, and if anyone makes a deal with these fools again, I will hunt them down and destroy them. Do you understand me?"

The name of the being popped into her head without thought. Somehow she knew having his name gave her power over him. Gwen did not know how she could follow through on the threat she had just made, but in that moment she knew she would. A door in her head had ripped open. Should she need the power it would be there for her.

Insidious straightened out of his lunge and lowered to the floor. He was still a good ten feet tall. He bowed deeply to Gwen. The threat was no longer in his eyes. Insidious knew a bigger fish when he saw it. In the Spirit World there were no fish bigger than a functional Lady of the Dead.

"Yes, my Lady. I understand and will abide by your command." Then he was gone.

When she heard several curses, Gwen's tunnel vision broke. Both Marco and Barrett stared at her, slack-jawed. It seemed like half the building had jammed itself in the doorway and out into the hall.

When Gwen looked at Viking, he bowed to her. Poet bowed deeper and from his waist. The snake watched her with respectful interest before it flickered out of sight.

"Okay, I have no idea what the hell just happened. Yet the shock is so thick I couldn't cut it with a chainsaw."

Gwen heard Vincent, but couldn't see him from where he must have been out in the hall.

Poet smiled as he spoke. "The Lady of the Dead just commanded a very powerful being not to kill Barrett. Then told him to go home and not help the rogues again. She called him by name. He bowed to her and without any anger or resentment did exactly what she commanded."

There were curses from out in the hall, then silence again.

August continued to watch her, blank-faced as he turned to Viking. "Now is as good a time as any for Native and Deuce to storm the castle. Let them know we want at least one rogue Were alive and we need to speak to the Hawks they took."

Viking pulled out his phone and pushed through the mass of people. Roman quickly followed suit. Gwen guessed he had left to update Apollo. The group at large began to disperse, giving one reason or another.

August never took his eyes off Gwen. "I would like to speak with you upstairs, please."

Gwen could tell he was making an effort to keep the commanding authority from his voice, and failing. She appreciated the effort though, so she nodded and flashed herself up to her apartment.

It was disorientating. She just thought 'my apartment' and suddenly she was there. It made her a little dizzy but she was sure that would go away with practice.

Gwen was not there long before male arguing voices entered the hallway. One of them had a key, she heard it in the lock, but had no idea who August would let follow him. When the door opened, more people than she expected filed into her living room.

August strode in like he lived there and came to stand next to her. He did not appear happy to have this many people with him.

Poet dropped his keys into a front pocket of his jeans, but stayed near the door. His eyes gave Gwen the distinct impression he knew he now made her uncomfortable and was being courteous enough to give her space. Gwen felt really bad about that. Poet was a good friend and despite the blasé front he put up, she knew he cherished having a place to belong. She needed to talk to him alone, soon.

Rounding out the group were Lucia and her boys. She entered first, followed by Barrett. Marco brought up the rear, shutting the door behind him. Lucia's gaze continually shifted from Gwen to Barrett.

Lucia was never one to endure silence. "How did you know that thing was after Barrett? It killed Stanger. Strangled him to death, but you only warned Barrett. Why?"

Gwen wasn't sure how to answer. She could see why the thing would kill Stanger. The MP wanted him silenced. Stanger had been spilling information. At the time, all she knew was whatever came through that wall wanted to kill Barrett. Gwen focused on Barrett instead of Lucia when she answered. His eyes flashed surprise.

"I was raised mostly by a man who protects what is his with a ruthless passion. That thing wanted to kill my friend and it was in my power to stop it."

It was all the answer she had. Gwen didn't know how she had forced Insidious to stand down, she just knew he had to be stopped. There wasn't anything else to it.

Barrett and Marco exchanged looks Gwen couldn't understand. Then they turned to her, and in unison, bowed from the waist. Lucia looked just as surprised as Gwen felt.

When Barrett straightened, he looked Gwen in the eyes. "I owe you my life, Lady of the Dead. From here on in, should you need my services, you alone shall have them free of charge."

Everyone else in the room was stunned. That offer was unheard of in the Night World. Only MPs within their own Strata performed free of charge. Yet neither Marco nor Lucia argued with him.

The situation made Gwen uncomfortable. "Don't say that, Barrett. I know for a fact you would have done the same thing for me and probably have. I think we are pretty even."

Barrett gave her an indulgent smile that told Gwen he wasn't about to rescind his statement.

"As much as I want to know what exactly I missed, I get the feeling that I will not like the answer. So instead I am going to go see if I can track how the rogues caught a being this strong." Lucia shook her head. "Insidious is such a stupid name. Where do they get these names from?"

Since that last part had not been to anyone in particular, no one answered her. When Lucia walked out of the apartment, Marco followed her. Barrett on the other hand, gave Gwen a glance before leaving.

August gave a heavy sigh. "I am not sure how I feel about an MP pledging his services to my mate." He turned to Poet. "Leave us, I need to speak with her alone. Please tell the leaders they can send their people home. The Warriors can keep the lookout for now. I will want to meet with the leaders before they leave."

Poet inclined his head before grabbing the door. Panic shot through Gwen. She needed to talk to Poet now, and she wouldn't get another chance for a while.

"NO!" It came out louder and more panicked than Gwen intended.

Both Warriors looked at her in surprise.

Before August could get upset, Gwen pushed on. "You can tell them all that yourself. I need a few words with Poet alone."

An angry possessiveness filled August's face. Gwen held up her hand.

"I promise to explain all of it to you when this blows over and if we get you through this Maddening thing."

The anger stayed in his eyes, but she saw curiosity as well.

"I cannot stay away from you long," August growled through clenched teeth.

Though her power was severely drained, she pumped more calm energy around August. "I know. Can I have five minutes, please?"

She could see August was warring with himself.

"Fine," he growled angrily and stormed out of the apartment.

Poet cautiously watched her and didn't move from the door. "That wasn't a good move, Gwen."

Gretchen S. B.

She sighed and flashed herself down onto the couch, and somehow she wasn't falling through to the floor. "I know, but it's a necessary evil. He needs to understand his rules do not apply to me."

She heard Poet snort before he came into her line of sight and sat in the chair across from her. "You mean you won't let his rules apply to you."

Gwen shrugged. "Same thing."

Poet watched her with curiosity and amusement but there was also a guardedness to his eyes she was not used to seeing. He knew what she wanted to talk about.

Gwen wanted to say the right thing, but she knew she would probably mess it up anyway, so she took a deep breath and looked her friend in the eye.

"Tell me about the snake."

He looked amused by her bluntness. "That would take longer than five minutes. Think of it like Jacob Marley's chains. It is a reminder to me of deals I've made and some things I've done."

Poet spoke with a seriousness Gwen rarely heard. He wasn't joking with her. She put that information away for later.

"Will it hurt me or anyone else?"

Poet gave her a mocking smile. "You mean other than me?"

When she didn't laugh, he sighed. "No, it will not hurt you because it knows the power you have. As for hurting others…I can't guarantee that one way or another. If it is not provoked it does not seem to bother itself with others."

"Could we rid you of it?"

Poet gave her a bitter laugh. "No, and I don't suggest you try. It is a punishment I deserve."

She could live with that, but she didn't like it.

"You're not allowed to leave me, then."

Poet blinked at her in complete surprise. "Excuse me?"

Gwen smiled. "When this ends, if I can still mate August, I will. You and I both know he is going to try to relocate me, and change my detail to Warriors he finds more suitable. Storebror won't leave me and as long as he is there, Raider will always be his second in command. I'm picking you, no matter what August says. I demand you stay with me."

The look Poet gave her was of mixed amusement and a small flicker of hope. That hope made Gwen's chest hurt.

Most of the older Warriors had been so long without family and something to belong to, something not out of Warrior obligation, that she could usually see the need for it in their eyes when they thought no one was looking. Gwen wanted so badly to give that to the Warriors around her. That was why she kept in touch with most of the Warriors sent to her detail over the years.

Poet was her good friend and that made her want to keep him all the more. It wasn't just the Warriors that wanted stability.

"You're family, Poet. You're the trouble-making cousin and if I'm going to be mated to the king of anti-modernization, I need you with me to raise hell and break out of that ridiculous compound of his."

He grinned and it was the grin Gwen was used to seeing. "Rebel against the king and not have to deal with the consequences because I am the Queen's pet. How could I say no to that?"

Gwen grinned back before shaking her head. "Good. With that settled, I need your help."

Poet raised an eyebrow at her.

"Don't think I didn't notice you didn't need to activate your pendant to see me."

His face grew serious again and Gwen raised her hands.

"I'm actually not going to ask about that. I'm just assuming it means you might know more on such subjects than I do."

Poet relaxed, leaning back in the chair. "Without a doubt."

Gwen rolled her eyes. "I need to find a way to help August with the Maddening. He cannot be away from me long and despite appearances, I won't be able to throw energy at him much longer. I need a way to mate with him soon. He is just about out of time. From my understanding, he is fighting it off better than expected."

Poet watched her thoughtfully. "I noticed you pooling energy around him. What have you tried thus far?"

A heavy blush rose in her face, but Poet just raised his eyebrows at her.

"I had Barrett put a sleep spell on the bed. I jumped into his dream and tried to seduce him."

Poet's lips twitched. "I take it that didn't go as planned."

"No, he is hell-bent on being a gentleman about the whole thing. He wants to court me."

Gretchen S. B.

Poet burst out laughing. "I'm sorry. It's just you said that with such disgust. Oh Gwen, this is why I find your company so enjoyable."

She wasn't sure how to take that so she didn't say anything.

Shaking his head, Poet narrowed his eyes in concentration. After several beats he seemed to come to a thought he did not particularly like. "I have an idea, but I do not like it…I would not wish it on you. The king, I couldn't care much less about, but you I don't…" Poet ran his tongue over his canines.

That concerned Gwen.

"I would need to consult Sivia and maybe Barrett to see if either of them could and would do it. We would need to poison the king."

Gwen stiffened.

"Not in the traditional sense. We would slip a poison into his food that would heighten his lust. There would need to be a sleeping potion in there because obviously he cannot take you bodily. If you could get into his dreams again, you would not have to persuade him take you, but he would be half-mad so I cannot promise he would be gentle. Once he sates his lust, because of what you are, I do believe that would satisfy the Maddening."

She knew what Poet was telling her. Sex would hurt. They had waited too long and now things wouldn't be pleasant. She couldn't see a choice. If the Night World went to war it would need its king, even if that king was hell-bent on making things difficult. Gwen knew August would be furious with her. Doing this would, in his mind, be a disastrous start to their life together. They were out of options. She took a deep, shaky breath to solidify her resolve.

"Would you do it if I asked?" Her voice sounded small.

Poet was silent before nodding. "Yes, for you I would. As long as you understand what you are asking."

Gwen sighed. "I do. This is me asking. Find out if anyone can do it and keep it as quiet as possible. Tell Roman, though, as he should know what we are doing. If he sees another way around it or thinks August will last long enough on his own, then we can postpone it."

Poet stood. "You're much stronger than Viking gives you credit for." Then he left to go about the business of poisoning the king.

Chapter 26

His mate was sad. Cesar could practically feel it coming off of her. He saw it in her face when he entered the apartment. Since he could not touch her, Cesar tried to pacify himself by pacing the floor in front of the couch. She sat there watching him as she had been for the last ten minutes. Cesar wanted to know what she had needed to discuss with Poet that would upset her so. Cesar knew instinctively she would not tell him, and he wasn't sure he could coax it out of her.

It did not help matters that since seeing her endanger herself for the MP, the Maddening had filled his brain with lustful rage. He was barely in control of himself. He practically yelled orders at everyone downstairs and thankfully no one yelled back. He couldn't hold Gwen and that made things worse. She was there and that soothed him marginally, kept him from losing his unraveling control, but it was not going to last much longer.

Before running upstairs, Cesar had pulled Roman aside while the other man was still on the phone with Apollo. Cesar informed his two generals it had been an honor to fight alongside them, and that he had another six hours at best. He promised them he would spend that time planning ways to save the kingdom from attack before letting the other kings and queens know about the change in leadership. He told Roman he expected his friend to kill him at four a.m. Neither man said a word.

Cesar knew it would be a difficult time for his generals. The other rulers had been hesitant to accept Cesar's leadership. Roman would have a much harder time. The two of them had been fighting alongside each other since before puberty. Every step of the way, Roman was there to argue with and bounce ideas off of. Roman would have no such council.

He knew he was leaving his people at the worst time, but there was nothing Cesar could do about it. It was best for all that he be taken out now before he could do any damage. But now that it came time to tell Gwen of his plans, Cesar couldn't bring himself to do it. As much as he did not want to leave his kingdom, he didn't want to leave her more. His Warrior instincts screamed for her at a deafening volume.

Gretchen S. B.

"You wanted to talk, August. So talk. We need to get back downstairs and meet with the leaders. Once they clear out maybe you could coordinate everything from up here. I need to sleep badly and I'm worried about popping out on you when my batteries empty."

Cesar stopped pacing long enough to take a good look at his mate. He looked past the sadness and cursed himself. Gwen was exhausted. Fighting off that creature must have taken all her reserves because she looked as if she hadn't slept in days. His Warrior instincts roared at how he abused his mate. Cesar knew for the next several hours he would work from her bedroom. He owed her those hours of sleep.

"Of course, my love, whatever you need."

She gave him a face that told him how much she did not like that nickname. It made him smile.

"What did you need to talk to me about?"

Cesar shook his head. He wouldn't tell her. Gwen didn't need to know. He now knew her well enough to know she would fight him about the deadline he could feel approaching. Then she would not get the sleep she so desperately needed. Without him there to protect her she would need all the strength she could get.

"I just needed some uninterrupted time with you, but I find my mind won't let that happen."

Gwen gave him a concerned look. "Then let's go downstairs and get this meeting over with."

———————————

The so-called meeting had been almost counter-productive. By the end, Cesar yelled at everyone to get out. He couldn't handle this crazy democratic way of doing things. After an hour, all they had accomplished was sending two of Carter's best noses to track the elusive third rogue Warrior and everyone was to yank some strings to see just how many Night Worlders were in on this plot. They were to report to Viking or Roman with every scrap of information they received. Cesar would also be contacting the kings and queens, informing them of what might turn out to be an international war.

Viking received a call from Native informing them that four of the Tigers were in custody but the Hawks were too heavily drugged to be of any help until morning.

That had not helped Cesar's mood. Gwen progressively looked worse. There was no doubt in Cesar's mind that she was at the end of her rope. Once he had commanded every non-Warrior from the premises, he turned to Gwen and growled at her to go to bed. She did not even argue with him. That scared him. She flickered a little, but disappeared and Cesar growled at every being that tried to speak to him as he made his way upstairs.

When he entered the living room he growled to see Gwen standing near the couch. "I told you to go to bed."

She didn't even bother to make a face. "Don't be a jerk, August. I just wanted to ask if you would lie with me a while, just until I fall asleep. It shouldn't be more than ten minutes."

Cesar felt his chest ache and his voice softened. "Yes, of course."

He knew he did not have a lot of time but at the moment there was nothing more important to him in the world. As Cesar went toward the bedroom, there was a knock at the front door. Cesar growled and ripped the door open.

Poet and Roman pushed past him and strode into the living room. Cesar slammed the door behind them and glowered.

"What do you two want?"

Neither man seemed affected by his furious tone.

Roman walked toward him, holding out a glass of some foamy orange liquid. "Poet remembered something he saw once centuries ago. We talked it over with Sivia and we think it might help relieve the symptoms of the Maddening. It isn't the safest thing in the world, but at this point what is?"

Cesar snarled at his friend. "You just don't want to kill me."

Roman shrugged. "That too."

Out of the corner of his eye, Cesar saw Gwen's shoulders slump in relief, but there was also apprehension. The fact that she seemed worried about him touched Cesar on a level he had not realized existed.

"Drink, August. If it gives us more time with a functional king, it's worth a shot. We need you clearheaded on this," she pleaded.

If only she had said she needed him. Cesar mentally shook himself. Gwen barely knew him, and thoughts like that were useless. His kingdom needed him. If Poet ran the idea by both Roman and Sivia, it must be sound if they were willing to chance it.

Cesar snatched the glass from Roman. "How long until it takes effect?"

Poet shrugged. "That I don't remember."

Cesar grunted and tried not to think about all the things that could go wrong. Then he downed the contents of the glass and shoved it back at Roman. "I want to be alone with Gwen for the next fifteen minutes. You and Viking come up here so we can come up with a plan. Bring Native too, I want a report."

Roman just nodded before he and Poet left.

When Cesar turned back to Gwen, she looked ever sadder than before. It hurt him like a physical wound to see. He was directly in front of her in a second.

"What is wrong, my love?"

Gwen sighed and turned toward the bedroom. She mumbled something under her breath about forgiveness. She didn't say another word as they climbed into bed.

Chapter 27

August dreamed of her bedroom again. Gwen couldn't help but feel flattered. Thessa hadn't even asked why Gwen had called her, just sent Gwen to August's dream. Gwen had not fully believed Poet until she dropped into August's dream to see him growling and ripping apart the furniture.

When she hit the bed, he turned to her and stilled. His expression was on the verge of insanity as he stood at the foot of the bed.

"What have you done?" The question was so guttural Gwen barely understood it.

"You need to have sex with me, August."

She tried to put authority in her voice. Which was hard, as he was downright scary.

August roared and leapt onto bed. His face was two inches away as he loomed over her.

"You think to drug me into taking you? You think I can't smell your fear?"

She couldn't deny it. He scared her, but some part of her was also turned on. All that male power was inches from her. Gwen wanted to take. To take him. She focused on that. If she focused on the attention and affection August put into their first dream, then she could handle him this out of control.

"Then maybe you should sniff again."

Before he could answer Gwen dug her right hand into his hair and pulled. It caught him off guard enough that by the time he reacted, they were already kissing. August growled into her mouth and the vibrations from his chest tightened her nipples.

When Gwen felt his hand tugging at her pants, she knew she had him. Only this time she needed to maintain control. Neither of them could afford August getting the upper hand again. August ripped her clothes off with enough force her hips jerked, making her gasp.

August growled into her mouth again as his hand dipped between her legs and began rubbing. Gwen put all her concentration into ignoring how good his thumb felt against her clit and moved her hands to his pants.

Gretchen S. B.

He was wearing jeans, which were harder to get off than the sweatpants would have been, especially with him plastered to her body. Gwen gasped as a finger slid inside her. All she could think was how good it felt.

She ripped her mouth from his. August growled angrily and fought to get her lips back. Gwen turned her head away. He began nipping at her neck. Gwen found herself momentarily distracted by the spikes of lusty pleasure shooting through her system. She fought to clear her head again.

"PANTS! OFF!" was all she managed between breaths.

August growled again before his hand moved.

Gwen whimpered with the loss of contact but a second later he was back, screwing her with two thick fingers. Little sounds escaped her throat as she climbed toward orgasm. Her body heated. Gwen came so quickly she felt as if the orgasm had been ripped from her body. The sensation was dizzying.

Just as she began to come back down, August shoved his thick, rock hard cock inside her. The pleasure and pain of the act overloaded her body. He was too big to have thrust in that quickly, but at the same time, it felt good. August moved fast, yet managed to hit her g-spot with every stroke. Her body was heating up again, getting hotter with each thrust. August moved fast and fluid inside her. Gwen dug her nails into his lower back in an effort to keep up with him. She was panting heavily and could feel the sweat starting to slick her skin.

This time when she came it was like bursting a balloon. She felt her body becoming too full, felt too much sensation. She was screaming and thrashing. Her inner muscles squeezed August, milking him in an already tight grip.

Even with her fuzzy hearing and the pleasure coursing through her, Gwen heard August bellow in triumph as he came. The Warrior claimed his mate and wanted the world to know. August's body collapsed to the right of Gwen's shoulder. Though he was still inside her, August was making an effort to keep his weight off her. Gwen found that sweet.

They lay like that for several minutes, not speaking or even looking at each other. The sex had been fast, hard, and fantastically mind-blowing. But Gwen wasn't sure she could do it again anytime soon. Her inner muscles were starting to ache a little and she knew she would hurt in a few hours. There had not been enough prep work for a man of August's size. Not that Gwen would change anything, but next time she would know better.

"I am furious with you."

He was pissed, but at least his voice was back to normal. August propped himself up on one shoulder, dislodging himself and rolling the rest of the way off her. He lay on his side facing her.

Turning her head, she looked up into his now sane face. His eyes convinced her, despite the bruised feelings, that she had done the right thing. They were clear of any sign of the Maddening. They were, however, not in the least bit pleased with her.

"I know you are."

Her answer only seemed to make him angrier.

"Can you not understand why I would not want to take you to bed so quickly?"

Gwen felt her own temper flare. "Can you not understand people need their king? You were being selfish…"

August let out an angry yell and leapt off the bed. His pants, it turned out, were around his knees and he fumbled for a moment before kicking them across the room. "Selfish? I wish to treat the woman I am destined to take care of with the respect she deserves and that makes me selfish? So to solve the problem you drug me to make the Maddening unbearable. What world do you live in? That logic makes no sense woman!"

He had been pacing but stopped to glare down at her. "Gwen, I didn't even remove my clothing for you. Even you are still half-dressed." He began pacing again.

Gwen stared at August, slack-jawed at the frustration in his tone. She couldn't believe it. He was blaming himself. He might be yelling at her, but she could hear the lack of conviction in his voice.

"You can't actually be angry with yourself about this?" Her voice held all her disbelief.

August turned to glare at her again. "I am a gentleman, damn it, and the king. I should be able to control myself. I should know better than to drink unknown substances…even if they are given to me by friends. I should have been able to fight the drugs, and barring that, I should have at least had the decency to remove all our clothing."

Gwen couldn't believe it. Without thinking, she rolled off the bed and walked up to him. August eyed her warily. When Gwen was about an inch away, she reached up, wrapped her arms around his neck, and laid her head on his chest. She felt August stiffen and stay perfectly still, but Gwen held on. After several beats, his large masculine arms wrapped around her waist and he relaxed.

Gwen decided to hold the rest of the conversation pressed against his gorgeous chest. "We tricked you. You are not to blame at all and if I catch you blaming yourself again, I'll start rebelling in nasty and wholly unnecessary ways just to drive you nuts."

She felt him sigh. "Why do I believe that?"

Gwen ignored his put-out tone and continued. "And if it's all the same to you, I'm going to take your ripping my clothes and keeping your own on as a compliment."

"How in the world do you see that?" August's voice was full of disbelief.

"I'm thinking of it more along the lines of you wanted me bad enough that speed was the determining factor."

He snorted, but she could almost hear a smile.

"Though I am going to have to talk to the people who put the drug together. I was under the impression you would jump me on sight and would be rough with me. Yet, you got me off first. Clearly not what was advertised."

August grunted. "Ignoring your…colorful language, I know I hurt you. I could tell by the noises you made, so I'd say that is about right."

Shifting her head so she could look up at him, Gwen snorted. "There are so many things wrong with that statement, I don't know where to start. Basically it comes down to more foreplay when we play that hard again."

"Have I mentioned how much it bothers me that you talk like that?" His eyebrows pushed together as he looked down at her.

Gwen snorted. "Deal with it. Pick your battles, August, because you aren't going to win that one."

"How about the alcohol?"

"Try again."

"How about having more conservative sleepwear for when we have company?"

Gwen grinned. "That I will give you, but you'll have to come with me to pick it out, to make sure it meets your standards."

She felt his deep chuckle. "I think I would actually enjoy that."

Gwen snuggled in closer. She couldn't smell him like she would have in the real world, and that bugged her. That and there was no body heat.

"I don't know how much longer we have until the drugs wear off."

There was a thoughtful pause. "I would assume not too long. There are far too many things to do. Until then we are laying down to rest. We will table the rest of our conversation for later."

"What?"

August turned her and began moving them toward the bed, stopping at the edge long enough to remove both their shirts. His eyes heated at the sight of her breasts. He appeared to force his eyes up to meet her gaze.

"You heard me. You need rest. Yes, I know we are in a dream, but I'm pretty sure you are not getting the rest you need so we are remedying that now. We will lie together until the drugs wear off."

He sounded so sure of himself that Gwen itched to argue, but she didn't. Instead she crawled into bed, with August right behind her. Gwen sighed. It felt good, but not as good as her actual bed. Would sex would be better in the real world too? Gwen dismissed that thought and concentrated on the moment, this calm and peaceful period she and August were sure not to see again for a while.

Chapter 28

Cesar's eyes opened and for a split second, he panicked, but then he saw her non-corporal form and he relaxed, marginally. She still wasn't strong enough to be there physically. On the plus side, the crafty woman had come up with a plan to get around the Maddening.

It had worked. The barely controllable anger and red fog were gone. He could, however, feel what he assumed was the first stage of mating.

He craved Gwen's touch and needed to touch her. His lust rested at a low boil that Apollo had once told him never fully went away. His general had informed both Cesar and Roman during the first stage he craved his mate at all times. Once the first stage passed, Apollo jokingly told them he only craved her when he saw her.

Letting out a groan for the headache caused by the drugs, Cesar rolled off the bed and gave Gwen one last look before heading downstairs. He glanced at the kitchen clock. One in the morning. The drugs had stolen three hours. Cesar prayed nothing dire had happened while he slept.

Cesar yanked open the lounge door and headed straight for Roman. Everyone in the room tensed as Cesar threw a punch directly to Roman's face. The crack told Cesar he had broken his friend's nose. Roman's head jerked from the impact and he fell back a step. Cesar stood calmly as Roman straightened back up and checked his nose.

When Roman saw the blood, he grinned like a madman at Cesar. "One? Just one punch? So her plan worked, then. Thank God."

Cesar narrowed his eyes. "You are never to do anything like that again. You hear me?"

If anything, Roman grinned wider. "You mean side with the young lady to save you?" He snorted. "Good luck with that."

Cesar snarled before stepping back. "Someone start reporting now!"

He looked around at the room's other occupants. Viking and Raider sat at the table across from where he and Roman stood.

Deuce, Native, and Poet were sitting in chairs against the far wall. Carter was there for some reason, and he strode toward Cesar.

The Wolf stopped about two yards away. "You mated Gwen. I can smell it. How is that possible?"

"Wait! The King of the North American Kingdom has mated our Gwen. Why was this not mentioned earlier?" Native interjected.

Poet snorted. "Yeah I know, it's pretty damn creepy."

Native mumbled his agreement.

Cesar ignored the exchange and looked at Native. "Tell me about the Hawks."

Native gave him an appraising look. Apparently, everyone wanted to look after Gwen.

"It did not take us long to track them down. We went to the children's school and from there, Walker and Orlando were able to track the scents to a vacant house in the middle of a housing development. By the time Deuce showed up, we had the surrounding area mapped out.

"We waited until Viking gave the signal and stormed the place. It was surprisingly easy. The four Tigers are young, inexperienced and did not keep watch like they should have.

"The adult male, Soaren, is heavily tranquilized. The drugs should clear his system within the next few hours. His mate is in terrible shape. She was beaten and frightened, and the poor girl has no idea of our world. What she experienced has traumatized her. The Hawks asked that we leave her with them. That way they can look out for her until Soaren wakes.

"The oldest children are twelve years old, Fern and Dale. Fern is human while Dale is a Hawk."

Native began to sound sheepish, which interested Cesar.

Native cleared his throat. "It would appear Fern is Dale's mate."

Raider folded his arms over his chest and frowned. "That is not possible. Neither is old enough to have gone through second puberty. Were males don't know their mate until then."

Native shrugged. "You didn't see him. When we came through the door he was on his feet and bracing for a fight. The girl had the younger Hawks right behind her. As if anything that could get through the boy couldn't rip through her. When the four younger ones saw Amy, the human mate, they ran at her and she steadied herself for their sake. But Dale wouldn't let any of us come near Fern, let alone touch her to see if she was wounded. Hawks only do that with their young and their mates. It was the damnedest thing. So we gave Skye a heads up. He promised to bring them and Soaren by first thing in the morning."

Cesar knew Native was right. That was not normal behavior for a Were who had not even started puberty. He couldn't help wondering if the Tigers had given the boy something.

"It is not completely unheard of."

All eyes turned to Carter as he shrugged.

"If a young Were finds himself in a position where the female destined to become his mate is in danger, his instincts will recognize her and respond accordingly. Odds are the boy will not fully understand why. His instincts will either fade with time, until second puberty hits, or he has a very rough decade ahead of him."

Carter focused on Cesar. "When you question them tomorrow, you must keep them together, act as if they are a mated pair and you should not have any problems."

Cesar nodded. He felt sorry for Dale. The poor boy's instincts were in hyper-drive and there wasn't anything he could do about it. At least Cesar understood and had a little bit of control with the Maddening.

"Can I ask about Gwen now?" Native's voice was filled with curiosity.

Cesar glared at Native. The other man was known for his obsessive need for knowledge.

Native shrugged. "All right then, can I ask what we plan to do with the room full of rogues? The four Tigers brought the count to twelve. It is getting crowded in there."

If he had been thinking clearly the last few days Cesar would have thought of that himself. "When this wave dies down, I'll have them escorted back to Montana. We have a permanent holding facility where they will be kept."

"Being mated is softening you. I remember the day when you would have simply killed them."

Cesar glared at Deuce, who shrugged.

"They might still be of use to us. I don't want to have them killed while they are still useful."

Deuce shrugged again, but this time there was a gleam in his eyes. "You could let me talk to them. That way you get all the information out of them at once."

"No."

Cesar knew once he gave the order to have them killed, these rogues would be, and there would be no taking it back. Cesar refused to use Deuce the way other leaders had. He wanted America to be safer, and the last thing we wanted was to encourage Deuce's brand of law enforcement.

No one questioned him, much to Cesar's surprise. "Let's question these Tigers and get some sleep. In the morning we will interrogate the rest of the rabble. Carter, since you are still here, help Deuce interrogate these guys. Native, you are welcome to head back home. Poet, find out where the hell the pirates are and why they haven't checked in. Raider, you are now in charge of the prisoners until we ship them out. Keep them incapacitated, but separate them out. I want Warriors guarding the rooms. If there is a repeat of what happened earlier with whatever that thing was, it is your head. Viking, set up the Warriors still hanging around in three man shifts. I want men on guard until this is taken care of. "

As Cesar headed out the door to watch the interrogations, he heard Native's voice.

"All right, someone tell me what is going on with him and Gwen. This is killing me."

Cesar smiled at the confusion in the other man's voice.

He was alone in the tiny room for less than a minute before Roman joined him.

"It is good to see you back to your old self."

Cesar grunted.

His friend grinned. "Oh come off it. You would have done the same to me. Don't forget I know you better than you know yourself. You are proud of Gwen and thrilled to have a mate that will stand up to you."

Knowing his friend was right did not make Cesar want to agree with him. Instead he changed the subject.

"I am worried about this Warrior using an alias. I fear he might be bringing reinforcements to come and take Gwen."

Roman's face stilled. "I thought the same thing, but I also think that by taking their reinforcements, we have forced them to

Gretchen S. B.

rethink their plan. I believe these rogues will think twice before going after a strong Lady of the Dead, one who happens to be mated to the King of North America. And believe me, both of those stories will be common knowledge by this time tomorrow. The people out here are in everyone's business. It is quite…odd."

Cesar wholeheartedly agreed, but was saved from comment by Viking's entrance. The young general nodded to both of them before speaking.

"It seems the pirates got into a fight up in Canada with some Immortals and now all four of them are sitting in jail overnight. Scotia also told Poet that a few rogue MPs approached him several months ago. When he turned them down they threatened his pregnant wife. He said, in light of that, he is more than willing to lend a hand should we need it."

That was good news. Cesar knew having other rogue Warriors on his side could be nothing but a benefit. Shaking his head to clear it, Cesar turned his attention to the interrogation room where Carter and Deuce had just dragged in the first Tiger.

All four Tigers were one step away from being completely useless. None of them older than twenty-six and none of them was truly Pride Leader material. They were all young and stupid. The only information they had was that the three Warriors recruited them and two Tigers in their Pride had, as one of them put it 'pussied out', and refused to help the rogues. The Tigers had no idea where their orders came from and didn't seem to particularly care.

After almost three hours of Tiger stupidity, Cesar finally returned to Gwen's bed for some sleep. Though his body needed the rest, Cesar knew his motive was to spend more time with Gwen, not to let his body recuperate from the Maddening.

As he stood over the bed and watched Gwen's ghostly form, Cesar felt all of the tension leave his body, and his dick became hard as a rock. Sighing, he crawled into bed next to her. Laying there, watching her back, Cesar promised himself that as soon as this mess ended he would take Gwen away. Not to Montana, but out to where nobody knew them. Where they could be alone and he could make love to her whenever he please. With that decided, Cesar smiled and he let himself drift off to sleep.

Gwen did not join him in his dreams that night. That put Cesar in a surly mood. After several more hours of interrogation this morning, his mood was not improved. Everyone was recruited or threatened into service by the three rogue Warriors.

The MP who had caused problems the day before, with the help of Barrett, gave them a little bit more information about the Frenchman going by 'Stetson'. The MP, Gehrig, at one point overheard Marvin talking about the Frenchman to Ellis. Apparently the man was a new player and Marvin did not trust him, because he did not know the Warrior's motives. But Marvin was told by the higher ups that 'Stetson' was the man to report to.

The idea that there were people higher up on the food chain than this MP, Marvin, did not sit well with Cesar. He was used to little rebellions here and there over the centuries. Now he was beginning to worry this might play out to be the war the rogues meant it to be.

He needed to get his hands on Marvin. Through Poet, Cesar instructed the pirates to bag the visit to the Yukon Pack and bring the MP to the fortress in Montana for questioning. Cesar knew if they could crack Marvin, then the situation could be headed off.

Cesar was in the lounge, working on ways to track Ellis with Roman and Carter, when he felt Gwen enter the room. It was something Cesar had never experienced before; suddenly he just knew she was there. His lust spiked over the top.

Cesar bolted from his seat and spun to look at her. He stopped in mid-step. She was corporeal again. The possibilities of what he could do to her now that she was in the flesh raced through his mind. Cesar balled his hands into fists to stop himself from yanking her to him, bending her over the table and taking her right here.

"I am assuming since I can see you that you are healed now."

Cesar jumped at Carter's voice. He had completely forgotten the other two men were there. Gwen gave Cesar a mischievous smile before looking at Carter and Roman.

"Yes it does, and I have some information you gentlemen might want." As she spoke, Gwen moved to sit in the empty chair between Cesar and Carter.

Gretchen S. B.

Cesar flexed every muscle in his body before taking his seat again.

Roman watched both of them, not bothering to hide his amusement. "And what would that be, young lady?"

"The MP, Marvin, is dead."

All three of them stilled, the pleasant mood vanished.

"What did you say?"

"The MP who gave orders to your rogues was murdered this morning."

Cesar frowned at his mate. "How do you know this?"

Gwen looked him square in the eye, and Cesar knew he wouldn't like the answer.

"I did some searching in the Spirit World this morning. I knew roughly where he lived, geographically. I knew once I reached the Fairy's house I needed to take a sharp left. It took me a while but I found it."

Her eyes were unfocused over Cesar's shoulder and she frowned.

"He was keeping some very powerful things hostage. They let me know what happened to him this morning before I freed them to go about their business. I don't know how he did what he did, but somehow he got the attention of the Strata-Enforcers. The seven of them came to his house this morning. The being who showed me this didn't know who they were but I figured it out from watching them.

"I've already informed Barrett that the Strata-Enforcers are in the area."

Cesar didn't like that, any of it. The Strata-Enforcers were the only group who could move through his Kingdom and kill without his approval. He had never trusted them and had only met them on two occasions. If they were in the area, it was not good. Even worse when he considered how long it took for them to solve any one problem, they would have heard about Marvin's dirty deeds months ago and didn't inform him. Cesar and Roman were working with Aztec to figure out ways to bar the Strata-Enforcers from entering their kingdoms without prior permission. So far, they had not come up with anything.

He moved past the fact that Gwen had probably endangered herself again. He took her advice to heart. Picking his battles meant leaving this one alone. Cesar didn't like the idea but knew he couldn't do anything after the fact.

"Did you find out if they have any other targets?"

Gwen shook her head. "They did not mention it one way or the other."

Roman grunted disapprovingly. "I do not like this development. The Strata-Enforcers are too much of a wild card."

Cesar agreed. The last thing they needed in a time of war was the MP council's watchdogs hunting in his kingdom. He made a mental note to contact the council. Not that they would return his call, but he would make the attempt anyway.

Viking cleared his throat from where he stood in the lounge doorway. He must have followed Gwen in.

"By the way, the Hawks are here, and I mean the entire nest."

Standing, Cesar held out his hand for Gwen. Now that he could touch her, he would be taking every opportunity. She looked from him to his hand with an amused expression before laying her hand in his.

As the group of them walked down the hall, Gwen tugged to get Cesar's attention. Not that his entire body was not already fully concentrated on her, but she wanted to say something private so he bent his head toward hers, knowing full well Carter would hear the entire conversation from where he was a few feet behind them.

"May I suggest that you let me interrogate the two young Hawks?"

Cesar growled. He was not putting her in the interrogation room alone with an unstable Were.

"Hear me out, August. If what Poet tells me about the boy is true, then he will not see me as a threat to him or the girl. I will be more likely to get information from them than a male would."

It was a good idea and Cesar could not help the feeling of pride. With it came the irritation at knowing she spoke with Poet before coming to find him, but he knew better than to mention it. "Fine, but if something happens, we are storming that room."

She looked up at him inquisitively. "You gave into that much easier than I would have thought."

A smile tugged at Cesar's lips. "I am picking my battles, but it is a good plan."

She continued to watch him warily as he escorted her to the interrogation room door. Gwen gave him one last look before stepping inside.

Carter had informed the rest of room of Gwen's plan by the time Cesar walked into the observation room. Cesar went to stand beside Poet.

"I hear you've been chatting with my mate." Keeping his voice as bland as possible, Cesar glared at the other man.

Poet grinned and turned to the glass. "Just doing my job. From now on I answer to my queen above everyone else. She asks, I answer."

There were several muted laughs from the other men. Skye at least had the decency to fake a cough.

Cesar held back his smile. He liked that Gwen had her allies. It meant she was better protected when he could not be around and that his life was about to be more interesting.

"Good morning, Dale, Fern." Gwen's voice held comfort and safety.

They all watched as the young male's body relaxed a bit as he assessed Gwen as non-threatening. The girl still gave worried glances to Dale. She clearly didn't understand her friend's rapid change in behavior.

Gwen smiled as she sat across from the couple, her back to the glass. Her calm demeanor seemed to fill the interrogation room.

"My name is Gwen."

Fern straightened in her chair and her eyes widened. "You're the Lady of the Dead, aren't you?"

When Gwen simply nodded, the girl turned her attention to Dale. "She's a VIP in the Night World."

Cesar noted the boy almost seemed to preen at the fact that he warranted such attention.

Skye snorted. "My son does have quite the ego. I fear this will only make that worse."

"All young male Weres have that same ego. Don't worry, someone will come along and smack it down a few notches." Carter laughed.

The Hawk's lips twitched. "We can only hope. As my wife is always telling me, 'at least he's not a cat. Their egos can't fit through doorways.'"

Carter snorted.

"I would be ever so grateful if the two of you could tell me about this whole event. Even the smallest detail could be of importance to us," Gwen continued.

Fern's shoulders slumped a little, as if trying to make herself smaller. The gesture was not lost on Dale. The young male sat up straighter and yanked her chair even closer to him so he could wrap his left arm around her shoulders. The girl relaxed.

"Yeah, that boy is screwed," Carter mumbled.

When Skye didn't say a word, Cesar looked at the Hawk. He was watching his son with pride, worry, and pain on his face. Cesar knew, though Skye was proud of his son for protecting Fern, he wished the boy hadn't needed to. Skye clearly agreed with Carter's assessment.

Dale looked Gwen in the eyes. "We attend a private school, Shore Side Academy. Any of our nest is authorized to pick us up. Soaren came to the school around the time the younger kids have their first recess, about ten-thirty. He told us something was wrong at home and none of us questioned it."

Dale scowled. "I should have questioned him. I am the oldest and the first child of the lead couple. It is my duty to protect the others and I failed." The boy sounded bitter for someone so young.

Gwen laid one of her hands on the metal table. She was trying to soothe without actually touching either child. Cesar was even more impressed by his mate. She knew enough about Weres not to touch them, but she didn't have it in her not to help them.

"That is not true."

Dale looked as if he might argue, but Gwen raised her other hand. "Think of it this way: are your parents fair and just leaders?"

The boy straightened again, his eyes sharp with determination. "Yes. They do more for their nest and our kind than the other leaders do. They protect their nest but do not hesitate to punish when it is due."

Gwen nodded as if it was the answer she expected. "Would you ever question their judgment or rulings?"

"Never!"

She nodded again. "And have your parents told you that you were at fault for any of this?"

"No." Dale's voice grew small.

Gretchen S. B.

"Then clearly you are not to blame for this and should not dwell on such a ridiculous idea. Instead focus on what really happened."

The boy eyed Gwen suspiciously. He clearly wanted to argue with her, but could not find a way to do it.

Skye laughed and leaned around Poet to slap Cesar on the back. "Congratulations, King. You have chosen very well for your kingdom and taken all hope of rebellion from your future offspring."

Cesar smiled but didn't respond. He was in whole agreement with Skye, Gwen was his perfect mate.

After another moment the boy sighed. "Soaren took us to a van. Inside it were three Tigers. All of us Hawks were drugged, and then they took us to that house and shoved us kids into the room you found us in. I told Fern to keep the younger ones as far from the door as possible. I could faintly smell Amy's perfume somewhere nearby. I kinda put two and two together and figured that was how the Tigers got Soaren. The Tigers tried to split us up but I wouldn't let them. I might not be at second puberty yet, but at least I know how to fight. The younger ones don't. They brought us food a few times but I wouldn't let anyone eat it. We couldn't risk something being in the food.

"When the Warriors brought Amy to us, I knew we were free, but I could see she was in worse shape than us. Soaren was not even conscious."

Gwen waited to make sure Dale was finished before she spoke. "Did you ever overhear any conversations? Hear any voices other than the Tigers?"

The young Were sat silently thinking for several moments. "I'm not sure. My hearing isn't any better then yours. So unless there was shouting, or they were right outside the door, I couldn't hear them.

"I know there were Wolves at one point because for a while the Tigers were bickering with them. Someone said something about a Warrior coming but that was about it. They were careful not to talk much when they were in the back half of the house where they were keeping us."

"Um." The girl's voice was barely more than a whisper.

That one noise gained everyone's attention and all eyes zeroed in on Fern.

"When they were fighting the last time before the Wolves left, one of them mentioned something about a meeting with a French guy. That he would know what the next step was because some Roman screwed with their plan. That if whoever was on the other end of the phone hadn't been so obvious the plan would be moving along as planned."

Gwen turned to look at the glass. She knew what that meant and Cesar realized in that moment that no one had told Gwen that grabbing her had been part of the rogue's plan. Cesar cursed. His mate was not going to be happy with him.

Gwen turned back to the young Hawks. "Did they say where this meeting would take place?"

Fern shook her head. "No, just that it had been moved south."

Nodding Gwen stood. "Thank you very much. The two of you have been most helpful." Then she smiled at them and walked out of the interrogation room.

When Gwen didn't open the observation room door, Cesar cursed again and swung the door open in time to watch the back door shut behind his mate.

Gretchen S. B.

Chapter 29

Gwen had not been outside for more than ten seconds before she heard the door open behind her. She knew it was August. She didn't want to talk to him right now. She had too many thoughts running around in her head, too many emotions swirling.

Just as she thought she was falling for the overbearing but painfully sweet king of the Warriors, he would do something to change her mind. She understood why he had kept this specific fact from her. He didn't want to frighten her.

Gwen got that, she really did, but she refused to have a relationship with someone who thought her weak. Gwen always imagined that when she did settle down it would be with a man who saw her as an equal. A partner, not a responsibility.

She loved Storebror more than any other person in the world, but he had been her protector for twenty years. Viking saw it as his job to look out for her and Gwen was fine with that, enjoyed it even, but she refused to go from one protective custody to another. Viking had always kept scary things from her whenever possible growing up. It had only been in the last few years that Gwen was able to wean him from that habit. Now fate had placed her in the arms of a man that would hold her tighter than Storebror ever had.

Gwen wanted to scream in anger, and she wanted to cry. Mostly she wanted to be left alone with what little freedom she had left.

Sighing, she addressed August without even turning to look at him. "I don't want to be near you right now."

"Gwen, I..."

She cut him off. Gwen couldn't listen to the confused hurt in his voice. She just needed to be alone.

"I'm not mad at you. I get it, I do. Just because I get it doesn't mean I have to like it."

August must have heard something in her voice because there was a moment of silence, and then she heard the back door open, and he was gone. Part of Gwen felt bad. She didn't mean to hurt him, she just wanted to be able to run her own life.

Gwen was surprised when she heard the door open a few seconds later. She turned to see Poet leaning against the wall, watching her with a pleasantly bland expression.

"Did he send you out her to watch me in case I run off?"

Poet snorted. "No. I would be the worst pick for that. I would let you leave and he knows it."

Gwen put her hands on her hips and looked at her friend pointedly.

Poet smiled. "His exact words to me were 'fix it, then explain it to me.' So out I came while they question the other Hawks."

Rolling her eyes, Gwen snorted. "Why you and not Viking?"

He shrugged. "He needs Viking in there. Plus Viking is not stupid. He knows why you are upset and that there is nothing he could do to cheer you up. See, as your pet I'm already making myself useful."

She scrubbed at her face in an effort to hide the smile Poet's comment produced. "And why exactly does Viking think I'm upset?"

Poet raised an eyebrow at her. "It's fairly obvious, even moreso because you have called him by his name twice now. You only do that when you're upset with him."

That hadn't occurred to her, but as he said it Gwen knew it was true.

"You're upset because one of the things you so crave from this life is control. Viking is in control, but he gives you room to wiggle because he cannot stand to see you miserable. The King, however, will stifle you. You dread what will happen when he whisks you off to Montana, away from the life you have built. Away from the small things you are able to control." Poet shrugged. "I get it, Viking gets it. I'm pretty sure Raider gets it, but with him you really never can tell. Lucia and Sivia get it because they strive for the same thing in their own lives. Your friend Sin will never get it simply because she cannot imagine not doing what she wants."

Gwen watched him for a moment. "So why didn't you explain it to him?"

Poet grinned. "I enjoy seeing him squirm. After centuries of ruthless composure, it's fun to see him so completely at a loss. Plus you needed to know we are well aware of how you feel. Don't worry, Gwen, we will straighten the king out for you." His grin grew mischievous. "Or make the whole thing hell for him. I'm fine either way."

Part of her relaxed at Poet's words. But having others aware of it didn't solve the problem.

"I can't live in the Warrior fortress. It would kill me."

Poet's smile disappeared. "I know. I dread living there as well. Don't worry. Worse comes to worse, the Pirates and I will break you out and hide you. You know as well as I that the Night Worlders out here would have no qualm about hiding you from the king." His lips twitched.

Gwen took a deep breath. That was good to know. If August did trap her in his isolated fortress she would have an escape plan. She didn't know what it was about escape plans, but they always made her feel better.

"Why are you so willing to look out for me?" The words were out before Gwen could stop them.

Poet's smile grew sad. "Like Deuce, I would not have joined the King in his American empire. I am not one for structure or following anyone else's rules. But Deuce and I are both too much of a threat for the King to have living as rogues in his kingdom. So I took the path of least resistance and joined him. If I can do anything to buck his authority without crossing the line, I will. Plus, I think you're kind of swell." He smiled wide enough to flash his fangs at her.

Smiling, she walked over to Poet, rolled to the balls of her feet and kissed his cheek. There was a split second where Gwen couldn't read Poet's emotions but as she leaned back down his usual smile was in place.

"Now my queen, why couldn't you do such a thing where his highness could see? Such displays are wasted when there is no audience."

Gwen rolled her eyes and tugged the back door open.

Chapter 30

Soaren had not given them anything useful. That frustrated Cesar. But what really bothered him was how Gwen stuck close to Poet. She should be near him, not her guard. Viking and Raider didn't seem to mind. It drove Cesar up the wall. As much as he hated it, Cesar was smart enough to realize that griping about it would only make matters worse. So he ground his teeth and kept his mouth shut.

At a quarter to one, Roman's cell phone rang. When Roman showed Cesar the caller ID read Apollo, Cesar made eye contact with his third general and the three of them left the lounge for the relative privacy of the stairs.

"What do you have, Apollo?" Cesar asked gruffly as Roman flipped open his phone.

There was silence on the other end for ten seconds. "Roman hasn't killed you yet."

Cesar felt a pang of regret. None of them had remembered to call Apollo and tell him the Maddening was over.

"I am sorry, my friend. No, Gwen figured a way to outsmart the Maddening. You are stuck with me now."

There was silence again. "Roman, you will bring this girl to me so I may thank her in person." The relief flooded Apollo's voice.

Roman smiled. "Yes Greek, you will get the chance to meet her. For now, though, I believe you have news for us."

Cesar could almost hear Apollo reining himself in. "Yes. I received a call from Stetson. I left a message on his voicemail this morning and he just now got back to me. He told me someone using his identity had royally pissed him off but it also explained a few things."

"What things?" Viking interjected.

There was a huff. "Let me finish. I guess San called him a few days ago, razzing him for coming out to the west coast and not paying a visit. Since San lives in southern California and Stetson hasn't left his place in eastern Texas in twenty years, he had no idea what San was talking about."

Apparently one of the younger Warriors out in L.A. told San that Stetson had gone rogue and was heading north to Olympia. I guess the fake Stetson was in Northern California at the time. The young Warrior couldn't figure out what could possibly be of interest this far north. San was so surprised he called Stetson to see if it was true."

Cesar's mind began to work in overdrive. If the meeting was in Olympia they had a chance to intervene.

"Did he know exactly where or when?" He asked his general.

"No. But I figure you know what the Warrior he's meeting looks like so at least you will have a heads up."

Cesar exchanged looks with his generals. Even with all the Warriors in the area out searching, there was no guarantee they could find the rogues.

Roman thanked Apollo and hung up.

The one most plausible option was to call Lucia and ask the MPs for the same spell they used earlier. It would cost him, but he couldn't afford to waste the time or manpower it would take to search the entire state capital.

He turned to Viking. "Call Lucia and tell her I need her to do that searching spell and I need her to set it up here. When she needs to negotiate cost she can call me. Until then I am rounding up men to go down to Olympia."

Viking nodded. "That drive will take you over an hour."

Roman snorted. "Not if we speed."

———

Cesar couldn't remember the last time Roman let him drive. Usually he made some snarky comment, but not today. Roman spent the first half of the drive getting Lucia's price down from an arm and a leg to just a leg. She asked for money this time and Roman got her down to five grand. Cesar was never happier to have accumulated wealth than when he needed to deal with MPs.

After the call, the SUV fell into silence. With Poet and Carter in the back seat, Cesar was somewhat surprised. Carter opted to ride with them so they could strategize, which they had wrapped up by the time Roman got Lucia's call.

"Would you like me to explain Gwen to you now or would later be a better time?"

Sighing, Cesar cracked his neck. He knew the silence had been too good to be true. He also knew Poet was baiting him. The other man knew how much Cesar wanted to understand his mate and Poet deliberately picked the worst time to explain.

"Hell, now, why not?"

Cesar could practically hear Poet smiling from the back seat.

"It's quite simple, actually. Freedom. Give Gwen freedom and she will choose to stay."

Cesar grunted. That didn't even make sense. "I don't understand."

There was laughter from behind him and it wasn't just Poet. Cesar felt himself become annoyed.

"She wants the freedom of making her own choices. Think about every time she has become cross with you. Were you keeping something from her? Making decisions for her? Were you taking away her choices?"

Carter chimed in. "Woman today do not want men to make decisions for them. I know all three of you come from periods where men took charge of everything, but for women Gwen's age, that's insulting. They see it as you telling them they are not capable of making their own choices."

Poet cleared his throat. "Food for thought. Did you ask Gwen how she felt about being moved to Montana away from everything she has ever known? Did you tell her about the Maddening? About the rogues? Did you ask her opinion on anything? Granted, she has spent most of her time incapacitated.

"She wants to be your queen, not just your consort. I know to us it seems strange, but Viking realized years ago that with Gwen, a little freedom goes a long way."

Cesar growled. "So I should leave her here and work out a schedule for conjugal visits?" That was the last thing he wanted. Cesar wanted Gwen lying beside him every night and waking up with him every morning.

There was a heavy sigh. "I would not phrase it like that when you mention it to her, but I do think asking her opinion and bringing up that possibility would go a long way. Gwen is not stupid or cruel. She would stay with you through the first stage of mating whether you asked her to or not."

Cesar didn't know what to say so he kept his mouth shut. He didn't like that Poet was right. He didn't want to have an absentee

Gretchen S. B.

mate. He wanted her safe and sound in the Warrior fortress for the rest of their days, but he wanted her happy more.

Chapter 31

Gwen sat and watched Lucia and the boys set up in the lounge. After a while, Storebror came to sit down beside her.

It was nice, their companionable silence. Gwen had missed that over the past week. Her alone time with him was something she treasured and she knew, with her mating August, it would probably disappear.

As if he could hear her thoughts, Storebror placed his hand over hers where it lay on the arm of her chair. She felt his necklace warm before she heard his voice in her head.

"Everything will be all right, Little One. I will always be here with you."

She smiled. *"Promises, promises."*

His chuckle filled her head. *"Someone is going to have to protect the king from you, and Poet and Roman sure as hell won't do it."*

Her smile grew at his words but disappeared as her earlier thoughts circled back around. *"It won't be the same, though. No more full moon nights out on my balcony with you telling me about the constellations."*

Viking snorted. *"You've known all those stories by heart for years."*

Gwen looked at him. *"That isn't the point."*

Viking returned her gaze with a sad smile. *"I know, Little One. Cesar is a good man, though. The two of you will take some time to adjust to each other. You may be surprised at how much the two of you could get along."*

Gwen was about to respond when Storebror's phone rang. He gave her an apologetic smile before removing his hand to grab the phone from his pocket.

After a few non-committal noises he looked over at the MPs. "The King wants to know if you are ready. They just exited into Olympia."

When Lucia nodded Viking hit speakerphone and August's voice filled the room.

"I am going to need a broader picture than last time. We will not know the street from a verbal description. Can you get me a slightly larger picture?"

Gretchen S. B.

Gwen saw Lucia's eyes flicker with annoyance. "Of course, King."

"Good. Let me know when you have something."

Then the line was dead.

Lucia snarled. "I liked him better when he was crazy."

A smile tugged at Gwen's lips but she kept it at bay and turned to Viking. "Is he always that demanding?"

He smiled down at her. "Absolutely, and most of the time, no one gives him problems."

Gwen rolled her eyes and turned back to the MPs, who now seemed to be starting. She had not seen this particular spell before. Exercising her newfound power, she focused her mind to watch the use of the MPs' powers. Gwen noticed a lot of Lucia's energy pouring into the small pot in front of her. After almost a minute of heavy concentration, Gwen saw Barrett turn to the wall at Lucia's back and after a few movements, a picture of the rogue appeared.

Ellis paced what might have been a warehouse. He was obviously agitated and talking fast. But everything around him was blurry, as if they were looking at a moving watercolor.

All three MPs bent over the small pot, squinting, each of them tapping the lip and expending more energy, but the picture did not grow any clearer. After about a minute, Barrett looked up from the pot to Viking.

"Get the King on the phone."

Storebror didn't even question, he simply made the call and hit speakerphone again.

"Where are they?" August asked without preamble.

Barrett stepped around the table so August could better hear him. "He is in a warehouse of some type, but someone with a decent amount of power is blocking either the building he's in or the others in that building. We can see him clearly but the world around him is hazy and I'm not sure we can clear it up."

August's frustration came through the phone clearly. "Try zooming out or whatever and see if there is anything that can give us a general location."

Nodding, Barrett walked back to the pot, where Lucia and Marco were already working. The image expanded at an almost dizzying pace. Gwen watched in fascination as the wavy lines began snapping into clarity.

224 | P a g e

Then the picture stopped moving and Lucia let out a sound of triumph. "Got the little pricks."

Suddenly the picture was zooming in on a street sign several blocks down. When the picture froze again the letters were visible to all of them.

"They are meeting in a warehouse four blocks south of 48th and Crest!" Lucia yelled.

"Good, we are still about ten minutes out. Let us know if they move." Then he hung up.

Within moments, the picture on the wall blurred and all three MPs jumped back from the pot, arms waving. Gwen could see a black mist seeping up from the brim of the pot and she knew whoever had set the spell around Ellis was on to them. Lucia and the boys' hands all moved rapidly through the air. Storebror stood, moving in front of Gwen, pulling out his sword.

The world spun out of control fast and several things happened simultaneously. Viking called for Raider to bring backup, Lucia crumpled in a heap on the floor, and Barrett raised his arms, slicing at the air. Then the room went pitch black.

The dark was oppressive, stuffy, and thick. Adrenaline shot fireworks through Gwen's body. She and Storebror had been through this kind of dark before, when she was nine. He had almost died. Flashbacks shot through her head.

This couldn't be the same MP, it couldn't. Gwen felt her panic grow with that thought. She tried desperately to control her shallow breathing. With one shaky hand, she clutched his necklace, and the other reached out to where he had stood when the light was sucked from the room. She felt the brush of a shirt against her. Unconsciously her fingers curled around the fabric.

"Storebror, please tell me I have your shirt." Even Gwen could hear the panic in her voice.

"Yes, Little One, I'm right here. But I do not know where our MPs are and I have yet to hear Raider come into the room." His voice sounded guarded but calm. If he was remembering the same event she was, he didn't show it.

Relief flooded her. Gwen wasn't letting him leave her side this time. She refused to stand by and let the past repeat itself. Still clutching the bottom of Storebror's shirt, Gwen stood and pulled the

Gretchen S. B.

knife from the sheath on her leg. Holding the knife calmed her panic, but the adrenaline continued to bounce around her system.

Raider's voice sounded from the direction of the door. "What the hell is going on in here, Viking? The air is like ink. Stay where you are, boys, no one is going in until we know what's happened."

"Stay put! I don't know what's in here with us!" Viking hollered back.

"I've made it so no one can leave the dark, only come in. That way whatever it is has to stay in here with us."

It was Barrett's voice coming from the far left but Gwen knew better than to fully trust it. When she and Storebror were stuck in this black last time it was with an MP that could fake others' voices. That was how he had injured Viking, pretending to be Gwen. Storebror had killed that MP.

What were the odds that another possessed the same ability? Storebror didn't answer.

"I did no such thing. I simply put a sealant spell on the room so none of this could seep out. We can't leave but neither can he." That, Gwen would bet, was Barrett.

"He can mimic our voices. Lucia, poke the door so we can get out of here," came the voice from the left again, but it was moving closer.

Gwen heard what sounded like Lucia snort. "Not likely, moron."

There was silence then Gwen heard movement just past Viking's shoulder. She felt him swing and heard metal on metal.

"Damn Viking, you nearly took my head off." It sounded like Raider.

"And how the hell did you get in here?" It was Lucia's voice but something sounded was off.

"I used to raid tombs for a living. The oppressive night is my friend."

Gwen reached out to Storebror. *"Is that really Raider?"*

There was movement in Viking's shirt. *"Yes, unless whoever it is can sword fight and change his body as well."*

"So little Gwennie is in here, is she? How excellent, I can take out a top Strata and the Lady of the Dead. Good, I was very upset that I missed you last time." The voice was downright creepy. He was mimicking Gwen's voice when she was nine.

She felt Viking tense. "I killed you." He sounded like he didn't quite believe his own words.

"Yes, and up until a few minutes ago I thought I killed you. Fortunately for me there are more interesting things on the planet than just living and dead."

Gwen shuddered at his real voice. They had to do something. Staying here, they were all sitting ducks. There was a thud and sounds of fighting.

"MARCO!" Panic filled Lucia's voice.

"Stay put, Lucia. If he can't see you he can hit you by accident." Barrett's voice was assertive but at the same time Gwen swore she heard him moving toward the fight.

Gwen's panic grew. These where her friends, and she couldn't just let this dead MP terrorize them. He had nearly killed Viking the first time, and given the chance, he would try again. Anger shot through her so white hot she swore the world snapped into view. Then she blinked. It had. Gwen could clearly see the room—well, it was a bit hazy. In front of her she saw Marco on the ground, blood running in rivulets down his stomach. He fought to remain conscious. Barrett was sending wild punches into the dead MP's form, but it wasn't doing any good; his fists continued to go right through. Barrett was chanting something Gwen couldn't quite hear.

"GWEN!?" Storebror's panicked voice rang out across the room.

The fight stopped momentarily as Gwen's disappearance registered. The ghost of the MP noticed her and grinned wide and leapt up toward her. In that moment, she realized she had gone non-corporal again. She didn't question it, calling as much power as she could she gave all her attention to the man trying to kill them.

"Enough!"

Her power flowed through her voice and the ghost looked at her in confusion but continued moving.

"You will stop!"

The MP stopped dead. He began tugging at his legs, but they wouldn't not budge. Gwen felt herself smile. This being had made a deal with something worse than himself to be able to keep practicing after his own death. Unfortunately for him, the Spirit World was something she could control.

"Who recruited you?" She put power behind her voice so he would be compelled to answer.

"An Immortal who goes by Adonis." The words held venom. He did not want to answer her.

"Is he one of the ringleaders of this rebellion?"

The MP struggled but Gwen knew her power would win. "I don't know."

"What were you sent here to do?" Gwen could feel her recently recuperated power beginning to drain. This was too new of a skill and the MP fought back too hard for her to keep her hold much longer. Not good.

"I was sent with the French Warrior to rein in these three young Warriors who jumped the gun on their assignment. We were to collect them and do damage control."

The power was slipping. Gwen could almost feel the reins of her power being yanked from her hands. She had a choice. She could either strain to get all the information out of this ghost, or she could force him back as she had the being attacking Barrett earlier.

August might disagree later, but to Gwen, safety trumped answers. Pushing what remained of her power into her voice, Gwen focused on the dead MP. "You will leave here immediately and never return. You will not harm any of us and you will never help these rogues again. Go back to where you came from."

The ghost screeched and began to fade, continuing to fight her. "You do not have sway over those who made me. They will send me back stronger."

Something in his voice made Gwen know this was no idle threat. She panicked but pushed all she had into her last statement. "You are of the Spirit World. That is my domain. I release the bonds that keep you here. You will go to wherever your destination would have been before this deal was made." Gwen wasn't entirely sure she had the ability to do that, or the power to back it but at this point she was out of ideas.

The last of her power drained before her command could be fully carried out. She felt the MP returning, clawing toward her. He was going to kill her and there wasn't a thing she could do about it. Suddenly Storebror's pendant heated, almost burning her skin and she felt foreign power race through her. Gwen didn't question it. She yanked the new energy and threw it straight at the ghost. She felt her commands click fully into place. The MP snapped out of the room, and along with him went the dark.

Gwen didn't pause, she used the foreign power to become corporeal, then released it. She didn't know where it came from and she wasn't going to use more of it than necessary. Her corporeal hand must have dropped the sword before changing over the first time because she just registered its absence. She felt her knees buckle and cave beneath her, her body simply lacking the energy to stay up right. But her hands never hit the floor. Storebror was there, grabbing her and cradling her to his chest a split second before she fell. Gwen's body felt as if she hadn't slept in days.

Lucia ran across the room to Marco.

Viking yelled to Rochester, who stood in the doorway "Rochester! Call Sivia tell her to get down here as soon as she can. Call Raine and tell him we need the Pack's doctor as soon as he can get here."

Lucia's hands pressed on Marco's chest as hard as she could, and she chanted in a language Gwen had never heard before. Glancing up, she saw Rochester still standing there staring at her in shock.

Anger ran through her. "Rochester, do as I say or I will beat you to a pulp while you sleep."

Raider's usual threat to the rookies seemed to get the other man's attention because he blinked, nodded, then ran from the room, yelling orders and pulling out his phone.

Gwen felt Raider drop down beside her and Storebror. His face was blank, except for his eyes. They were shaken. The man who had risked his life for treasure for centuries was looking at her with worry. Gwen lifted the hand not trapped under Storebror's powerful arms and grabbed Raider's hand. He squeezed back before simply holding on.

They had become a family over the last ten years, fighting for the peace they wanted so badly and for all three of them any hope for peace officially ended. From here on out they would be fighting for everything again. Though there would be more people on their side this time, the other side was bigger too, and had a head start.

When she turned back to the MPs, she saw the devastation on their faces. Their Strata was their family. Barrett began some kind of chant. Lucia looked at him with worry before switching her chant to something else, something calmer. Gwen could see their energies surrounding the now unconscious Marco. Most of Lucia's concentration seemed to go into keeping pressure on the stomach wound. Marco's shirt was covered in blood.

It was all Gwen could do not to give into her panic. She didn't even notice Raider's hand slipping from hers until he came into view, kneeling over Marco's body and ripping Marco's shirt to tend to the biggest wound. Next to him sat the first aid kit they kept in the lounge. With Raider moving in, all of Lucia's attention went to working her magic. Her left hand grabbed Barrett's right and Gwen watched their power intensify. The pool of blood covering Marco's clothing stopped growing.

Viking held her to his chest as they knelt less than a yard away. They were so close and yet there was nothing either of them could do. Gwen looked up at her lifelong protector and memories of every time she had ever come close to losing him paraded through her mind. Both she and Storebror knew exactly how the MPs felt. When she heard Raider curse, she used the opportunity to look away.

Raider's hands suddenly stilled as he looked to Viking and Gwen. "They've stopped the wound from bleeding. That's dangerous magic. Not exactly safe with the Strata-Enforcers around." He gave the two chanting MPs a look before going back to the wounds.

Gwen wasn't sure how long they all knelt there before Simon, the Pack's doctor, jogged into the room. Viking stood and tugged Gwen to her feet as Simon dropped the handle to his large rolling bag. The doctor gave Marco a once over before looking at Raider. "You have medical experience?"

Raider nodded. "Very little. I was a medic in the Civil and the first World War."

That was news to Gwen, but it made sense. Raider had bandaged her up from time to time.

Simon gave Raider an appraising look before turning to Lucia. "What are you using on him?"

Lucia's large pain-filled eyes looked up from Marco. "I've used a pain spell. He'll stay unconscious as long as you need and Barrett is preventing him from bleeding out. He can hold that spell for maybe fifteen more minutes."

The doctor looked from one MP to the other before opening the back pocket of the bag next to him. "All right then. Everyone who isn't necessary, clear out. You," He pointed to Raider, "will assist. And someone send in Sivia when she gets here because I sure as hell can't stop an infection like she can."

Gwen was only half aware of Storebror leading her from the room. She heard cursing from inside as Rochester closed it behind them. She could vaguely hear Viking giving the younger men orders but only one sentence got through.

It was Kegan. "Poet's been calling like crazy the last ten minutes. None of us answered. We figured if you and Raider were ignoring him, we sure as hell weren't picking up."

Viking gave the other Warrior a look before turning to Gwen. "Let's get you to bed. Then I'll come back down."

Gwen nodded even though she wanted to disagree. She was drained of power and now that the doctor was here, the adrenaline in her system waned. She was crashing despite her worry for Marco.

Simon possessed a better poker face than anyone Gwen had ever met but he did not seem worried about Marco's chances of survival. Gwen grabbed that thought and held onto it as tight as she could. When she and Storebror were halfway to the stairs, Gwen turned to the two Warriors standing by the closed door. "When Marco is stable tell them my spare bedrooms are open to them. He can recover here as long as he needs."

Both men nodded and one answered, "Yes, my queen." But Gwen couldn't tell which.

Viking shooed Gwen into her bathroom with instructions to change. She didn't have it in her to argue. The sooner she recovered, the sooner she could get back downstairs. She needed to get hold of these new abilities. With the coming war she could not afford nap breaks.

Viking sat on the edge of her bed when she came back into the room. The way he was sitting with the half empty glass of

Gretchen S. B.

Monk's poison in front of him let Gwen know he was not heading down as soon as Gwen would like.

   She sat down across from him and felt worry gnaw at her belly. "How is Marco doing?" She knew if he had the time to get a drink, then time was moving faster than she thought.

   Viking swirled his glass. "I called down about two minutes ago. According to Roch, Simon's saying Marco shouldn't die, unless there is an added spell he can't scent or there is another attack. Barrett saved him by blocking the blood flow. As soon as Simon finishes stitching him up and Sivia can clean his wounds, they are moving Marco up here to rest for about a week, or until he is out of the woods enough that Barrett and Lucia can take him home. I guess Lucia is trying to barter services with a White MP to speed Marco's healing. Roch says it isn't going too well. Lucia's temper keeps flaring."

   Gwen's shoulders slumped with relief as she plopped onto the bed next to him. They were all very lucky, much luckier than they had the right to be. MPs were human, just like her. That meant Marco wouldn't have the advanced healing of other Night Worlders, and it made his survival more impressive. Gwen took a deep breath before looking at Storebror again. He was hiding something. She knew it. Years with him made even his blank face readable to her.

   "And?"

   He continued to watch his swirling drink. "When you went non-corporeal Cesar felt it and went nuts. It almost caused an accident when the pendants flared. When they calmed him, he, Roman, and Poet began calling us to find out what the hell happened. I called Roman back and gave them a heavily abridged version. I told them you went non-corporeal to fight something, and though drained, you were fine now."

   There was a tightness to his voice that bothered Gwen. He wasn't lying, but something wasn't quite right. She could almost feel anxiety rolling off of him. "What is bothering you, Storebror?"

   Viking took a deep breath and in one gulp downed the rest of his glass before slamming it on the table. Only then did he look at her. "That shouldn't have worked!"

   Confusion filled her. "What shouldn't have worked?"

   "I watched you drain your power. Without even thinking I thrust you some of mine. All I thought was 'Little One is going to die'. It shouldn't have worked, Gwen. My powers are not compatible with the powers of the Lady of the Dead. I've tried to give you power before when you were little. That's how I know it doesn't work. My energy should have splashed against you and returned. But instead you absorbed it, used it. You shouldn't have been able to do that."

Gwen felt a sense of dread. This was big. Then she heard the words of that ghost about a door in her head. Gwen felt herself grow cold. "Why? Why shouldn't it have worked?"

Pain trickled into Storebror's eyes. "Because the only ones I have ever seen do that were my family. All of my family is dead. I've only ever met a handful of people with powers similar to my mother's."

Gwen shifted on the bed. She could already feel her body starting to recover, but she still needed rest soon. "Remember what those ghost MPs told me about the door in my head? Could that be it? Maybe my powers as Lady of the Dead simply shut down abilities I would have possessed anyway."

Viking nodded slowly. "Yes, it would also explain several things. Lately you have been displaying abilities that are not strictly those of the Lady of the Dead. I had chalked it up to our poor record keeping, but this…this makes sense. You show hints of the abilities my mother and sisters displayed before they died." His eye flashed with his last sentence.

She knew he felt a spike of pain when his family came up.

"I will train you more appropriately from here on out. When we get the chance I will train you as my mother trained us. You must be able to use all the abilities at your disposal."

There was so much resolve in his voice that Gwen knew she couldn't convince him otherwise. Even if she was getting training elsewhere. It wasn't in her it burst his bubble.

"Did you mention this to August or Roman?"

Viking's face blanked again. "No, and nor will I until I am sure these powers are the same as my own. Though they both know there are things I can do that are out of the norm, they have never pushed to find out more than that."

Gwen nodded and laid down on the bed. "Let's put it aside for a bit so you can go downstairs and I can sleep. Come get me in about a half hour. I want to see Marco for myself and I think we

Gretchen S. B.

need to speak with Lucia about our wards. Too many nasty things have managed to make their way in here recently."

At first Viking looked to argue but as she finished, he nodded. "Agreed."

Breathing a sigh of relief, Gwen rolled over and fell asleep before he even left the room.

Chapter 32

The car was silent except for Cesar's occasional growl. He could not help it. His mate had put herself in harm's way, again. Cesar couldn't decide whether he wanted to kill her or never leave her side. The fear that ran through him when his pendant throbbed made his body turn to ice. The SUV nearly crashed into a sports car. Even now, knowing she was safe, Cesar could not keep his Warrior instincts in check. Everything in him screamed to turn the SUV around and see to his mate's safety himself. Cesar knew he couldn't; his knuckles on the steering wheel were paper white from the effort to stay on course.

Viking had been incredibly vague in his description of events. Cesar knew the other man had not shared everything, but he knew Viking would not lie about Gwen's well being. Cesar was getting tired of the Seattle Night World and their way of doing things. It shouldn't have rubbed off on Viking; the man was more than a thousand years old. He shouldn't be so easily swayed. Cesar had half a mind to kidnap Gwen now and carry her away to the Montana stronghold and not let any of these insane beings near her.

Cesar took a deep breath. He was letting his temper get the best of him. His mate wasn't entirely unreasonable. If he sat her down and explained things to her maybe they could come to some agreement that would not have him wanting to rip throats out every few hours.

Carter cleared his throat from the back seat as they turned onto fourth. "You know chances are they ran when their Spirit World protection disappeared."

Cesar knew this, and worried that the advantage they had was gone. "It's a good thing we have a nose with us, then, isn't it."

The Wolf snorted. "I can't track from inside one car to another, King."

"Then they better not have gone very far," Cesar responded.

No one said anything else as they drove up to the warehouse. The place seemed deserted. There were no cars, no rogues patrolling the perimeter. Cesar turned to the Alpha. "What do you smell?"

Shaking his head Carter frowned. "I don't, that's just it. I don't smell or hear anyone. The only tracks I smell are several hours old."

"That does not make sense," Roman interjected.

Carter's frown deepened. "I know."

It was a trap of some kind, Cesar knew it, but it was also their only lead, which did not give them much choice.

"All right, everyone pull out weapons and prepare for a fight because we are going to walk right into their hands."

As he approached the door, Cesar yanked the gun he was carrying from behind his back, then activated his pendant in case the trap was a spell. He glanced over his shoulder to make sure the other men were prepared. He came in low and pointed toward the opposite corner of the building. As a Warrior it was pretty hard for anything to kill him, so he wasn't worried about getting back out the door should there be an ambush.

But there wasn't. The wide open building was completely empty. There wasn't even a place where someone could hide. There were no alcoves or separate rooms. The only furniture was a single tall table, similar to the ones he had seen at Starbucks. Cesar stood up and motioned for the others to follow. As they entered, he made his way to the table. He could see something on it.

"We're clear, they are long gone. Carter, what do you smell?"

Cesar heard the Alpha holster his gun from somewhere behind him.

"Three beings. The two Warriors were toward the door, similar to how Lucia described them and the third…" The Wolf trailed off.

"I wasn't aware Weres could smell the Spirit World." The skepticism was blatant in Poet's voice.

Cesar reached the small table. Roman was standing to his left, and they looked down at the hand-held digital recorder in front of them with a sticky note next to it with 'Play Me' in big scrawling letters.

"We can't. I just don't know what the third being is. It smells like several species and yet none at the same time. It's coming from the far corner over there past the King and Roman. I've never smelled anything like it before." Cesar watched Carter walk by them and continue to the far corner of the warehouse.

Roman looked at him. Cesar simply nodded in response. His lieutenant hit the play button and a thick sixteenth-century French accent filled the air.

"This message is for the King of North America. If you are not he, I recommend you stop this tape and hand it over to his highness." The last two words dripped with disdain. After a sizable pause, the voice continued.

"Now, I believe I can safely assume that I have been handed over to the King, seeing as how loyal his subjects are. So highness, I wish to apologize on behalf of the movement for these four young Warriors and their alarmingly large band of misfits. They were not following our orders in this endeavor of theirs, and it would appear that the MP Marvin did not like our way of doing things or our time line, and grew impatient and decided to go off on his own. I hear you have most of these misinformed souls in your custody. I thank you for doing most of my work for me in this instance. Know that I will take care of the stragglers and you should not experience any further trouble on this matter. Once again, I apologize on behalf of the movement. We feel quite shamed that these little nuisances ruined our element of surprise. No matter, we would never have been so obvious in our endeavors anyway. Now that we know you will be looking out for us, we will simply lay low for a while and cling more to the shadows. Au revoir, highness."

The silence in the warehouse was palpable. There was a rebellion and it was much bigger than anyone realized. Cesar experienced cocky leaders before, but this man wasn't a leader. For a lower man on the totem pole to hold such confidence was a bad sign.

"Roman, take the recorder and get me Aztec on the phone. There is no foreseeable way this is contained to North America."

Roman grabbed the recorder and nodded, flipping out his phone as he strode out of the warehouse for better reception. Cesar then turned to Poet.

"Get someone important with the Shapeshifter agency on the phone now. I want the kills sanctioned in case they are not all from this Kingdom."

Poet nodded before following Roman out.

Cesar turned to Carter. "Now tell me in exact detail what you smell."

Gretchen S. B.

The other man shoved his hands in his pockets and made his way toward Cesar. "I smell a being with magical abilities but I can't tell the flavor. The aspects to the scent that would state either MP or Immortal are absent. It's the same with the smell of a Warrior or Were, a distinct smell of 'other' but not any specifically and there is something else. Something I can't put my finger on. It's sweet like blood. I'm not sure how else to put it."

Cesar felt dread set in. "Could it be a spell to mask a scent?"

Carter shook his head. "No, those eliminate the being's smell completely or disguise them as another race, but I would still be able to smell the spell. I don't smell any spells."

There had been rumors for hundreds of years that with people of the Night World free to interbreed, the offspring could resemble a new species entirely. That would mean his Kingdom's enemy had an unknown advantage over him. There was no real way for him to know what cards they held. Those thoughts only made Cesar want to talk with the other Kings and Queens more.

"Since this was a dead end, we'll head back north and regroup." Cesar turned and walked straight out the door.

He still had no idea how Lucia's spell could show the rogues here and yet Carter's nose said they had left hours ago. It didn't add up.

"Get Lucia on the phone I don't care whose phone you have to call to do it. Ask her why her spell was wrong and let her know she won't get paid for such sloppy work," he barked to Carter over his shoulder.

As he walked past Roman, his lieutenant handed Cesar his cell phone. Grabbing it, Cesar tossed Roman the car keys.

"Aztec?"

"Cesar, my old friend, I've been hearing rumors about you." There was a joking quality to Aztec's voice.

"We can discuss that later. Right now I have a serious problem you should be aware of."

"Proceed." The other King's voice dropped all familiarity.

Cesar gave an abridged version of events as they made their way back to the freeway. He was to the part about Marvin's death when he heard Carter's raised voice from the backseat.

Aztec must have heard it too. "I will let you get that while I hunt down my two lieutenants. They should be made aware of this as well. I will call you back on this phone when I have them."

Grunting his agreement, Cesar turned from the phone to the backseat. "Put her on speakerphone."

Carter pressed a button and the SUV filled with Lucia's angry voice. "...Paid for services rendered! His highness cannot make himself an exception simply because he pleases. There will be consequences!"

Cesar felt his own temper spike. This MP thought much too highly of herself. "His highness will not pay for a spell that did not work and if you insist on continuing your tantrum I will have Carter hang up with you and I will call the council personally to see that you are disciplined for your actions."

Silence. They both knew the only form of discipline the MP council had was the Strata-Enforcers, and there was no bargaining with them, just death.

"What do you mean did not work?" Her voice was much calmer. It was good to know she had some common sense.

"When we arrived no one had been there for hours. The two Warriors left hours before we even reached town. How is that possible?"

There was silence again. "Let me check something."

There was no response for several minutes before she came back on the line. "I have an idea, but I don't think you'll like it." Lucia's voice was wary.

"Tell us anyway." Cesar sighed. There was nothing about this he did like.

"I think it was a trap of some kind. The thing that attacked us. It used to be an MP. I can't be sure without seeing the site, but I think he cast a recording spell to make it look like the Warriors were still there, probably only long enough to find and attack us, and take out your MPs. But what I don't know is if they knew they were luring you down there and why."

"I know. We will discuss your compensation later, Lucia." Cesar nodded to Carter and the other man pressed a button and returned the phone to his ear.

Cesar let out a heavy breath and leaned his head onto the headrest. This week had spun out of control fast. He gained a mate and a serious rebellion. The Pacific Northwest needed his attention. It was far too unorganized for the trouble heading its way. The low boil in Cesar's system had spiked after Gwen endangered herself, which was not helping him concentrate. At least the cocky voice on the recording told him he would have some time to plan before the next attack. Cesar firmly believed that was due to them depleting the key people in the area.

He would use that time to prepare his kingdom for the coming trouble and to woo Gwen through the first stage of mating. Cesar wasn't going to let his clever little mate get one over on him again. Now would be the time to win her properly and hopefully when the next wave of rogues came the first stage would be out of his system.

"I've touched bases with Apollo, got him up to speed." This from Poet in the backseat. "He wanted me to ask you if he should come out here or if you will be coming there."

Cesar turned to frown at the other man. "How do you have the Greek's number?"

Poet grinned. "I'm on Gwen's detail. All three of us have the number to your secret lair, just in case something happens."

Assuming Poet meant the private office he and his generals shared, Cesar nodded. "Call him back, tell him to stay put and let him know I want a guard detail sent in the next day to pick up our prisoners and take them to the fortress to be dealt with upon my return."

"Will the Lady of the Dead be with you?"

The car went dead silent at Poet's question. Cesar ground his teeth to fight from saying yes. He knew forcing her would only give him more grief and a less happy mate. Cesar wanted her happy more than almost anything else "I don't know. That will be her decision, not mine."

The silence continued until Roman's phone rang. Cesar jumped, forgetting he still held it in his hand.

"Aztec."

"Yes, I have you on my office line so both lieutenants can hear you."

Cesar started where he left off and was able to get to the end without one interruption from anyone, either in the car or on the other end of the phone. After playing the recording into the phone, so Aztec could hear the snide voice, Cesar gave a brief pause before continuing with what he knew would be a somewhat troubling request.

"This tape only convinces me further that this rebellion is worldwide. If this rebellion is as big as I believe it is, there is no way they would settle for just North America. I believe we should do everything in our power to prepare with the little time this slip up has given us. All ten of us should meet."

There was a long eerie silence on the other end of the phone. Cesar knew what he was asking, getting all the Kings and Queens in one place was unheard of. The most was four. They used to meet regularly centuries ago when there was only five of them. It would take months to put together, but Cesar's strategic mind knew it was their best option.

"My friend, do you know what you are asking?" Aztec's voice was completely blank.

"I do." Cesar kept his voice just as blank.

The other King might be almost five centuries younger than him, but Aztec had been the uncontested King of South America three hundred years before Cesar had even begun to claim the North American throne. The younger man knew far more about inter-kingdom relations.

"I am with you on this being more than an idle threat. Something about it feels real to me and it would explain a few missing persons in my kingdom. You and I should collaborate without question since we control most of this hemisphere.

"The others will take some convincing unless they are successfully hiding the cracks a rebellion would make. Europe would come, Amadour is always curious, and the French voice on that tape would intrigue him. Bakalanga takes any threat seriously, so you will have Africa. But the rest would be hard to convince. Especially Greenland, hell, it's hard enough to get a hold of Red as it is. I can't imagine him leaving his kingdom."

Cesar figured as much. No one was big on collaboration in the older kingdoms. They were too used to keeping eyes on each other. Though there had been no land disputes since before Cesar was King, old habits died hard.

"I know this, but so do the rogues. They will rely on our divided natures to conquer us one at a time."

A heavy sigh came through the phone. "I know this is best, Cesar. Just don't expect it to be easy. If you do manage to coax in most of them, the meeting won't take place for months if not a year. I will help you in this any way I can, but you must make the initial contacts. Find a place to hold this meeting that could be secure, preferably neutral ground. A word of advice, though, don't call them rogues. Use the term rebels when you speak to the others. You don't want their old paranoia getting to them, thinking every rogue Warrior is out to get them. I know it's semantics, but it's better to be on the safe side. Many rogues simply want a peaceful existence, and they wouldn't want to rebel against the way of life they've built.

"I have a few issues that need attending but let me know how the communication goes and keep me updated on this rebellion. As always let me know if there is anything we can do to help."

Knowing that was the close of the conversation, Cesar returned the offer of help and ended the call. There were several seconds before anyone spoke. Cesar had not expected it to be Poet who broke the silence.

"I have been through more regime changes than I care to count. I am not at the moment eager for another. I enjoy my current place in society, so to speak. Know that should things become messy I would take Gwen and hide her so she could not be used against you or Viking."

Cesar contemplated that for a few moments. His baser instincts roared at the idea of being without his mate, but as king, he knew if anyone could protect Gwen in hiding during a war it would be Poet. The man had been an outcast before Cesar was born. Viking would need his attention on the war; he would be reluctant but would eventually agree.

"That is much appreciated."

Roman snorted. "Not so much as a growl against the idea. Do not worry, old friend, we will not let it get to that point."

Cesar certainly hoped so, but he did not hold the confidence of his lieutenant. If the kingdoms worked together they would win without a doubt, but not alone. At least with the Americas united, they could protect themselves. But his kingdom was still the largest population of criminals and outcasts. He had no way of knowing where the majority of them would side. Needing the rest of the ride to think, Cesar leaned back in his seat and closed his eyes.

Chapter 33

When Gwen woke up, Marco was stabilized and resting in one of her extra bedrooms. Gwen approached Lucia and Barrett about enforcing the wards on the store. Though the current ones did a good job of keeping out the Spirit World, they could not stop beings wreaking havoc once inside. They both whole-heartedly agreed that upgrades were needed and they had spent the last hour checking each of the existing wards.

Gwen and Lucia stood on the outside pushing and testing the ward while Barrett did the same from the inside. Reinforcing and modifying as they went. These new wards would prevent unfriendly magic from being performed from inside the building as well as around it. They were sealing the building when Lucia's phone went off a second time. She ignored it while she and Barrett finished sealing.

When Lucia finished, she took a deep breath and shook her body out before turning to Gwen. "Okay, that is the best I have for now. Let me do some research. Then I'll run it by you and discuss each individual addition."

Gwen nodded. "Okay, what will all that cost?" Lucia sometimes gave her discounts when no one was looking, simply because of their friendship.

"Nothing." Lucia held up her hand before Gwen could respond. "Hold on, let me finish. I say nothing because this is a safe haven for most of the Night World and as the last few days have shown us, it's best for everyone that it is fully protected."

"Thank you, Lucia."

Lucia waved her arm dismissively. "Thank me when it actually works." Then she checked her phone. "Oh, this might pertain to you too. I asked one of my sources about the spirit MP. He would know more about that kind of thing than Barrett or I." Then she held up a finger and stepped out of earshot. "Hello, Perry?"

That name rang a bell, but before Gwen could find it in her memory, a needle plunged into her neck and less than a second later the world swam. "Lucia!" Gwen wasn't sure how loud her voice had been but she didn't get a chance to repeat it before everything went dark.

Chapter 34

Cesar's mind went red a second before his pendant throbbed. Curses filled the SUV. All Cesar could do was growl. Gwen was in trouble. It was almost as if his mate connection to her had faded.

"WHAT?" Carter's wary voice hit Cesar's ears.

But Cesar was already calling Viking.

"I don't know what happened!" Viking yelled as a greeting through the phone. "Last I saw her she was discussing security with Barrett and Lucia." Cesar could tell the other man was running.

"Why weren't you with her?" Cesar growled.

"I was, but stepped inside to verify something for Apollo. He was updating me on the current situation." A string of ancient curses flew from his mouth. "Hold on, I see Lucia."

Cesar could hear the muffled voices but couldn't make out what they were saying.

A second later Viking was back on the phone. "They were finishing the wards and Lucia took a call from an associate who had information on the attack earlier. She heard Gwen mumble something, turned around and a guy, looking a lot like our last rogue was running down the street with Gwen slung over his shoulder. Lucia screamed for Barrett to find us and took off after him but he was too fast for her to keep up. She lost him five blocks down, but knows she can track him if we get the ingredients together fast enough."

"She should not have been alone, Viking!" Cesar knew he sounded lethal.

"I know this, my King." He could hear Viking struggling to keep his voice in check.

"We are maybe fifteen minutes away. She had better be fully prepared when I get there." Then he hung up.

Poet must have explained things to Carter because the back seat was silent. Which Cesar was grateful for.

"She must be taken from here. At least for a while. It is not acceptable that anyone can get to her at anytime."

"Agreed," Roman stated.

"And this rogue must die."

"Agreed." His friend's voice had taken on a lethal quality.

"Good."

Cesar concentrated all his anger on the rogue that would dare take his mate. That calmed him some, and his hot anger turned to cold vengeance. His mate was a good woman, loved by many. Only a suicidal idiot would kidnap her.

"So the rogue is not as obedient as the Frenchman thinks. I wonder what he thinks young Ellis is doing right now." Poet made a good point.

Cesar wasn't sure if the rebellion's lack of control over its lower levels was to his advantage or not.

"What makes you think this wasn't exactly what the Frenchman wanted in the first place?" Carter asked.

Roman shook his head. "Because the idea of taking the Lady of the Dead never really made sense in the first place. Think about it. She is well loved and even with minimal power, she is an asset to the Night World. Warriors worldwide would hunt her down, on top of all the locals. Unless the rebellion had a very strong foothold, which it clearly doesn't, going after Gwen does not make sense. A snatch and grab where there is no bigger plan is one thing, but if your aim is domination you wouldn't want to draw that much attention to yourself so soon."

If Cesar had been thinking clearly the last few days that would have occurred to him too. The Maddening's lingering effects on him impeded heavily on his job. It was not what he needed right now.

"So, it's revenge then?" Carter responded.

Roman nodded. "Most likely or he wants to follow through on Marvin's plan."

His blood ran cold. "If he's that stupid, he might try it on his own."

The silence that followed was so heavy with anger it was almost hard to breathe.

Gretchen S. B.

Chapter 35

Gwen didn't have any idea where she was. Her mind was groggy, so much so that the world felt heavy. It had been years since someone got the jump on her. Trying desperately to clear her head, to remember what Storebror had told her as a child, what she should do if she found herself in this situation.

First she tried to reach him, but it was a no go; she was far too foggy or too far away from him. Next she concentrated on body awareness to assess injuries. It wasn't easy. Her mind couldn't hold one thought very long, but she couldn't feel anything broken. The only pain was from the shot in her neck. Maybe she could get away. Then she felt the chains around her wrists and ankles as she tried to get up from the chair. Tugging as much as she dared, Gwen could feel there was no give. The drug, whatever it was, was wearing off, marginally. She could almost think clearly without taking what felt like ten minute breaks between thoughts. Maybe if she could wait it out her mind would clear enough to go non-corporeal and escape, providing her captor had not already planned for that.

Taking a deep breath, Gwen opened her eyes to narrow slits. She was in an unfurnished house, in what looked like a kitchen. It was extremely dark, but she didn't know whether that was because she had been out that long or because the windows were covered. Her mind wasn't quite nimble enough to connect if the coverings on the windows were that thick.

Movement caught her attention. At an island in the middle of the kitchen stood a man just under six feet tall. She couldn't quite make out more than that because his back was to her. She swore she heard him humming to himself. He started to turn and she slammed her eyes shut. There was no advantage in letting him know she was awake.

The humming got louder, and she could hear him coming closer. There was a clanking sound like a spoon hitting a bowl.

"Marvin must have gotten his doses wrong, either that or he really wanted you out until the last possible second. He is dramatic like that. Too bad he's not answering his phone. He's going to miss all the fun." The humming returned but moved away.

He didn't know the MP was dead. Gwen knew there was an advantage there somewhere but she couldn't figure out where. She

246 | P a g e

also didn't know how he would be able to complete Marvin's plan. He wasn't an MP. Odds were this was Ellis. Even though he was working alone, he planned to do magic with all the items she had seen on the counter.

They were originally going to strip her of her power, and that was probably still the plan, but how was Ellis going to execute it? Gwen couldn't think of an answer, so instead she weighted her options.

One, she could wait this out and hope the cavalry came in time. Two, she could use her power to get out of here. Option two won before she even finished the thought. Gwen was not the wait for the cavalry type.

Now that she could think clearly, her sense of dread lessened. Not completely, there was still a good chance she wouldn't be strong enough to go non-corporeal. It was still a new skill and took a lot of energy. She needed a backup plan. She could go invisible but that wouldn't help untie her. She could move herself from one place to another, but that wouldn't get her more than a few yards away. If she could flash somewhere and then go invisible, all she would have to do was hop on a bus and hope no one sat on her. That could work, but she just had to wait. The only problem was the Warrior in front of her. She needed a way to incapacitate him long enough to get August down here and take Ellis prisoner, but she had no idea how to accomplish that.

Sivia was the one who knew about potions and the like. Gwen wasn't betting on him having another nifty syringe full of drugs handy. She couldn't knock him unconscious because she didn't have the magic or Warrior strength to do so. She did have the two blades she always carried on her, but he was faster than her and Warrior healing would only give her a handful of minutes, tops. If her reinforcements were not far away, then it wouldn't be an issue, but Gwen knew that wasn't something she could rely on.

What if she could convince some Spirit World beings to hold him for her? If she could find several of them with some strength, it might work. But it would mean leaving her body unattended for who knew how long. Gwen knew she had to take the chance. Slowly she lowered her walls so she could see the Spirit World around them. She could feel that she wasn't strong enough yet to get very far but maybe it would be far enough.

Shooting out of the house, Gwen headed for the nearest power she could feel. She was surprised to recognize where she was. Gwen was traveling down East Lake Sammamish Parkway. She could feel a strong energy coming from a wooded area just off the road. As she got closer, she could feel several distinct beings. Hoping they were friendly she landed a yard from the tree line.

"Hello? I Would like to speak to you, if I could," Gwen called in the general direction of the trees.

She felt them almost flying toward her, three of them, male. Gwen tried to hold her calm. Panicking about their speed would only hinder her. What burst from the trees surprised her. Three gray, huge, almost solid Wolves came to a halt in front of her. This was the first time she ever encountered Shapeshifters in the Spirit World. She knew theoretically it could happen, but that didn't damper the shock.

The one on the left tilted his head. *"You are the Lady of the Dead, are you not?"*

"I am," Gwen responded.

At once all three of them began shifting into their human forms. Gwen had always been fascinated by the change from one form to the other, but watching ghosts do it was unnerving. When they finished there were three rugged looking men in their thirties wearing overalls and flannel standing in front of her. Though their 'bodies' looked fine, the clothing was singed. She could tell they died in a fire and knew better than to mention it. Traumatic deaths were still traumatic after the fact.

"How can we help you? I can feel your distress." This from the spirit in the middle.

Gwen found some spirits were like that. They could carry their personalities over to the grave with them. She sensed no deception coming from them and could see the genuine worry on their faces. Gwen couldn't help the pang at the thought that such nice men died so young.

"I have been kidnapped by a Warrior who wants to drain me of my power. I can escape on my own but I do not want him getting away. I ask for your help. Are the three of you strong enough to keep a Warrior captive or baring that staying with him so the King can find him later?"

The one on the left spoke again. *"We believe we can do as you ask. We have never tried to hold on to someone before but we know we can follow him for you. We are not attached to these woods."*

Relief soared though her. *"Oh thank you so much! If after this is done there is anything I can ever do for you, find me and let me know."*

The one in the middle shook his head. *"That is very kind but nothing we want you would be able to give us."*

There was nothing to say to that so Gwen kept her mouth shut.

The middle one waved up to the sky. *"Lead the way, Lady of the Dead."*

Gwen pushed herself up and back toward her body. She could feel more than see the three spirits behind her. She had confidence this plan would work, as long as these spirits were as trustworthy as they seemed. Otherwise, she was in trouble. Pushing that last thought aside, Gwen went over her plan again. There were so many variables she hoped she could handle them all.

Gwen found herself thinking of August. After they found Ellis, maybe they could go on a long weekend away. She liked him, August was a good guy, even with his goofy self-destructive ideas on chivalry. Gwen knew she could grow to love the gorgeous, overbearing Warrior. They had a few kinks to work out with the whole living arrangement thing. There was no way she could stay in Montana. Why couldn't August move here with her? That struck her as she re-entered the house. Why couldn't he move here? Or they could split their time, switching every few months? She felt hope that this could all work out.

Before entering her body, Gwen turned to the three Spirits as they landed in the kitchen. *"You don't really need to hold him. Just prevent him from leaving the house."*

One of them smiled. *"This might be fun."*

Gwen thanked them one last time before landing back in her body. When she returned to the house, she paid attention to the neighborhood around her. If she could get herself outside on the street and one house down she figured she could make a break for it. Now came the hard part. Normally when she did this, she pivoted to activate it. She was relying on her new powers to get her where she needed to be. If this didn't work, she didn't have a backup plan.

Concentrating on nothing else, Gwen pictured the street in front of the house, filling in every detail she could think of. When she had the picture as complete as she could get it, Gwen pivoted her feet as much as she could in the chair.

A second later the chains were no longer around her. She immediately began chanting the invisibility spell and opened her eyes. Panic flowed over her. To her horror, she was still in the house. In fact she was only down the hall from the kitchen. Adrenaline shot through her the same time she felt the invisibility kick in. There was an angry roar from the kitchen. Fear gripped Gwen as she made a mad dash for the front door. She had to beat Ellis there. It wasn't like she could go through him and clearly her transportation magic didn't work well.

As she reached the front door she heard him enter the room on her heels. Gwen knew he couldn't see her but he would see the door open and he was heading right for it.

"Go! We've got him!" said a faint male voice in her ear.

Taking the voice at its word, Gwen ripped open the door and dashed out onto the street. She hadn't ever leapt off the porch before she heard the door slam and lock behind her. Pleading and thanking the spirits, Gwen took off down the street. Her heart was beating so hard and so fast she could hear it in her ears. She only had a vague idea which direction to go. She swore she had seen a park and ride nearby. If the ghosts could keep Ellis away, and if she could get there, she could get home. Then it dawned on her. She had her phone, and she could probably reach Storebror now as well. At least she hoped so; she had never tried for this far away.

"Storebror!" she shouted, holding his necklace as she ran. She didn't stop, just in case Ellis was anywhere behind her. He had a vehicle after all, and she didn't know what magic he had at his disposal. Gwen would rather be safe than sorry.

"LITTLE ONE!" The relief and fear in his voice was palpable.

"I need a ride."

"Where are you? Are you alone?"

"Yes, I escaped but I don't know how far Ellis is behind me."

"Raider and I will be right there in the rover. Just tell me where you are."

Relief flooded Gwen's system chasing away all the adrenaline. *"I'll be on East Lake Sammamish Parkway a mile or so up from a park and ride here in a minute. Where are you? Where is August?"*

There was a pause and Gwen held her breath. Had something happened while she was gone?

We am turning onto the parkway now. August is maybe five minutes behind us."

Gwen exhaled. *"How?"*

"Tracking spell, but I will tell him that we are picking you up."

Gwen panicked. *"No! Tell him to go to the house I was being kept in. If we are very lucky Ellis will still be there for August to handle."*

She felt worried amusement. *"Little One, what did you do?"*

"I'll tell you later. I just made it to the street." She rattled off the signs she saw.

"I see them. We are one light past you. I am turning into a parking lot."

Gwen cut the connection and kept an eye out for Viking's SUV. There was no way she was becoming visible in the middle of a store parking lot when she still didn't know where Ellis was. She finally recognized the black vehicle as it pulled into a bookstore parking lot.

It rolled into one of the back spaces and the back passenger side door opened. Gwen sprinted to the car, still maintaining invisibility. It wasn't until she slid in and slammed the door behind her that she relaxed.

"I say we don't do this again." She was still out of breath from running at top speed for the last ten minutes.

"Agreed," both Warriors affirmed.

"Let's get you home, shall we?" Raider smiled as he put the car in reverse.

Gwen sat up straight. "No, we can't yet! If Ellis gets out of the house before August gets there, I'm the only one that can track him."

The car stopped moving. "What?" Raider turned.

Viking's brows came together as he looked at her. "What exactly did you do?"

"I charged three spirits with the task of keeping Ellis in the house until August got there and if they couldn't do that than they were to follow him so I could lead August to them."

"That's ingenious." Raider didn't even try to hide his surprise.

Viking's expression didn't change. "What sort of spirits were these?"

She only hesitated a second. "Werewolves."

There was silence again as they stared at her. It was a little unnerving.

"I'm not sure I want to know any more than that." Raider turned to face forward. "Just do your floating thing and see if the King needs our help."

Gwen didn't respond. Instead she leaned back, lowered her walls and floated away from her body. She wondered, as they were officially mated, could she find August?

As she concentrated on picturing her Warrior, she felt a tug moving her in the direction of the house. It wasn't like the tug to return to her body, but oddly similar. Following the line for about a minute she found herself floating above an SUV. Concentrating, she sunk in to the backseat, hoping to land between Poet and Carter, since Gwen would put money on Roman and August refusing to sit in the back.

As she hit the seat, she adjusted so she floated at the same speed as the car.

"Good to see you, Gwen." Poet smiled down from her left.

The tension escalated and the car jerked.

"What?" Astonishment filled Carter's voice.

"Her little astral-self just joined us in the car," Poet supplied happily.

August practically turned all the way out of the passenger seat. "How can you tell?"

Poet grinned at her again and winked. "I put the pendant on when Gwen disappeared. Figured it might come in handy."

She knew that was a lie. He could see her anyway. August fumbled with his shirt to activate his pendant. Gwen knew the moment it worked because his shoulders relaxed and an affectionate smile filled his sexy face. Gwen's heart fluttered a little.

Chapter 36

"There you are. I just hung up with Viking." Cesar's lips twitched. "An interesting plan you've concocted."

Emotions swirled within him, warring between pride for his mate and anger for Ellis. Though he loved that she was with him, if they did have to hunt Ellis down, he didn't want her using up her reserves now.

"Go on back to your body. No use in wasting energy if you don't need to. I'll call Viking and let him know if we need you."

Gwen nodded once before she stood up and disappeared through the roof.

"Man, you just got a goofy expression on your face." Roman laughed. Only Roman would have the audacity to say such a thing.

Cesar frowned. "I am not above making you a eunuch."

Roman only laughed harder.

"Turn right at the stop sign. This is the street the house is on," Cesar commanded as he read the street sign. They were two houses away from where Gwen had been taken. "17472 should be the second house once we turn the corner."

Cesar didn't even have to read the numbers to know it was the right house. The second house glowed with Spirit World activity. Cesar wouldn't have seen any of it if he hadn't activated his pendant. From the looks of it, Gwen's ghosts were still in the house. Roman pulled up to the curb and parked.

"Do you see that?" Cesar asked Poet without turning.

A back door opened. "Yes and I'm quite curious as to where she found these spirits."

He was wondering the same thing. Cesar knew when Roman activated his pendant because his friend gave a low curse.

"Let's go then." Cesar didn't wait for the others to follow. Instead he marched right up to the front door, raising his voice to the house. "I am the King of North America. The Lady of the Dead sent me here to collect the Warrior traitor from you, and on behalf of the Kingdom I thank you for your help."

There was no answer except the power around the house disappeared and the front door unlocked and opened.

"Well, that isn't at all creepy." Carter said from somewhere behind him.

Cesar ignored the comment and walked in. It was as if the ghosts Gwen enlisted had left. Again he found himself wondering where Gwen had found them.

"He's upstairs." Carter said before walking over to the staircase. "And he's whimpering like a child."

Cesar exchanged a look with Roman before following Carter up.

The Wolf stood in a doorway halfway down the hall. Cesar could hear the whimpering now. *What had Gwen's spirits done, exactly?*

When he stood by Carter, Cesar could see Ellis curled in the closet sitting in a fetal position with his head buried against his knees, rocking. It was a disturbing picture that brought unwanted memories to the forefront of Cesar's brain.

Shaking his head clear, he strode over to Ellis and put authority in his voice. "Ellis, for crimes against your kingdom, I, King of North America, arrest you."

"Okay." It was soft, barely audible.

Cesar motioned Roman over and the two of them got Ellis to his feet. The boy was stark white and didn't take a decent breath until he was in the car and seated between Poet and Carter.

Roman and Cesar hung back so they couldn't be heard.

"What on Earth did the young lady make a deal with? That was a lot of power to bring a Warrior, albeit a young one, to hysterics. She did not seem worried about them having that kind of effect and I very much doubt she gave them explicit directions." His friend's expression was as worried as Cesar felt.

"I do not know, but frankly they were on our side so I can't bring myself to hunt them down. Am I worried about that kind of power being out there? Yes. But we have bigger issues to deal with for the time being. When this is all over and we have stabilized things then we will look into these Were Spirits, but until they cause us problems I'm hesitant. We want all the powerful allies we can get."

Roman's expression told Cesar he agreed but he didn't entirely like it.

"In the meantime I want you in charge of moving all the prisoners to the fort. Once I arrive, I want everything settled so I can concentrate on contacting all the other Kings and Queens."

Gretchen S. B.

Roman inclined his head. "Of course. Let's get you to your mate."

Chapter 37

The next two days went by so fast Gwen wasn't quite sure what actually happened. She returned home with Raider and Viking in the early evening and went straight to bed. August had been right, she was drained. Gwen hadn't even realized she had fallen asleep until August woke her up by sliding into bed behind her. It was the most comfortable, natural thing in the world to fall back asleep with August curled around her.

When she woke the next morning, he was already in the shower. Feeling a bit mischievous, she joined him. The scandalized look on August's face had her falling against him, laughing. She coaxed him into more fun things they could do in the shower and to her surprise, he had no qualms.

When they finally got downstairs, almost an hour after her usual time, the truck with the inventory for the café had come in and she had to run off to handle it. August got waylaid by Roman with some kingdom business and she didn't really see him the rest of the day. He gave her a peck on the top of her head as he and Roman came out into the store to grab their lunches, which gained her some razzing from her staff.

Being a Saturday, there were events all afternoon and evening which kept her busy. Then there was a party at night which August insisted he was going to. Roman tagged along to make fun of his friend. She and August crawled into bed after midnight and fooled around until Gwen drifted off from sheer blissful exhaustion.

When the alarm sounded on Sunday morning, Gwen groaned, gaining a chuckle from behind her. She smacked him. It didn't have the desired effect. Gwen rubbed her face. Ever though Sunday was her half day, the thought of getting up was not at all appealing. All she wanted to do was lay in bed with August all day.

"You get your spare room back today." August had the sexiest morning growl she ever heard.

"Hmm, do I now?" she purred at him before stretching.

Lucia was able to barter services with a White MP, who had sped up Marco's healing process considerably. But Marco had left last night.

"Your ability to make me want you is unfathomable. But yet some of my men will be here by noon to collect the rebels…"

Gretchen S. B.

Gwen shot up in bed. Noon! She had an author doing a book signing today from noon to two. How had she forgotten? It was already eleven and she was supposed to give an introduction.

Leaping from the bed and running to the bathroom, she explained over her shoulder. "Can't talk, so late!"

She was actually grateful when August didn't join her in the shower. He wasn't in the bedroom when she sprinted into the closet at eleven-thirty. She needed to be downstairs now. As she bolted out of the hall, an arm snaked out and grabbed her, sending her into the sexiest chest she had ever had the pleasure of sleeping with.

"Whoa there." August chuckled.

"Not now, I'm supposed to be downstairs handling the set-up."

Moving away from her, he kept his grip on her arm. "I know about the book signing, but bear with me a second." His beautiful face smiled down at her as a blue travel mug popped into her view. "This is your coffee."

He let go of her so he could move her hand to take it. Gwen was so touched by the sweet, homey gesture she was actually speechless. Then a red travel mug came into view.

"And this is what you think passes for breakfast." He was still smiling as he shook his head.

A feeling so close to love she couldn't tell the difference bloomed inside her. With her free hand, instead of grabbing the red travel mug, she grabbed his neck to bring him down to her, and gave him a scorching kiss that conveyed every emotion she was feeling at that moment. Before he could really kiss her back she backed up and took the second mug from him.

"You are one amazing guy." Gwen gave him one last lingering look before dashing out the door.

The book signing went off without a hitch, thanks to her fantastic staff. Leaving Sissy in charge of the actual signing part of the event, Gwen left the store. She wanted to see the prisoners being removed from the building. She was worried something might go wrong without her there to preempt it.

As she entered the back hall, she saw the rebels being taken out in some heavy duty shackles one by one, to black tinted passenger vans behind the building. When August saw her come out of the store he broke away from Roman and another man Gwen didn't know and strode over to her.

"Hey, do you have a few minutes to spare?" He actually looked nervous.

"Yeah, a few."

August nodded and grabbed her hand, leading her over to the staircase. Gwen wasn't sure how to feel about him wanting to talk in private. He didn't say anything until they were up in her apartment and he had locked the door.

"I need to get back to Montana after I wrap a few loose ends up with the locals tomorrow morning." He wasn't even looking at her.

Gwen's heart dropped. She knew it was inevitable but she still couldn't help the sadness that engulfed her. "I see. So we are discussing the living arrangements then."

August nodded, still not looking up from the floor. He started pacing. "I want nothing more than to have you with me but over the past several days I've come to understand that isn't possible. I want to negotiate your…visits to the stronghold." He said visits like it was a vile word and her heart broke for him.

"August, I…"

He interrupted her. "Don't worry, they won't be longer than two weeks at a time and once the first stage is over, it can be less."

Anger spiked through Gwen, now he was just being ridiculous. "AUGUST!"

His gaze shot to her and he stopped pacing.

"I don't particularly want to be away from you either." She waved her arm as he opened his mouth. "Hear me out. Why can't you live here? Not at first, of course, but I've been thinking about this. For the first year we switch every month or so back and forth, until you are comfortable enough to work here. That way the kingdom's capital isn't the be all end all of the government because it will be in two different places. Harder for the rebels to take down. Just take a minute to think about it."

August's expression was one Gwen couldn't quite interpret. "You've spent time thinking about this?"

She couldn't tell if he was mocking her. "Yes."

Before she knew what was happening, August picked her up and they were locked in the most incredible kiss of Gwen's life. It was demanding, passionate, and a wild declaration of love. She didn't know how long the kiss lasted but when he moved away, his expression was glowing with excitement.

"I will build you a house. A house I can work from, far enough away to be almost isolated, but close enough that you are near the store. A house we will raise children in and teach them how the Night World truly works, and not the insane Northwest version. But first I will settle things in Montana and then we are going on what they call a honeymoon. Pick where you want to go and we will. Then we will organize from there." He was beaming by the time he finished.

Gwen laughed, long and happy. She had absolutely no qualms with August's plans for the future. They sounded perfect to her. The joy on his face was all she could see as he spun her around before pulling her in for another passionate kiss. Gwen couldn't help it, her heart filled with this man. Her man, her Warrior mate.

About the Author

Gretchen happily lives in Seattle, Washington, where she spends her time creating new characters and situations to put them in. She also enjoys cheering on her local sports teams, even though it sometimes seems they are allergic to winning.

You can visit Gretchen S. B. on the interwebs at any of the following:

Gretchensb.com

https://www.facebook.com/pages/Gretchen-S-B40293959350712/5

https://twitter.com/GretchenSB

Made in the USA
Middletown, DE
02 March 2015